COMMANDOS

Set Europe Ablaze

Book 1

COLONEL RICHARD D. CAMP

CASEMATE

Philadelphia & Oxford

Published in the United States of America and Great Britain in 2021 by
CASEMATE PUBLISHERS
1950 Lawrence Road, Havertown, PA 19083, US
and
The Old Music Hall, 106–108 Cowley Road, Oxford OX4 1JE, UK

Paperback Edition: ISBN 978-1-63624-008-4
Digital Edition: ISBN 978-1-63624-009-1

A CIP record for this book is available from the British Library

Printed and bound in the United States of America by Integrated Books International

Typeset by Versatile PreMedia Services (P) Ltd.

For a complete list of Casemate titles, please contact:

Casemate Publishers (US)
Telephone (610) 853-9131
Fax (610) 853-9146
Email: casemate@casematepublishers.com
www.casematepublishers.com

CASEMATE PUBLISHERS (UK)
Telephone (01865) 241249
Email: casemate-uk@casematepublishers.co.uk
www.casematepublishers.co.uk

"And now set Europe ablaze."
Winston Churchill

Prologue

Live Fire Exercise, Camp Pendleton, California, 10 June 1942—Machine-gun fire erupted from the edge of the treeline, shattering the morning stillness. Copper-jacketed .30-caliber slugs blanketed the fighting positions on the small, brush-covered knoll. A dozen riflemen stepped out from the treeline and converged on the hillock, ignoring the storm of fire that passed directly in front of their formation. A squat, broad-shouldered lieutenant wearing sweat-stained utilities and a helmet with a white band around the base followed anxiously behind them. "Stay on line," he shouted nervously, the dangerous crack of bullets focusing his attention. He was keenly aware that one mistake could get someone killed. A scant 10 yards from the bullet strikes, he tossed a smoke grenade, which quickly blossomed into a brilliant green cloud from the fist-sized canister. The smoke signaled a cease-fire to the machine gunners in the treeline. Under the lieutenant's tight control, the line of riflemen marched across the knoll, shooting into the fighting positions as they passed by. Suddenly, the piercing blast of a whistle penetrated the crackle of gunfire. "Cease-fire! Cease-fire!" the lieutenant shouted. A tall, slender officer in a sage-green herringbone twill field uniform stepped out of the treeline and strode purposefully toward the younger man.

"Good work, lieutenant," Marine Captain Jim Cain declared, congratulating the young platoon commander on the successful assault of the simulated enemy position. He was pleased. This was the first platoon from his company to have gone through the live fire exercise since he had taken command. While the tactical elements of the problem were relatively uncomplicated—two rifle squads and the machine-gun section served as a base of fire, while the remaining squad enveloped from the right flank—the devil was in the detail. The base of fire had to ensure they did not shoot the enveloping force; the green smoke, the cease-fire signal, had to be timed perfectly; and finally, the assault force had to maintain a straight formation or risk getting shot if a man got ahead or fell behind.

Cain had been watching the "canned" tactical problem from an observation tower. The newly joined second lieutenant had maintained good control over his 40-man platoon, and the young Marines, who for the most part were just out of boot camp, handled the exercise like veterans. As the platoon assembled for the "hot wash-up," Cain's senior staff non-commissioned officer, Gunnery Sergeant Leland Montgomery—a first sergeant had not been assigned—handed him a message: *Report to the battalion commander as soon as possible.*

"Can't it wait until after the debrief?" he asked Montgomery.

"No, sir, the colonel said he wanted both of us in his office most ricky-tick."

Thirty minutes later, the battalion adjutant ushered them through the saloon-style swinging doors into Major "Red Mike" Edson's office. The "old man," the traditional moniker for a Marine commander regardless of age, had the doors installed because he said they reminded him of all the slop shoots he had been thrown out of in his younger days. The major was sitting behind a battered government-issued wooden desk in the center of the room, backdropped by the battalion colors and the national ensign that stood in a wooden bracket. The two flags were angled so they crossed one another, with the national ensign on top of the overlap. A large plaque bearing painted skull and crossbones, the Raider Battalion's crest, was affixed to the wall between the two flags.

"Sit," the colonel ordered. He was not one for small talk. "I just received these orders from headquarters. Read them and then we'll talk." He passed the message flimsy to Cain. Montgomery looked over his shoulder.

> From: Commandant of the Marine Corps
> To: Captain James M. Cain 027192 USMC
> Gunnery Sergeant Leland F. Montgomery 1992845 USMC
> Subj: Reassignment and Temporary Additional Duty
> Ref: (a) Marine Corps Special Order 10-77 of 1 July 42
>
> 1. In accordance with reference (a), on or about 5 July 1942, you will stand detached from your present duty station and proceed and report to the commanding officer Commando Basic Training Centre at Achnacarry, Scotland for a period of instruction not to exceed 10 weeks. You are to report no later than 10 August 1942.
> 2. You are to proceed to the Port of Embarkation, Norfolk Naval Base, for operational government transportation to the Port of Southampton, Great Britain and subsequent civilian rail transportation to Achnacarry, Scotland.
> 3. Your Officer Qualification Record, Enlisted Personnel Record, Pay, Health, and Dental Records are entrusted to your care for safe delivery to your new command.
>
> T. Holcomb
> Lieutenant General
> Commandant

Cain's mouth dropped open. "Colonel, there must be some mistake," he pleaded. "I just took over the company and I need to get it ready for deployment."

Edson fixed the young officer with a piercing stare that could only be described as icy. "Captain, are you presuming that the commandant doesn't know what he's doing?"

Oh no, Montgomery thought, *now the skipper's in for it.* Cain swallowed the lump in his throat and finally found his voice. "No, sir, I merely thought that I needed more time to bring the company up to your high standards."

Montgomery inwardly cringed, waiting for the explosion. The old man was known for blow-torching anyone who tried to butter him up.

And it was not long in coming. The old man leaned over his desk and pointed his heavily callused finger at the younger officer. "Cain," he said threateningly, "you are the biggest bullshitter I've ever seen," and then he broke out in a loud guffaw.

Montgomery couldn't believe it. He had served with the colonel for several years and had never seen him smile. In fact, there was an ongoing bet among the staff non-commissioned officers in the battalion that anything other than a scowl would crack the old man's face! To add to the gunny's amazement, the colonel's whole demeanor softened into something resembling a human being instead of the lean, mean, fighting machine that he usually always projected.

"You two," he said, "are the best company commander and the best gunnery sergeant in the battalion, and I can't spare either of you … but, the commando school is so important that I decided to let you go." He paused and looked intensely at the two men. The two were in sharp contrast; Cain had a round face, deep-set blue eyes, and an easy smile that were in marked contrast to Montgomery's hawk-like, deeply creased face, and hard, cement-colored eyes that scared the shit out of any wrongdoer that crossed his path.

Physically, they could not have been more different—the officer's muscular 6-foot frame was in sharp contrast to the SNCO's wiry physique—but there the differences ended. They were professionals in every sense of the word; aggressive, strong-willed, and totally dedicated, with a deep respect for the other's capabilities. Those traits had enabled them to work together in building the best-trained company in the battalion.

"I'm depending on you and this poor excuse for a SNCO to come back and share what you've learned," the old man continued. "Now, get the hell out of my office and execute your orders!"

Part I

Commando Basic Training Centre, Achnacarry, Scotland

1

Waterloo Station, London, England, 1800, 5 August 1942—"Let's stretch our legs and get something to eat," Cain proposed, as their train pulled into London's Waterloo Station. They had just spent several uncomfortable hours on the train from Southampton, jammed in a coach with dozens of chain-smoking, raucous British soldiers, and they were tired, hungry, and badly in need of fresh air. They had time to kill—the London, Midland and Scottish train that would take them to Spean Bridge Station, seven miles from the Commando Basic Training Centre at Achnacarry in the rugged Highlands of northwest Scotland, was not scheduled to leave for another couple of hours. Cain slipped the elderly conductor a few coins to keep an eye on their seabags and stepped onto the platform.

"Look at that!" Montgomery exclaimed, pointing to the blackened and scorched steel girders at the end of the station. They walked closer to the boarded-off section.

"Incendiaries," Cain declared, pointing upward to the twisted beams that once held a large section of the demolished roof. "Looks like the bomb hit right there," he said, indicating to the most heavily damaged supports. "It exploded and scattered the incendiaries all over this end of the track. It's a wonder the fire crews were able to save the building."

Montgomery nodded in agreement. "Fucking Nazis," he exclaimed.

The station was a beehive of activity; trains pulling in and out, passengers laden with baggage rushing toward the platforms, porters pushing loaded trolleys, and the stampede of hundreds of uniformed servicemen scurrying to catch the last trains before nightfall. As the two Americans strolled across the busy concourse, Cain spotted a British soldier and his girlfriend in a passionate embrace, seemingly oblivious to the hubbub swirling around them. The soldier broke away and ran off to board a departing train, leaving the woman dabbing her eyes with a handkerchief. No one in the crowded station seemed to take notice of the parting; the scene was all too familiar, repeated hundreds, perhaps thousands of times a day. The men walked outside in the lengthening shadows, hoping to find someone who could tell them where they could get something to eat. They spotted a policeman standing near a wall of sandbags protecting the front of the station's World War I Victory Arch. "The King's Arms, corner of the second road on the right," the bobby told them, pointing up the street. "Be alert, Yanks," he warned, "Jerry may be around tonight." The two Marines walked along a shabby block of apartment buildings that had sandbags stacked as high as the second story in an effort to protect them from bomb blasts. Halfway down the street, a heap of rubble filled a massive hole between two of the drab buildings.

"Bomb," Montgomery uttered, pointing to the adjoining brick walls. A repair crew had installed temporary wooden trusses to shore them up. "See how the walls are scored and charred by the blast? It's a wonder they didn't all collapse."

The two continued down the street, passing other buildings that had been damaged by near-misses. One flat had lost its rooftop to an incendiary bomb. Two stirrup pumps that had been used to try and extinguish the blaze were still propped up against the side of the building. Remarkably, its taped windows were still intact. An iconic poster of a grim-faced Winston Churchill making a "V" sign with his hand was framed in one window, while a photo of the king and queen was displayed in another. Further along the road, Montgomery spotted a plaque bearing the English royal coat of arms suspended over an ancient oaken entranceway.

"Must be the place," he said, "I can smell the beer from here."

Montgomery pulled open the heavily carved, multi-paneled door and groped his way through the heavy blackout curtain. Inside, a smoke-filled narrow room ran the length of the building. A scuffed oaken bar and several wooden tables covered with bottle rings filled the room. The bar itself was on the right, tables and chairs on the left.

"My God, it's a museum," Cain mouthed, crowding in behind Montgomery. It was like being transported back in time. Shadow boxes held period British military uniforms and scores of regimental cap badges and shoulder flashes; framed paintings depicting long-ago battles lined the walls; and captured battle flags hung from the low-beamed ceiling.

"Have you ever seen so many weapons?" Montgomery said, staring at racks of swords, pikes, and halberds. "No wonder the place is called the King's Arms." An early crowd of boisterous soldiers and older men in dated suits occupied the stout wooden tables, drinking pints of ale. A cheerful fire blazed in a fireplace against the back wall.

The level of conversation dropped as the patrons turned to stare at the newcomers making their way through the thick, smoke-laden air to a vacant spot at the ancient oak bar that bore the dents and scratches of thirsty men.

"What'll you have, mate?" the bartender asked Montgomery in a heavy Cockney accent.

"Beer," Montgomery answered, "and anything you have on hand to eat."

"Sorry, Yank," the man replied, "ale we have, but food is rationed and I don't know how long the ale will last either." The two Americans were taken aback by the comment. They hadn't realized there was a food shortage.

"How bad is it?" Cain asked the man, as he filled two mugs from the draft pump behind the bar.

"Let me put it this way," he replied, handing them the tankards, "there aren't many fat people left in England."

They found a small table near the fire that had been conveniently abandoned by a couple of the locals, and sat back to enjoy the drinks. A radio played the current hit song, "We'll Meet Again," by Vera Lynn. "The Forces Sweetheart," as she was known, was mostly ignored by the boisterous crowd intent on their own conversations.

The Marines were halfway through their second pints when the throaty wail of a siren cut through the hubbub. It shrieked and howled, unrelenting in its urgency. The patrons stopped talking instantly and unconsciously looked up at the ceiling, as if they could see German bombers overhead. There was a long moment of silence.

"Air raid," the bartender announced matter-of-factly, "please make your way to a shelter." Cain and Montgomery followed the line of patrons into the pitch-black street. Off in the distance, a searchlight probed the clouds in an attempt to catch a raider in its beam.

"Where the hell is the shelter?" Montgomery voiced.

A man in civilian clothes appeared out of the darkness. He had on an armband and wore a flat helmet painted with a white "W," signifying he was an air raid warden. "This way, lads, and be quick about it," the warden told them nervously. "Jerry is on the way." The deep rhythmic note of powerful engines accentuated his warning. A nearby battery of QF 3.7-inch antiaircraft guns began firing their 28-pound high-explosive shells at the German bomber formation three miles above their heads. Parachute flares suddenly blossomed over the railroad station, followed by the mechanical scream of heavy missiles hurtling toward the ground.

"No time," the warden shouted, "get down!" A series of shattering explosions erupted all around them. Clusters of incendiaries burst into dazzling white pinpoints of intense light. Yellow flames leaped up from a house at the end of the street. Burning embers rose into the sky, carried by the wind from building to building until the entire block was on fire.

A young boy spotted the men and ran toward them screaming hysterically, "Mummy, Daddy … please help them."

Cain grabbed the wild-eyed youngster and called out, "Where are they?" The panic-stricken youngster pointed to a three-story apartment building halfway down the street. Its upper story was fully engulfed in flames.

"Come on, Gunny," Cain yelled, "let's see what we can do!" The two Americans ran toward the searing heat. They reached the building and found a man lying halfway out of the doorway. Montgomery grabbed the limp form and pulled it out of the building.

"I'm going inside!" Cain shouted, and darted into a hallway that was thick with black smoke. He sucked in a lungful of it and was immediately racked by a spate of coughing. He dropped to the floor where it was easier to breathe and crawled further into the house. A body lay on the floor. He reached out and pulled it toward him, straining with the effort. The heat was intense and he feared he would not get out before he was overcome. He slowly inched back down the hallway, dragging the body, but his strength was giving out. Flames filled the end of the corridor. He was losing consciousness. "Can't breathe," he muttered, and passed out.

"Skipper, where the hell are you?!" Montgomery shouted, trying to spot the officer in the dense cloud pouring from the entrance. He took a deep breath and plunged blindly into the smoke-filled hallway, determined to rescue Cain. He took three steps and stumbled over Cain's body. He grabbed his ankles and started pulling the limp form toward the doorway. "Damn you're heavy," he grunted, and then realized that the officer had wrapped his arms in a tight embrace around the figure of a woman and wouldn't let go. Montgomery redoubled his efforts and managed to slide the two bodies to the doorway before he blacked out. A member of the Auxiliary Fire Service that had just arrived saw him emerge from the burning building and called for help. Several rescuers loaded the three bodies onto stretchers and carried them to a mobile first aid post a block from fire. Women Red Cross volunteers administered first aid.

Cain slowly regained consciousness. He opened his eyes and peered into the face of an angel.

"I must be dead," he rasped. "But if I'm dead, how come I feel like shit?"

The face broke into a smile. "You Yanks are never at a loss for words," the pretty volunteer replied. Cain tried to rise but she pushed him back down. "You need to rest," she said. "You've had a close call."

"How come he gets all the attention?" Montgomery chimed in. "I'm the one with smoke in my lungs."

The girl laughed. "You soldiers are all alike," she answered cheekily, with a toss of her head, and started to walk away.

"Wait," Cain called out. "What about the woman?"

The volunteer turned around; her smile was gone. "She's been taken to the hospital with severe burns," she replied solemnly. "All I know is she's still alive."

Minutes later, a fire warden appeared and told the two Americans that they would have to evacuate the area. The conflagration was out of control and the firemen were pulling back. Cain looked down the street. The entire block was a raging inferno. The heat was so intense that telephone poles were bursting into flames. They looked like huge torches. A gray fire truck slowly backed down the asphalt street that was already starting to buckle and melt from the heat. A smoldering fire hose lay where it had been abandoned by firemen in their haste to evacuate.

"Come on, Skipper," Montgomery said, "there's nothing we can do here, except get in the way." Cain simply nodded, overcome by the tragedy he was witnessing. They shakily made their way back to the train station, which miraculously had escaped destruction. Their coach was still sitting at the platform. "Might as well go aboard," Cain suggested, as the all-clear sounded. The conductor told them that the train was now not scheduled to depart until daylight.

"Settle in," he told them, "it may be a long night."

2

London, Midland & Scottish Railway, Waterloo Station, Dawn, 6 August 1942—The shriek of an air whistle jolted Cain awake in the middle of a nightmare. He had been dreaming of being caught in the open during an air raid. He jerked upright, confusion registering in his eyes. It took him a moment to realize it was the LM&S's way of reminding everyone that the train was getting underway. The whistle sounded again and the car lurched forward with a crash of its heavy metal couplings. A cloud of gray-black steam and smoke belched out of the powerful engine's stack as it slowly pulled the 12 packed coaches out of Waterloo Station. The passengers, mostly servicemen and women, were quiet, either asleep or simply too tired to talk to one another after the exertions of the night. The only sound was the *clack-clack … clack-clack* of the metal wheels passing over the tiny gaps between the steel rails.

The train cleared the covered station into a scene of utter destruction. Block after block of bomb-damaged and shattered buildings came into view. Piles of rubble partially blocked the streets. "My God," Cain murmured to himself, shocked by the devastation. Flames still flickered through jagged gaps of half-destroyed walls. Firemen played streams of water on the smoldering debris, while exhausted rescue crews sifted through the wreckage searching for trapped survivors. The spires of a bombed-out church stood as a somber memorial to those who died in the raid. He spotted a solemn-faced stretcher party carrying a blanket-clad body toward an ambulance. Further along, he saw a gutted street car teetering on the edge of a huge bomb crater. The worst sight was perhaps the dozens of numbed survivors wandering aimlessly through the destruction pushing carts loaded with a few pitiful possessions they had salvaged from their demolished homes. Cain nudged Montgomery and pointed to where the King's Arms had once stood. The street was nothing but a pile of rubble.

Within a hundred yards, the train was flagged down. A group of railroad workers were busy clearing the track of bomb debris with hand tools.

"Look, they're all women," Montgomery said, pointing out the window at the husky girls dressed in filthy coveralls and billed caps that covered their hair.

The train's conductor, who happened to be passing by, explained, "There's such a shortage of men that women are doing much of the repair work. The rest of us are either too old or disabled." Cain spotted the World War I service pin on the elderly man's uniform. "Chlorine gas, damaged my lungs at Ypres in 1915," he said, noticing the Yank's curious look. "The Huns launched the gas attack at sunrise. We saw a strange green cloud wafting toward us. We didn't know what it was until the men started dropping, unable to breathe. I was fortunate that I only got a little whiff but it was enough to scar my lungs and keep me out of the current dustup."

After 20 minutes, the train was cleared to proceed. Once out of the city, it picked up speed. The Tommies immediately adhered to the old soldier's maxim that one should take advantage of any and all opportunities to eat and sleep. Cain was amazed that so many men could actually find a place to doze amongst the jumble of rifles, packs, pouches, boots, and bodies that filled every available cubic inch of space. There was barely enough room to squeeze through the aisles. He and Montgomery were lucky to "rescue" two seats across from a pair of curious Royal Marines.

"Are you Yanks?" the large, red-faced corporal asked in a rich, rolling brogue while staring directly at the eagle, globe, and anchor insignia stenciled on the left breast pocket of Montgomery's herringbone twill jacket.

"U.S. Marines," the gunny answered, sticking out his hand and introducing himself and the captain.

"Blimey, what's an officer doing in the 2nd-class car?" the Brit asked incredulously, surprised by the American's friendliness.

"The gunny sergeant and I always travel together," Cain responded casually. "And you are?"

"I'm Corporal Finch and this here is Marine Hawkins from No. 40 Commando," Finch said, pointing to a fresh-faced youngster sitting next to him. "We're on our way to the Commando Depot."

Montgomery nodded. "That's where we're headed," he said.

Six hours after leaving Waterloo Station, the train slowed. The conductor came through the car announcing there would be a change of locomotives at the next station, giving everyone the opportunity to stretch their legs and get some food from a Red Cross canteen that had been set up close to the tracks. The news was greeted by a rousing cheer from the soldiers. They had not eaten since the previous evening and were starved. When the train stopped, they made a mad dash for the food carts.

"Queue up, lads," a huge Red Cap sergeant bellowed, stopping the men in their tracks. "There's enough food for everyone."

A formidable-looking matron held court over the serving line. "Now, boys," she said sternly, "behave, I don't want to have to tell your mothers." The admonition worked. The men each gratefully accepted two corned beef sandwiches and a mug of tea, with a respectful, "Thank you, Mum," and quietly moved along. Within minutes, they were surrounded by curious youngsters from the village, much to the delight of the soldiers; some of the senior NCOs had children of their own.

A whistle blast summoned the riders back aboard the cars. After the refreshments, the men were in high spirits. Card games flourished and lively chatter filled the carriage. At one end of the car a group of Welsh soldiers started singing and before long the entire car was belting out the favorites—"Pack Up Your Troubles," "We'll Meet Again," "There'll Always Be an England"—with a gusto that surprised and amused the two Americans.

Finch noticed the two were not singing. "Hey, Yanks," he chided, "join us." Cain was game but Montgomery looked like he had swallowed a lemon.

"Come on, Guns," Cain encouraged, "singing won't hurt your image."

"I don't know the words," Montgomery offered in defense, just as the inhabitants of the car broke into, "It's a Long Way to Tipperary."

"It's your song," Cain said, knowing the older man had enlisted a few years after World War I, when the tune was in its heyday. Cain was taken aback when Montgomery started singing in a rich baritone voice.

"Church choir," Montgomery sheepishly admitted later.

Finch, the inquisitive Royal Marine, peppered the gunny with questions about everything under the sun, which gave Cain the opportunity to scrutinize the passengers. Except for a sprinkling of older NCOs, most of the men were young. He guessed their ages ranged between 19 and 20. Physically, they reminded him of his own Raiders, whipcord lean—no fat men in the infantry—and medium height. Most of them had survived the evacuation of Dunkirk and had the confident bearing and look of seasoned combat veterans. They wore heavy brown wool, two-piece uniforms. Most had shed their blouses in the overheated car for a khaki wool shirt, but kept their trousers tucked into gaiters. They all wore the heavy ankle-high hobnail "ammunition" boots. Cain was particularly interested in the bewildering array of cap badges—forage caps, service dress caps, berets, and many Tam O'Shanters—that seemed to represent every unit in the British Army.

Finch finally ran out of questions, which gave Montgomery an opportunity to ask him about his service. "My first posting after training was HMS *Royal Oak*," Finch began. "I was a rear rank Marine and spent my first six months just learning the ins and outs of battleship duty." Montgomery nodded knowingly. He had served on USS *West Virginia*, *Wee Vee* as she was known, and had suffered the usual "fun and games" that were played on new men. He remembered scouring the ship's engineering spaces for a left-handed monkey wrench, much to the delight of the old-timers.

Finch grew serious. "Sergeant Montgomery, you are the first person I've talked to about that night," he said. "I feel miserable when I think of my friends who were lost. It has unsettled me and left me with nightmares. I was aboard *Oak* the night she was torpedoed in Scapa Flow."

Montgomery had heard about how a German submarine managed to slip inside the anchorage and put four torpedoes into the huge ship.

Finch continued, "I was on the midnight to 0400 watch when I heard a muffled explosion in the forward part of the ship. All of the plates in the ship rang against each other and the whole ship shuddered."

Montgomery thought about *Wee Vee* when the torpedoes slammed into her hull on 7 December, and the pandemonium as she started to settle. *Thank God for the ship's first lieutenant*, he thought. His order to counter-flood kept the ship from rolling over. Instead, she settled into the mud right side up, saving hundreds of men from being trapped below.

"I ran forward to the Marines' mess deck," Finch continued. "Several of my mates were turning out of their hammocks but most stayed where they were. I guess they didn't want to get up in the middle of the night. I went from there to the quarterdeck where there was a faint smell of cordite. Suddenly, there was another explosion and a flash. The entire ship shuddered and debris shot into the air. It was followed almost immediately by another explosion and the ship started to heel over. Dense flames and acrid smoke swept over the quarterdeck, choking me."

Montgomery identified with Finch's description. He vividly recalled his own experience as smoke and flames swept over the forward part of *West Virginia* from burning fuel escaping from the sunken *Arizona*. He was the captain's orderly on the bridge when the attack started. A bomb exploded on *Tennessee* moored 50 yards away on the starboard side. Jagged shards of shrapnel flew across the divide and scythed through the men on the bridge, barely missing Montgomery, who was standing behind a steel girder. The captain fell mortally wounded, with a hole in his chest big enough to put a fist in. Other dead and dying men sprawled on the deck. It was a scene right out of a horror movie. He knew exactly what Finch had experienced.

Finch's voice cracked with emotion. "The ship was heeling over to starboard and I couldn't keep my footing on the deck. I ran to the port rail and tried to hang on. The ship started to roll over, so I climbed up on the rail and ran down her side. Men were trying to scramble out of the portholes, but couldn't get clear. It was awful." He paused to catch his breath and then began again. "I could see flames inside the ship. We could only help a few before the ship turned over. I scrambled onto the keel and jumped into the water as far as I could, but as she sunk, the suction dragged me under. I kicked and struggled and finally made it to the surface just as I was about to pass out." Montgomery stared at Finch. He had a faraway look in his eyes. The youngster was reliving a nightmare.

"The sea was thick with heads and there were cries for help all around," Finch recounted. "I swam to get away from them, and found a piece of wood to hold onto. The water was so cold that I began to lose the feeling in my legs. Finally, a boat came near and someone spotted me. They picked me up more dead than alive. I spent two months in hospital before I was released back to my unit."

Damn, Montgomery thought, *no wonder the youngster has nightmares*, and although he wouldn't admit it, he had a few flashbacks of his own, but nothing like Finch's. His dreams usually involved wrapping his hands around a Jap's neck and squeezing the shit out of the bastard!

Their conversation tapered off as they both gazed out the window while the train thundered northward, mile after mile through the sparsely populated Scottish Highlands. The roadbed followed a route across the center of the country toward the west coast, past tiny isolated Highland villages—Crianlarich, Tyndrum, Bridge of Orchy, Loch Treig—rugged, snow-covered mountains, across fast-flowing rivers, and large open expanses overgrown with colorful heather and gorse that swathed the Rannoch Moor. The skies were gray, threatening snow, and filled with low-hanging clouds. Cain shivered, remembering other godforsaken places where he had frozen his ass off.

"The moor is a beastly place, cold and dangerous," Finch said. "It's not a place to wander around. There are ghosts."

"You're bullshitting me," Montgomery scoffed.

"Nay, sergeant, it's true, just ask the Jocks," he replied earnestly, pointing to two Highland soldiers at the end of the car. "They grew up on the moor and know it like the back of their hands." Montgomery shook his head in doubt.

"Hey, lads," Finch called out to them, "come talk to the Yanks about the ghosts on the moor." The two readily agreed and clambered over the gear piled in the aisles and rearranged the packs so they could sit down.

Finch introduced them. "This is Corporal McTavish, King's Own Scottish Borderers, and Lance Corporal MacDonald, Scottish Rifles."

The two seemed to be made from the same mold—solid, an inch above average height, with broad shoulders and heavily muscled arms and legs, which Cain thought was the result of working the hard-scrabble Highland farms. Finch repeated that the moors were haunted and asked the Highlanders to back him up.

"Aye, it's true," McTavish affirmed, in a thick Scottish brogue. "I've seen many a ghost on the moors."

"Give me a break," Montgomery sneered. He'd been around the block too many times to be taken in by a Scottish bullshitter. The Highlander didn't take offense; he had come up against many skeptics in the past.

"I'll tell you what happened to me," he began. "I was on my way home from the pub one night and stopped to pee," he said in a low, measured voice. "Suddenly, I heard the sounds of men walking through the gorse," he added, masterfully building up suspense. "The sounds got closer and closer." His tale attracted soldiers from the surrounding seats, who leaned closer to the storyteller. They were fascinated by his account. "And right in front of me stood four ancient Highland warriors in kilts waving two-handed broadswords." He raised his voice in emphasis. "Scared the hell out of me, I can tell you. Before I could run away, they charged, roaring their battle cries," he said, pausing while he scanned the face of each of the listeners.

"What happened?" one of the soldiers asked impatiently.

"Why, they killed me," the Jock barked, roaring with laughter at the surprised look on the youngster's face. Montgomery joined in the laughter and congratulated the Jock for "a story well told."

3

Spean Bridge Railway Station, Scotland, Late Afternoon, 6 August 1942—The train slowed and the conductor announced that Spean Bridge Station was the next stop and they would arrive in just a few minutes.

"This is us," Finch said enthusiastically. "We get off here and hike to the training center." A ripple of excitement passed through the car. The aisles were quickly filled with men hurrying to don their marching order. Cain glanced out the window as the train rumbled down a slight gradient into the picturesque little station. Seven British NCOs were standing on the raised concrete platform adjacent to the station master's building. A welcoming party, he guessed by their look. They were arranged in two ranks behind a powerfully built soldier bearing three stripes under a small crown insignia on the sleeve of his uniform blouse.

"Colour sergeant," Finch explained. "He's in charge of the detail." Cain took another look at the NCO. The man cut an imposing figure; tall, at least 6 foot 6, and barrel-chested with an outsized head that seemed to sit directly on his broad shoulders. His most striking feature, however, was a beautifully waxed handlebar mustache that extended at least 2 inches on either side of his mouth.

The train came to a complete stop in a squeal of brakes and a cloud of steam. Out of the mist stepped a kilted pipe major skirling "Scotland the Brave" as he marched smartly up and down the platform.

"My God," Montgomery exclaimed, "what the hell is that noise?"

"That, my friend," Cain replied, seeing the effect the piper's music had on the troops in the car, "is music to get your blood stirred up." All the Tommies were jammed against the windows staring at the impressive figure in his regimentals—feathered bonnet, blue tunic with gold piping, Royal Stewart tartan sash, horsehair sporran, and kilt, complete with dirk tucked in the right sock.

"Och, look at the bugger strut," Corporal McTavish exclaimed admiringly. "He's a credit to the Kosbies."

"The what?" Montgomery inquired.

"'Tis the nickname of our unit, the King's Own Scottish Borderers," McTavish replied. "The best outfit in the army." His statement brought a chorus of hoots and jeers from the other soldiers.

The good-natured ribbing was interrupted when one of the NCOs on the platform stepped aboard the car. "Get off the train, you lazy sods, and form up on the platform!" he shouted. "Last man will be returned to unit!" The car exploded with motion. Men tumbled out of the exits in various stages of readiness—some in full kit, others carrying their gear in their arms—while desperately rushing to get in formation. No one wanted to be the last man. The NCOs harried them every step of the way. "Kitbags on the truck and get fell in quickly!"

The two Americans watched the antics with a professional eye. "Remind you of anything, Gunny?" Cain asked.

"Parris Island," Montgomery answered. "Just like new recruits." Both men had served at the Marine Corps recruit depot at Parris Island before the war. Montgomery spent two tours as a drill instructor, while Cain was assigned to oversee the training. The recruit depot experience had gained them an appreciation of the value of quickly establishing control over new men.

The two Americans quickly gathered their gear and stepped off the train into the cool air—but not in the frenzied manner of the British soldiers. Their seemingly casual manner attracted the attention of the colour sergeant, who dispatched one of his underlings to "hustle" them along.

The corporal marched purposely up to the two and, in a loud voice, inquired, "What the bloody hell do you two think you're doing?" At an inch over 6 feet, Montgomery towered over the diminutive NCO, who barely stood 5 feet, 5 inches in his ammunition boots.

"Corporal," Montgomery addressed the midget, as he later referred to him, "you will come to attention and address my officer as 'captain' or 'sir,' and you will address me as 'sergeant,' is that clear?" he said, in a tone of voice that was more statement than question. The corporal did a double take. No new trainee had ever questioned his authority. He looked to the colour sergeant for backup but the NCO chose to ignore him, with a look that spoke volumes—*You got yourself into this, now get yourself out of it.*

Deciding that discretion was the better part of valor, the corporal stood to attention in front of Cain and saluted. "Begging your pardon, sir," he began, "would you and the sergeant be good enough to join the formation?"

"Certainly," Cain replied amiably, returning the salute. The two walked over to the extreme right of the formation and took position as their seniority dictated. They outranked everyone in the formation. Truck engines coughed into life. One of the men mistakenly thought the lorries were for them and mentioned to his mate that their transport had arrived. Unfortunately, his comment was overheard by a cadre member. "Transport, transport? Good God," he bellowed contemptuously, "they're for your kit, you twit," and turned away in disgust.

The colour sergeant stepped forward. "We are going on a little stroll," he roared, his size and booming voice instantly gaining attention. "Anyone who drops out will be returned to unit."

Finch, who had placed himself directly behind Montgomery, whispered, "Little stroll my foot, it's a 7-mile forced march." Without a further word, the colour sergeant ordered the formation to face right. "Forward march!" he hollered, and stepped out in front of the formation. He immediately set a furious pace that caused the formation to stretch out. Gaps appeared. The colour sergeant's NCOs dogged the column yelling "Close up! Close up!" The men struggled to maintain the pace, particularly the shorter ones. They were often forced to double time just to keep up. Cain and Montgomery were long-legged and were able to maintain the pace without difficulty. However, the soles of their feet had softened due to a lack of exercise on board the ship to Great Britain and so started to develop blisters.

The column passed through the village, past the Spean Bridge Hotel and over a wooden bridge spanning the Caledonian Canal. The road rose steadily in a back-bending, stamina-sapping climb through hills that seemed to go on forever. Finch declared that there were no down slopes on the hills; they just went up on both sides. Not one of the miserable soldiers disputed it; they simply shook their heads in agreement. Signs of civilization soon disappeared—no farms, no cultivation, just bracken, trees, and hills … never-ending hills. By the third mile, Cain could feel a blister forming on the heel of his left foot. "Shit," he mumbled quietly, pissed because he never got blisters. *Nothing to do but gut it out*, he told himself. Forty-five minutes into the march, the men were looking forward to a break. It was laid down in the King's Regulations that the army was to take a 15-minute break every hour while on the march, but it was obvious that the colour sergeant was going to ignore the regulations. He kept up the blistering speed.

"What's the pace?" Cain asked.

"It must be at least 6 miles an hour," Montgomery answered. "A real ball buster!"

The only sound from the column was the shout, "Close up!" and the crunch of boots on the unyielding roadway. The march began to tell. Faces turned red, breathing became labored. The men were too focused on putting one foot in front of the other to talk. A long line of stragglers followed the column, some limping from blisters, others too played out to continue, and a few who just plain quit. None of the colour sergeant's NCOs paid them any mind. Either the stragglers caught up, or they would be returned to unit. The march was the first of many tests to come. There was no time for slackers, no second chances. Only the fittest, most strong-willed, and daring survived to become commandos. Cain looked at the men's faces around him. They showed the strain of the march—expressions of pain and misery—and determination.

"How are your feet?" he whispered to Montgomery.

"Hamburger," he responded, "it's these damn new boondockers. They aren't broken in yet."

"You gonna make it?" Cain asked.

"It'll be a cold day in hell before I let that Limey bastard outwalk me," Montgomery declared angrily.

Twenty minutes later, the front of the column crested a hill and spotted their final destination laid out in the valley below. "Achnacarry," Finch uttered. A magnificent, centuries-old stone mansion stood on the bank of a river that flowed into a picturesque loch. A chain of daunting and desolate mountainous terrain flanked the low ground. One immense peak stood out, towering over the others. Montgomery pointed to the turrets and battlements running along the roofline of the two-story building. "It looks like a castle," he remarked.

"Just a wee place in the country," Finch jested, and then added seriously, "It's a Highland treasure. The chief of the Cameron Clan lived here for 250 years until the government appropriated the building and grounds to use as a training center for the duration of the war." He pointed to the large Union Jack that fluttered from a parapet. "It's the first time English troops have occupied the manor since the mid-1700s when they burned and ravaged the castle."

The mansion's previously landscaped lawn and gardens were cluttered with dozens of green-painted Nissen huts arranged in orderly rows that gave the place a decided military appearance. Dozens of soldiers were drilling under the watchful eyes of NCOs on an expanse of a tarmac parade ground in front of the huts. Other squads were double-timing to and fro, directed by cadre wearing distinctive green berets. The faint crack of small-arms fire and the dull thump of explosions confirmed the presence of firearms and demolition ranges.

The pace quickened. Cain didn't know if it was because of the downhill grade or just the colour sergeant's nastiness, but it made very little difference, for the end result was the same. The speed of the march had separated the men from the boys. The formation had shrunk by half. A long line of forlorn stragglers stretched as far as he could see. They had little chance of catching up before the column reached the training center. They would be "returned to unit" with no appeal. Cain risked a glance at the survivors. Their faces registered a grim resolve to keep going, despite exhaustion and pain. They were the type of men that the commandos wanted. He looked at Montgomery and saw the same look. "How are your feet?" he asked.

"They never felt better, Skipper," the SNCO replied sarcastically, "just like yours."

Cain grunted. "You lie like a rug, old man," he replied through clenched teeth. His foot hurt like hell and he had no doubt that his boondocker was filled with blood.

A quarter mile from the center's gated entrance way, the colour sergeant halted the column. "All right, lads, smarten up!" he bellowed. "We'll march into camp looking like British soldiers."

He dressed ranks while his NCOs blocked the road, keeping the stragglers from joining the formation. They were to be formed up and trucked back to Spean Bridge to catch a train back to their units. Satisfied with the appearance of the column, the colour sergeant ordered "Forward march!" The men stepped off as if they were on parade—heads up, shoulders back, rifles at the slope with the exaggerated arm swing of the British Army. The strike of the steel-shod heels of their ammunition boots on the roadway served as a cadence. They entered the camp in perfect formation. Only those men who had made the speed march on bruised and bloodied feet could understand what that last quarter mile had cost them.

Just inside the gate, along a treelined driveway, they passed a long row of well-kept "graves." Each grave was marked by a wooden headstone bearing a painted epitaph that began with, "This man," and ended with the supposed cause of death—"failed to keep his rifle clean," "showed himself on the skyline," or "was too slow to take cover"—all stark reminders that the training they were to undergo was designed to keep bad things from happening to them.

"Blimey," Finch despaired, "they've frightened me half to death already."

McTavish piped up, "Jesus, the bastards kill us on the march from the railroad, and when we get here they bury us!"

After being dismissed, the men hobbled off to their billets. The two Americans joined the procession, walking gingerly to a Nissen hut.

4

Commando Basic Training Centre, Achnacarry, Scotland, 1900, 6 August 1942—The Nissen hut was familiar to the Americans. It reminded them of the Quonset huts that housed the Marine recruits at the training depots. The hut was made of prefabricated steel bent into half a cylinder resting on a concrete slab foundation. The ends were closed in by a wooden frame that contained an entrance door and two windows. Inside, steel cots lined both sides of a narrow passageway. Grimy mattresses rested on metal bands attached to the cot by springs. An open wooden locker was positioned between each cot. There was no insulation; the only heat came from a pot-bellied, coal-burning stove that stood in the middle of the hut. A chimney pipe directed the smoke upward through the metal ceiling. Several bare light bulbs were strung from an electric line that ran down the center of the hut. They served as the only light. A small enclosed room was located in the far end of the hut. The room contained five "open seating" commodes and a long galvanized metal trough that served as the urinal. Five taps supplied cold water to a waist-high sink made from the same cheap metal as the "pisser." Accommodations were spartan to say the least.

The two Americans dropped their gear on an empty cot and sat down to unlace their boondockers. Cain eased the left shoe off first.

His white sock was stained with blood and he had a devil of a time trying to take it off. The sock was stuck to the raw flesh on his heel.

"Here, let me help you," Montgomery said, reaching over and yanking the sock off, without as much as a by your leave.

"Damn that smarts," Cain swore mightily.

"Don't be such a wimp," the gunny replied with a malicious grin.

"OK, your turn," Cain remarked. "Let's see those feet." Montgomery shed his boots. "Now we'll see who the wimp is."

Just at that moment, a soldier approached. "Need some help?" he asked. "I'm one of the CMTs. Medic," he added quickly, after noticing Cain's quizzical look. Without waiting for an answer, he knelt and examined Montgomery's feet. "Nasty," he muttered, and immediately went to work. After lancing the blisters, he applied an antibiotic ointment, dressed the area with sterile gauze, and taped it in place. "That should fix you up, mate," he remarked. He glanced at the gunny's boots. "Better work on those shoes, Yank. If you don't soften them up, you'll continue to have problems."

If looks could kill, the man would have been dead. The medic had touched a nerve. Montgomery prided himself on maintaining his feet, adhering to the philosophy that the infantry did not travel on its stomach, but on its feet. The CMT ignored the gunny's murderous look and attended to Cain before moving on to help the other sufferers.

"If this keeps up," Cain remarked, "he'll have quite a practice built up."

Cain sat back on the thin mattress and surveyed the room. Most of the men were busy arranging their equipment in the lockers but several were waiting patiently for the medic to tend to their feet. One or two others looked completely disoriented, as if they were trying to decide if commando training was right for them. Finch, the old salt, had already stowed his gear and was in the process of assisting his buddy when he noticed the two Americans were not unpacking.

26

"What's up, captain?" he asked innocently. "Waiting for your batman to set you up?"

Cain laughed. "Sorry to disappoint you, corporal, but we're expecting to move to the high-rent district tomorrow."

"Cor," Finch exclaimed, "just as I was getting to know you." At that moment, the door flew open and an instructor stuck his head in and yelled something that sounded like "Waffle" to Montgomery. "What the hell did he say?"

"Yaffle," Finch repeated, "food. It's time to eat."

The hut exploded with activity. The men were starved and rushed out the door, only to be met by a Colour Sergeant Bourne and several of his NCOs.

"Where the bloody hell do you think you're going?!" he roared. His shout stopped the men in their tracks. "Fall in," he commanded. The men quickly got into formation and the "colour," as he was called by the British soldiers, briefed them on the next day's schedule—"a little stroll after breakfast, followed by classes in the afternoon"—and then he marched them to chow. The cookhouse was located in a large Nissen hut adjacent to the parade ground. A line of hungry men stretched out the door.

"Blimey," Finch exclaimed, "the scran'll all be gone by the time we get inside."

"Worried are you, Finch?" Bourne asked sarcastically. "Afraid you'll miss supper?"

"No, colour sergeant," he replied contritely, "I didn't want the American Marines to miss out on our fine army rations." Bourne stepped closer and glared intensely at the younger man before turning and marching away.

"I'm in for it now," Finch muttered glumly.

The line of men moved steadily and in less than a quarter of an hour the two Americans found themselves inside the crowded cookhouse. Plywood tables and benches filled the center of the room, while a serving line ran along one wall. Finch led the way to a table stacked high with tin trays and stainless-steel flatware. They picked up eating utensils and moved along the row of vat cans.

"Great!" Finch exclaimed. "Bangers and mash."

"What the hell are you talking about?" Montgomery asked.

"Sausage and mashed potatoes," he replied, "with onion gravy and baked beans, just like my mum used to make." Cain chuckled at the remark and nudged the gunny to hustle along, as he was holding up the queue. As Montgomery moved along the line of servers, he received a scoop of lumpy mashed potatoes, two greasy sausages, a cup of baked beans, and a ladle of gravy that was dumped all over the concoction. At the end of the line, he reluctantly grabbed a mug of weak tea from a large urn.

"What kind of a mess hall doesn't serve coffee?" he groused.

The Americans found two seats and started eating. The noise from so many men in the small space was so loud that they didn't bother talking. They just concentrated on shoveling the barely eatable "slop," as Montgomery called it, into their mouths. Ten minutes later, they were on their way back to the hut when one of the training cadre stopped them.

"Gentlemen, if you would follow me, please, the quartermaster sergeant will issue your uniforms and equipment." They followed the NCO to a hut that contained bins filled with equipment. Uniforms were stacked on shelves that lined the walls.

A heavyset storeman carefully "eyed" them as they entered the building. "Forty-two long," he said, pulling a green-and-brown fiber, wool serge jacket off a shelf and sliding it toward Cain. "Thirty-six waist and thirty-six inseam should do it," he added confidently, handing the officer a pair of trousers. "Put them on," he ordered officiously. Turning to Montgomery, he looked him up and down and picked a jacket and trousers from the shelf and handed them to the gunny with the same admonition. The two undressed and shrugged into the uniforms. Surprisingly, they fit rather well.

"Come this way," the supply clerk ordered, leading them to a line of bins. He handed each of the Americans a haversack. "Put the equipment in it," he directed, "you can sort it out later." Pouches, gas cape, gas mask, bayonet, a steel helmet, water bottle, belt, suspenders, and gaiters soon followed and were stuffed into the haversack.

"Sit, please, and take off your boots," he instructed. "What is your shoe size?" He returned with two pairs of boots. Cain examined his pair. The unlined ankle-length boots had leather laces, steel heel-plates and toe-plates, and iron-studded leather soles. "They sure as hell aren't made for comfort," he said.

Montgomery agreed, thinking of his aching feet. "The damn things will last longer than my feet," he replied.

The clerk loudly cleared his throat, his way of registering his displeasure with the gunny's comment. "Gentlemen, would you be so kind as to gather the rest of your kit, I'm late for an appointment at the pub." The two Americans staggered to their hut, where their new-found buddies "put them together."

Cain was sound asleep when the hut's door was flung open and "one of those damn pipers came marching through, I thought I would have a heart attack!" as he later wrote in a report to his battalion commander. "The screech brought me right out of the rack." Montgomery swore that he'd get the guy if it was the last thing he did. Both men grabbed their shaving gear and rushed for the head, only to find it already jammed with their hut mates. It was so crowded that Montgomery swore that he shaved someone else in the crush of bodies. The water was so cold that washing up was done at the "double quick." Nature called, but Cain took one look at the exposed "crappers" and decided to hold it until a more convenient time. Within minutes, one of the cadre stuck his head through the hatch and shouted to get outside for PT.

—✦—

Commandant's Office, 1000, 7 August 1942—Lieutenant Colonel Rupert "Laird of Achnacarry" Moss OBE, Royal Welsh Fusiliers was bent over his desk studying a packet of record books when there was a thunderous bash on his office door.

"Enter," he said gruffly, his voice registering mild annoyance at being interrupted. The heavy oak door swung open and Colour Sergeant Bourne, wearing the standard wartime uniform—heavy gray-green woolen trousers, battledress blouse, and green beret with the commando insignia—marched in, his heavy ammunition boots thundering on the wooden floor. He came to a stop at the regulation three paces from the desk, stomped to attention, and rendered a crisp parade ground salute.

"Sir," he bellowed in a Scottish brogue so thick that Moss often despaired of ever fully understanding the man. "The American Marines are here," he announced, as if an invasion force was just outside the door.

"Bring them in, colour sergeant," Moss answered formally.

"Sir," Bourne boomed, acknowledging the order. He saluted, executed a textbook facing movement, and marched purposely out of the office, shutting the door with enough force to shake the frame.

Moss shook his head in wonderment. He had tried, without success, to encourage the colour sergeant to be more informal. "Commando headquarters is not Buckingham Palace," he had once pointed out. Bourne had acknowledged the comment with a snappy salute that would have done His Majesty's Life Guards proud.

Despite his failed attempt to rein in the colour sergeant, no one mistook Rupert Moss for being a shrinking violet. He was a tall man, heavily built, with a broad face and broken nose that tilted slightly to the right. A little scar tissue around his brows gave him the appearance

30

of a hard-edged brawler. His voice was soft unless he was angered, and then it changed to a roar that could be heard across a parade field. He was a highly decorated veteran who had survived the brutal bloodbath of the trenches of the Great War to become a drill sergeant in the fabled Coldstream Guards and regimental sergeant major in the Brigade of Guards. Along the way, his obvious military potential as an officer had been recognized and he was duly commissioned. He was hand-selected to be Achnacarry's commandant and took over the position with a vengeance. He demanded the highest standards and accepted nothing but the best. In his welcoming speech, Moss promised that by the time "you lot leave Achnacarry, you will have had the best training in the world. As graduates, you will belong to the finest troops in this war—the commandos. When the time comes for you to face the Hun and he sees the determined glint in your eyes and the cold steel of your bayonet, he'll drop his rifle and run like the hounds of hell are after him!"

Moss, anticipating another of Bourne's dramatic entrances, rose from his chair and started for the door but he was not quick enough. The door frame shook under Bourne's assault. "Come in," Moss said quickly, hoping to forestall replacing the 200-year-old oak door. Bourne started to march in but was taken by surprise because Moss half-blocked the entranceway. He recovered in time to come to attention and salute.

Before he could report, Moss calmly asked the two uniformed men behind him to, "Please come in and have a seat," pointing to an arrangement of chairs and an old stuffed sofa in front of a stone fireplace, alight with a cheery fire that barely took the chill out of his office. "Colour sergeant, I'd like you to join us," he added, beckoning Bourne out of the doorway.

The first Marine entered. "Sir, I'm Captain Jim Cain," the officer declared, "and this is Gunnery Sergeant Leland Montgomery."

The men shook hands. "Welcome to Achnacarry Castle, gentlemen," Moss greeted them warmly, and ushered them toward the seats.

"Captain Cain, I received a personal message from my old friend, Red Mike Edson, asking me to keep an eye on you two," he began. "In fact, his exact words were, 'Jim Cain and Gunny Montgomery will need close supervision at all times to keep them out of trouble.'"

"Sir," Cain stammered, "you know what a jokester Major Edson is."

"I didn't know that," Moss replied straight faced.

After Moss took a wooden chair with his back to the fireplace, the three junior men had to sort out who would sit where, which was no small feat. Cain quickly grabbed the other chair, which left the two enlisted men with a battered sofa that had seen better days. The old springs gave way under their combined weight, leaving them with their knees almost touching their chins. Cain smiled inwardly as the two uncomfortable sergeants struggled to maintain some semblance of soldierly deportment. He detected a hint of a smile on the colonel's face. *I believe Moss enjoys Bourne's discomfort*, he thought.

The colonel's batman entered the room. "Tea, colonel?" he asked.

"Will you gentlemen join me?" Moss enquired, although the invitation was a mere formality—who wouldn't say yes to a man at least two ranks senior to you in his own headquarters?

"Yes, sir," the Marines answered together, although both were dying for a hot cup of coffee. The batman quietly left the room.

"Let me tell you about this school," Moss began. "Training is designed to develop individual fighting initiative, and is based entirely on offensive principles. The training program seeks the development, to the very highest possible degree, of stamina and endurance under any operating conditions and in all types of climate. Its goal is to hone individual military skills, as well as to develop special skills, namely: combat marksmanship, close combat, demolition, breaching obstacles, and conducting raids." He paused. "I understand that you both volunteered to be here."

"Yes, sir," they answered in unison, although Major Edson had done the volunteering for them. "We were chosen by Major Edson to attend the school and pass on what we learn here."

"Excellent," Moss replied, "I believe you will find that my instructors are first-rate and totally dedicated. All of them are combat veterans and anxious to pass on what they have learned fighting the Hun."

The batman arrived with the tea. He passed out large steaming mugs and silently departed. *This should be fun*, Cain thought, as he watched the two enlisted men trying to balance the mugs without spilling the boiling hot tea in their laps.

"Now, tell me a little about yourselves," Moss requested. He nodded at Cain, who gave him a rundown on his Marine background.

"Colonel, I joined the Marine Corps in 1938, shortly after graduating from college. After officer training at Philadelphia, I was assigned to the 4th Marine Regiment in Shanghai's International Settlement."

The colonel leaned forward. "And Saint David," he said, reciting the traditional greeting between the Fusiliers and the Marines on the latter organization's birthday.

"Royal Welch Fusiliers," Cain exclaimed, recognizing the greeting. "I had many friends in the Fusiliers before they were withdrawn in '39."

"Yes, I fondly remember the Marine band playing as we boarded lighters for transport back to England," Moss said. "When did you leave?"

"I rotated in October 1941," Cain replied, "a month before the regiment withdrew to the Philippines."

"Yes, a terrible calamity," Moss declared sadly, recalling the loss of the 4th Marines when the Japanese captured the Philippines. "Almost as bad as Dunkirk," he added.

"After returning stateside," Cain continued, "I was assigned as a company commander in the 1st Raider Battalion."

"Ah, yes," Moss broke in, "I believe our Winston influenced your President Roosevelt to push for the creation of a commando organization."

"Yes, sir, and that's how I ended up in England," Cain explained. "The Marine Corps sent the gunny and me to go through the commando training course for possible incorporation into our Raider syllabus."

"Well, your timing is spot on," Moss said. "We have a detachment ready to start the training cycle. That's why I asked Colour Sergeant Bourne to sit in on our meeting. He will be the senior training NCO."

Oh great, Cain thought, seeing the evil glint in Bourne's eye. *This is going to be fun!*

Moss turned to Montgomery. "What is your background, sergeant?" he asked. The question caught the gunny just as he took a sip of the bitter-tasting liquid in his cup. He instantly wanted to spit it out, but decided discretion was called for—besides, there wasn't a spit cup around—and swallowed it.

"Colonel, I enlisted in 1925 and trained at the recruit depot at Parris Island," he said. "It was shortly before the Depression and I didn't have a pot to piss in, so the idea that I could get three hots and a cot appealed to me."

Cain turned pale, the colour sergeant turned purple, and the colonel sat wide-eyed for a brief moment and then burst out laughing. "You do have a way with words, sergeant," he remarked, making light of Montgomery's pithy comment. "Where have you served?"

Montgomery was on a roll. "Most of the shitholes in the Caribbean, sir—Haiti, Nicaragua, Panama," he continued. "I even pulled liberty in Aruba with you Limeys."

Oh shit, Cain thought, *now he's offended the colonel*. Limey was not exactly a term of endearment. Moss did not seem to take offense. However, Bourne turned several shades of red and puffed up like a toad.

"Well," Moss said, before the NCO could explode, "I certainly enjoyed our little chat, but I expect you gentlemen want to get settled. Colour sergeant, would you mind showing them to their quarters?"

"Sir," Bourne responded, leaping to his feet and saluting. "Come this way," he gruffly told the two Marines.

After the three men left the office, Moss sat down behind his desk and picked up one of the record books that he had been studying before the interruption. "Captain James Cain," he said out loud, opening the heavy paper stock cover of the Officer Qualification Record. His eye was drawn to the upper torso of the 2 ½ × 2 ½ black and white photo of Cain wearing a green uniform. "Certainly isn't a very flattering photo, typical military," he mumbled, considering the grim-faced image staring into the camera's lens. He looked at the photo more closely—it revealed a face that suggested self-confidence, a toughness, a man's man. However, it was his eyes that captured Moss's attention. They conveyed an intelligence, a determination, a strength of character that marked him as a man to be reckoned with. Having interviewed over 500 applicants for the school, Moss considered he was a good judge of character. *Cain will do very well at the school,* he decided. The physical data listed in the OQR backed up his evaluation—72 inches in height, 190 pounds—and not an ounce of fat on his body, he had noted during the course of the interview. He made a mental note to have Colour Sergeant Bourne "test" him to verify his assessment.

Moss picked up Montgomery's record book. The photo stapled to the book showed the face of a powerful-looking man—square jaw, closely cropped hair, broad nose, and eyes that seemed to bore holes in the camera's lens. *This man is dangerous,* Moss decided, *just the type of man for this duty. I believe Bourne will meet his match with these two.*

<hr />

McNeal Manor, 1100, 7 August 1942—"I have taken the liberty of having your gear taken to your billet," Bourne explained—twice,

35

because the Yanks didn't seem to understand plain English. "Follow me," he said, marching at the double quick along the cobblestone path; his steel-shod ammunition boots ringing loudly on the stony surface.

The two Marines looked at each other knowingly. *It's started*, they thought. *We may be Marine Raiders, but we're going to have to prove ourselves to the commandos.* The three men tramped out the gate and into the small hamlet. They made their way along the lane which Cain surmised was the main drag. It was lined with two-story whitewashed cottages roofed with thatch, fitting the perfect image of a quaint Scottish village.

Bourne gave a brief historic commentary. "Achnacarry has been here for the last two hundred years, ever since the chief of the Clan Cameron built the castle. Come along now, we mustn't keep his honor waiting."

He led the Americans toward an old-world, two-story stone manor house. "Captain Cain, this is your billet," Bourne said in his thick brogue. "Please come with me and I'll introduce you to the owner."

Cain got the gist of his meaning when the colour sergeant motioned at the house with his hand. They passed through the gated entranceway in the waist-high weathered brick wall that was covered with red and green ivy. A pair of rose beds lined the short gravel walkway leading to the front of the house. A magnificent oak door that looked like it had been there for centuries was flanked by two half-glazed windows. As they approached the doorway, it was opened by an older man dressed in gray slacks, crisp white shirt, with a perfectly knotted regimental tie, highly polished shoes, and a blue blazer. Cain guessed that the gentleman was in his mid-sixties, slight, with a deeply creased face and thinning gray hair. He lacked an inch from being as tall as Cain, but his erect posture gave him the appearance of added height.

"Sir," Bourne bellowed, coming stiffly to attention and saluting. The older man correctly returned the salute. "Brigadier McNeal," the colour sergeant said by way of introduction, "this is Captain Cain of the American Marines' 1st Raider Battalion." Cain hurriedly saluted after hearing the word "brigadier" and seeing how Bourne reacted to the older man.

"I was expecting you, captain," McNeal said in a voice marked by a slight Scottish accent. "Your bags were delivered an hour ago." Before he could say any more, a stunning young woman appeared at his side. Cain could not help but notice that she was quite a bit younger than the brigadier. *You old devil you*, he thought to himself just as the lady spoke.

"Daddy, invite the gentlemen in, you're keeping them out in the cold," she instructed with the soft lilt of a delightful Scottish brogue.

Oops, Cain chastised himself for thinking the woman was the brigadier's trophy wife. *She does bear a resemblance to her father*, he thought, after taking a closer look, *except she's a damn sight prettier!* She had flawless skin, green intelligent eyes, rich auburn hair that framed a strikingly pale face, finely chiseled features, and a shapely figure. A hint of freckles on her cheeks added to her attractiveness.

The old gentleman smiled at being scolded by his daughter and stepped back from the doorway. "Please come in," he said.

Bourne begged off. "I have to run the lad down to his billet," he interjected, rendering a salute. "Off we go, sergeant," he said to Montgomery, and stepped off at the quick march.

Montgomery swore to himself, *Where does the big oaf get off by calling me "lad"?*

"Captain Cain," the brigadier said, as the officer entered the foyer, "allow me to introduce my daughter."

"I'm pleased to meet you, Ms. McNeal," Cain voiced, sticking out his hand.

"Please call me Loreena," she responded politely, taking his hand in a surprisingly strong grip. "Welcome to our home."

She turned to the brigadier. "Father, shall we adjourn to the drawing room?" Loreena led the way down the richly paneled hallway, past a substantial staircase, and into the drawing room.

My God, Cain exclaimed to himself, *this room is a museum.* The walls were adorned with oil paintings of stern-looking men in colorful Highland uniforms, edged weapons ranging from spears to wicked-looking knives, and enough small arms to equip an infantry squad. Arranged among the various artifacts were stuffed animal heads, whose glassy eyes peered down from lofty perches. An intricately woven Persian carpet covered the middle of the floor. Cain's eyes were quickly drawn to a magnificent oak fireplace, above which hung a portrait of the brigadier in Highland attire, complete with kilt.

Loreena noticed Cain looking at the painting. "That's my father when he commanded the 1st Battalion, the Black Watch in the Great War," she explained proudly. Before Cain could say anything, the brigadier interrupted.

"Of course, I didn't retain command for the entire war, just for a few months at the beginning," he explained.

"Daddy was wounded quite severely," Loreena added, taking her father by the arm. "Why don't we sit down," she offered, gesturing toward the leather-upholstered wing chairs arranged in front of the fireplace.

"Would you like some tea," Loreena asked pleasantly, "or something stronger?"

The brigadier interjected, "I have some magnificent Glenlivet that I have been saving for a special occasion."

Cain considered the options for perhaps a split second—plant drink or single malt whiskey—and made a decision. "Sir, I'll take the Glenlivet."

"Why did I know that'd be your answer?" Loreena teased, walking over to a beautifully carved wooden serving cart. She carefully lifted the half-full bottle and poured an inch of the golden-brown liquid into each of three crystal glasses. Cain raised an eyebrow. *My type of woman*, he thought, as Loreena passed the glasses to the men and raised hers in a toast.

"*Mìle fàilte*," she spoke in Gaelic, and then translated, "A thousand welcomes." They took a sip—good Scotch is to be savored, not gulped, even a heathen Marine knew that. Cain raised his glass in salute.

"An Irish toast to my new Scottish friends," he said, reciting one that his father always used. "May God grant faithful friends near you always." *Damn*, he mused, feeling the effects of the Scotch, *this is one helluva assignment!*

"I'm sorry to put you out," Cain said. "I didn't know that I would be billeted in a private home."

"Nonsense, my boy," the brigadier countered. "We have the extra space and it allows us to do something for the war effort."

Loreena broke in, "And besides, it gives *Dadaidh* an opportunity to man-talk with soldiers."

The brigadier smiled. "You see, my daughter knows me too well." He continued, "From time to time, I would like to talk with you about your training."

"It's a deal," Cain agreed, "but only if you share your experiences during the Great War with me."

"You men can't have all the fun," Loreena said. "You have to promise to include me or you can fend for yourselves." Both men laughed and promised they would.

"Speaking of fending for myself," Cain said, "I'd better go to my room and unpack. I expect I'll have a busy day tomorrow."

The Cottage, 1700, 7 August 1942—The two enlisted men marched side by side along a quaint side street on the edge of Spean Bridge until they reached a small, two-story, whitewashed cottage.

"This is your billet," Bourne announced, the first words he had spoken since leaving the brigadier's manor. "Go in," he said, pushing open the unlocked door.

"Shouldn't we knock or something?" Montgomery asked.

"Why should we?" Bourne replied. "It's my home."

"Lord save me," the gunny uttered quietly, "what have I done to deserve this?" If Bourne heard the comment, he chose to ignore it and ushered the Marine into the entryway, where a comely middle-aged, gray-haired woman stood in a small comfortable parlor.

"Mrs. Mackinnon," he said by way of introduction, "this is Sergeant Montgomery of the American Marines. He is the one that will be staying with us."

"I'm pleased to meet you," the lady replied in a gentle voice, shaking his hand. "Angus mentioned that a Yank would be staying here."

Montgomery almost choked. *Angus, that's a helluva name*, he thought to himself, taking a quick glance at Bourne, *but it sure describes the big ox. The guy is a bull—large head, thick neck, and wide shoulders.*

"Mrs. Mackinnon is my housekeeper," Bourne explained. "She keeps the house spotless and my belly filled."

"Speaking of food, dinner will be ready shortly," Mrs. Mackinnon announced, "so why don't you show Sergeant Montgomery his room."

Bourne nodded and motioned for Montgomery to follow him up the stairs. "The room on the left is yours, mine is on the right. Mrs. Mackinnon lives downstairs in a back room. The loo is down the hall."

Montgomery hardly understood a word the Limey said—in his mind, the Scots fell into the same category as the English. *What the hell is a "loo?"* he wondered.

"When you're ready, come down to the kitchen, that's where we eat," Bourne explained. "The door to the left leads to the parlor and the one on the right is the kitchen." Montgomery went into the room and found that his sea-bag had been unpacked and carefully arranged in the dresser, and his extra dungarees hung up in the small closet. He hastily shed his sweat-stained HBTs and stood in the middle of the room in his skivvies wondering, *Where in the hell can I wash up?*

There was a knock on the door and before he could open it, Bourne stepped in. "Here are some civilian clothes that might fit you," he said, handing them to the semi-nude Marine. "You can wash up in the loo." *Ah*, Montgomery thought to himself, *that clears up that mystery.*

Montgomery joined the others in the kitchen, which was the hub of the cottage. Bright copper pans hung from hooks over a large oak table that had four solid wooden chairs arranged around it. The table and chairs were old and worn and looked comfortable. A separate oak desk stood against a wall. A Bakelite rotary telephone sat on top, along with a notepad and a glass jar containing several wooden pencils. A wood-burning stove took up one end of the room, where a delicious smell was coming from the pots simmering on its cast-iron top. "We're having Stoved Howtowdie with Drappit Eggs," Mrs. Mackinnon announced, lifting a large casserole dish from the stove.

Oh my God, Montgomery cringed silently; *they're going to poison me.*

"Sit, sit," Mrs. Mackinnon ordered, ladling huge portions onto the men's plates. Montgomery stared at the mixture in front of him and tried to decide whether to just gulp it down—devil take the hindmost—or play around with it pretending to eat. But then his saliva glands went into overdrive and his brain screamed, *Eat, you're hungry*. He raised his spoon and prepared to dig in.

"Angus, will you say grace," Mrs. Mackinnon announced, stopping the gunny's spoon in mid-stroke. *Oops*, he thought, trying to cover up his faux pas with a deft hand maneuver.

Bourne closed his eyes, cleared his throat, and began, "Some hae meat and cannae eat. Some nae meat but want it. We hae meat and we can eat and sae the Lord be thankit." As he finished, Mrs. Mackinnon looked at Montgomery with a mischievous smile and announced, "Now we can eat." She had noticed Montgomery's sleight of hand.

"Do you have a favorite blessing, sergeant?" she asked innocently, her eyes sparkling playfully.

"Why of course," Montgomery quickly responded, taking up her challenge. "Lord, we know without a doubt you'll bless this food as we pig out," he solemnly recited. There was a moment of silence. Her eyes widened with surprise, Bourne's face reddened—and then they cracked up.

"Well done, Yank," the colour sergeant managed to spit out between hoots.

———◆———

"Delicious," Montgomery announced, taking the last spoonful of casserole on his plate. "I can't remember when I had a more appetising 'How do you say it' with rabbit eggs." The remark was met with more laughter. The relaxed atmosphere of the dinner had turned it into a pleasant opportunity for the men to get to know one another. Their lighthearted banter broke through the macho barriers that existed between them—a promising start on the path to mutual respect and possibly friendship.

After the men helped Mrs. Mackinnon clear away the dishes, Bourne suggested a "wee dram" to finish off the meal. He quickly produced three glasses and a bottle covered with a thick coating of dust, which he wiped off with a hand towel, much to Mrs. Mackinnon's annoyance. "Special, are we?" she asked.

"It's not often that we have guests," Bourne replied, pouring a generous measure of the precious liquid into three glasses and handing two of them to the others. "A toast," he said, raising his own glass. "*Slàinte Mhath.*"

"Good health," Mrs. Mackinnon translated for Montgomery's benefit, and responded with, "*Do dheagh shlàinte*," "Your good health."

The three sat at the kitchen table, exchanging small talk and enjoying each other's company until Mrs. Mackinnon excused herself, claiming a busy day ahead. The men remained, not quite ready to hit the sack. Bourne poured himself another generous dram. "Tell me about your service," he asked, handing over the bottle.

Montgomery studied him closely to see if he was serious or just being polite. Satisfied that it was a genuine expression of interest, he launched into an account of his 15 years' service. Bourne sat back in his chair and listened intently as Montgomery talked about chasing the wily bandit Sandino and surviving deadly ambushes in the Nicaraguan jungle, of marching with "Red Mike" Edson on the famous Coco River patrol, guarding the U.S. Mail with "shoot to kill" orders, multiple tours training recruits, and his most recent assignment with the 4th Marines in Shanghai's International Settlement.

"I was lucky to get out on the last boat before the war started," he stated emotionally. "The regiment was captured when General Wainwright surrendered the Philippines."

Bourne could plainly see the pain on Montgomery's face when he talked about his friends who were now in the hands of the "murderous slant-eyed bastards."

"I was there in '37 when the Jap Marines slaughtered thousands of Chinese civilians," Montgomery explained. "They raped, pillaged, and burned their way through the city," he said, his voice rising in anger. "The Nips tied men to poles and used them for bayonet practice and lopped off heads just for the fun of it!" Bourne was taken aback by the hatred in Montgomery's eyes. "That's why I volunteered for the Raiders and why I intend to kill as many of the little bastards as I can before this war is over," the Marine said forcefully.

5

Commando Basic Training Centre, Athletic Field, 0630, 8 August 1942—"All right, lads, settle down," Bourne barked, "it's time to get to work." He carefully scrutinized the dozen prospective commandos standing in formation. They were all dressed in the standard British khaki battledress uniforms, except for the two Marines, who wore the two-piece, sage-green herringbone twill US combat uniforms. The two had been the subject of a great deal of intense interest by their classmates, who wanted to know what the Yanks were doing in the school. They were fascinated by the eagle, globe, and anchor stenciled on the left breast pockets of their uniforms. "Quite different from ours," Finch sniffed haughtily.

"Gentlemen," Bourne interrupted, "please sort yourself out in two files of six according to rank; senior man on the right of the first file." He waited impatiently while the dozen men sorted themselves out. Cain determined that he was the only officer and took the head of the right file. He had been told that his rank would be respected but he was still considered a student and should follow the orders of the instructors, most of whom were "other ranks." Gunny Montgomery, the highest-ranking enlisted man, took position on Cain's immediate left. The rest of the men, all corporals and sergeants, filled in the files according to their dates of rank.

Bourne, exasperated by the time it was taking, bellowed, "Don't make this your life's work; there's a war on in case you haven't noticed." Finally satisfied that the formation was correct, he welcomed them to the school, promising that the next seven weeks would be the most memorable experience of their lives. "When you leave here," he emphasized, "you will be exceptionally skilled killers!"

"The work day will begin promptly at 0830 and will end at 1740, unless there is a training exercise," Bourne continued. "You will have Saturday afternoon free, unless there is a training exercise."

Gunny Montgomery heard one of the British corporals mutter, "You may also be able to eat and shite, unless there is a training exercise."

"What's that?!" Bourne thundered, glaring at the offending NCO.

"Nothing, colour sergeant," the offender replied innocently, hoping that Bourne would forget his transgression. Not to be, however. The colour sergeant gave him a little nod, as if to say, *You're in for it!* "Training periods," Bourne explained, "will include small arms, explosives, field craft, map-reading, field problems"—he paused for effect, a nasty smile spreading across his heretofore severe expression—"and physical exercise!"

"Now we're in for it," the corporal grumbled.

"Lads, it's time for a little road trip," Bourne announced. Four instructors suddenly appeared as if by magic.

"Right," Bourne roared, "turn!" The command caught the two Marines by surprise and they were slow in reacting. In the Marine Corps, the command is, "right face," not "turn." "Oh shit," Cain muttered, embarrassed at being caught out. "Captain," one of the instructors called out before he could react, "if you would be so kind as to face to the right."

"Quick, march!" Bourne barked. Both Marines recognized the command "march," and managed to lurch forward without being critiqued. "Damn," Montgomery exclaimed quietly, "I wish these Limeys would speak English!" Fortunately, counting cadence was the same in both countries. "Left-right-left-right," the leather-lunged colour sergeant called out. Cain caught the rhythm and stepped out. Almost immediately, an instructor appeared off his shoulder. "Captain, if you would be so kind as to increase the pace," he said respectfully, and then added sarcastically, "We are expected to return before breakfast."

The first mile went fairly well, but then, as fatigue set in, the men found it harder and harder to keep in step, much to the annoyance of the instructors. They let the trainees know how irritated they were. They never raised their voices; however, they were quick to point out an offender's deficiencies.

"You are a poor excuse for a soldier if you can't even stay in step, my lad. Should we send you back to your unit?" The mere threat of being "cast out" brought renewed efforts. Cain tried hard to maintain a steady pace—helped along by Montgomery's whispered guidance. The gunny counted two tours on the drill field at the recruit depot among his many duty stations. They marched about 3 ½ miles before Bourne called a break.

"Gather round," he ordered. "Gentlemen," he began, as the men formed a school circle, "I want to explain why the training center insists on marching in formation. It is to instill teamwork, the essential ingredient in commando operations." He paused and looked each man in the eye. "In case you think that we are just doing this for harassment, I want to assure you that everything we do at this school has one purpose—to make you into the Nazis' worst nightmare!"

Cain was genuinely impressed with the way Bourne explained what he was doing and why. It was a good "teaching moment," one that Cain filed away for future use. His opinion of the colour sergeant changed. The man was not a tyrant, just tough, demanding, and determined to train the men to peak performance. Bourne's voice broke into his musings. "We're going to start back," he said, "and this time I want you to pick up the pace. The school's standard for 'passing out' is to complete a 7-mile march in one hour. On your feet and fall in!" he shouted. The march back was not a complete disaster but it certainly did not live up to the standards of the instructors, who spent most of the time patrolling up and down the column correcting defaulters. By the time they arrived back at the center, long lines of hungry men had formed at the entrance to the cookhouse. Bourne dismissed the section with a derogatory comment. "Sad, truly sad," he grumbled, shaking his head slowly in discouragement.

"Going my way?" Cain asked.

"Why, it just so happens…" Montgomery started to reply, when an instructor interrupted politely.

"Captain, may I remind you that trainees shall move at the 'double' aboard the base."

"Right," Cain replied, turning toward Montgomery and commanding, "Double time, march." The two Marines jogged off at the regulation 180 steps a minute until they reached the main gate. "Detail, quick march," Cain called out, using the British command to resume the normal marching rate of 120 steps per minute.

"Damn, Skipper, this is just like boot camp," Montgomery complained, as they walked through the gate and into the small village.

"Hey, Marine, ours is not to reason why," Cain jested.

"Yes, sir, I'll try to remember that when Bourne is breathing down your neck."

"He is rather a difficult man," Cain replied.

"Easy for you to say," Montgomery lamented, "I've got to live with him."

McNeal Manor, 1800, 8 August 1942—Loreena met Cain at the door. "Captain, dinner will be served at 7 p.m. in the dining room," she said. "You may want to freshen up." As she started to walk away, she added, "Father dresses for dinner."

Cain went up the stairs to his room, wondering what the hell she meant by, "Father dresses for dinner." *I didn't really expect him to eat in the nude*, he thought to himself. As he entered the room, the mystery was cleared up. A blue wool jacket, gray wool trousers, pale blue shirt, and regimental tie were displayed on a wooden clothing butler. He quickly tried the trousers on and found they were almost a perfect fit. *How the hell does she do it?* he wondered. He quickly took a shower, shaved the stubble off his face, ran a comb through his closely cropped blond hair, and dressed. With minutes to spare, he made his way downstairs to the drawing room. The brigadier was seated in one of the overstuffed chairs, sipping a pre-dinner libation.

"Ah, Captain Cain, won't you join me?" he asked. "I have a delightful single malt Scotch."

"I would love to," Cain replied. The brigadier poured a generous amount of the dark amber liquid into a glass and handed it to him. He hoisted his crystal glass in salute: "Victory over the Huns."

Loreena chose that moment to enter the room. Cain almost choked on his whiskey. The woman was transformed. She had changed from well-worn country togs into a tartan floor-length gown with a white ruffled neckline that accentuated her beauty. Her shoulder-length auburn hair framed her fair complexion and highlighted her green eyes.

"You men couldn't wait for me," she scolded.

"I'm sorry, my dear," the brigadier responded, and quickly poured a measure of whiskey into a glass and handed it to his daughter. Cain gaped at her and when she caught him staring, he turned red. She noticed his discomfort and smiled self-consciously. The brigadier saved them from further embarrassment. "Drink up," he said. "I'm sure Captain Cain is starving after a hard day of training."

The trio walked across the hall into the beautifully appointed dining room. A well-used stone fireplace took up one end of the rectangular space. A painted mural depicting a Scottish hunting scene covered one wall, while two large leaded glass windows on the opposite wall gave Cain an unobstructed view of the manor's grounds. Even in the fading light, he could see the old, waist-high, stone wall surrounding an ancient yew that was outlined against the backdrop of a heavily forested glen. He was mesmerized.

"Magnificent," he exclaimed.

"Yes, it's quite beautiful," the brigadier responded thoughtfully, "my ancestors chose well." Loreena broke in. "This land has been in our family for over three hundred years," she said proudly, "although the manor was not built until 1801."

"Yes, I noticed paint was hardly dry," Cain said with a laugh.

Dinner was served buffet style from an antique sideboard that must have been as old as the house. Cain held his plate while Loreena heaped it with a vegetable and lamb casserole.

"It's called Scottish Stovies with Lamb," she explained, noting the quizzical look in Cain's eyes, "one of Daddy's favorites." The food was delicious and Cain had all he could do to keep from making a pig of himself. He glanced up from his plate and realized that he was finished and the other two were only halfway through their meal.

"I'm sorry," he said, "it's been a long time since I've eaten in polite company."

"That's all right, captain," the brigadier replied, "I acted the same way when I came home from the war. It took me several months before I got used to eating from plates."

Cain was born in 1917, one year before the Armistice ended the Great War. As a youngster, he attended the usual Memorial Day commemorations but they didn't mean much to him until he met a local Marine vet who had fought in the Great War. He spent many a fascinating hour listening to the old man's account of fighting with the Marine Brigade in France.

"An excellent meal," the brigadier announced, saluting his daughter with his half-filled wine glass. Cain echoed the compliment.

"Thank you, gentlemen," Loreena replied modestly. "If you would be so kind as to adjourn to the drawing room, I'll join you shortly for a nightcap." Her tone of voice suggested that the issue was not up for debate.

The two men quickly rose and walked across the hallway.

"Will you join me for a drink?" the brigadier asked. "A little Drambuie, '*An Dram Buidheach*,' might be just the thing to top off a superb dinner." Cain looked mystified.

"Sorry, it means the drink that satisfies," the brigadier replied, starting to pour the whiskey and honey concoction into three crystal glasses. He filled each of the pear-shaped snifters with a good 2 inches of the potent liquor. He finished just as Loreena entered the room.

"Just in time, I see," she said. "Shall we sit down?"

"Captain, a toast," the brigadier proposed, "to the lady of the house."

The two raised their glasses—"To the lady of the house," they repeated.

Loreena blushed and responded with a polite, "Thank you." The three took seats facing the burning logs in the fireplace. Cain's overstuffed chair angled slightly toward the brigadier, giving him an opportunity to closely observe the older man.

"Sir," he began, breaking the silence, "what was it like in France?"

The brigadier stared at Cain for a long minute and then glanced briefly at his daughter, who nodded encouragingly. "I have not thought about the war for a long time," he said, trying to decide whether to talk about it or not. He reached a decision. "It was ghastly, no other way to describe it. The trenches, filthy with mud, constantly wet, the stench of rotting bodies, huge rats, and the constant threat of snipers." He stopped and took a long pull of his drink before continuing. "Hun machine guns spitting hell and devastating artillery bombardments—just awful! And now we're at it again," he said, his voice choked with emotion. Loreena stood, walked over to her father, and laid a hand on his shoulder, tears streaming down her face. "My brother was lost at Dunkirk."

Damn, Cain thought to himself, terribly embarrassed that he had opened old wounds, *why did I have to open my mouth?*

"I'm terribly sorry for your loss," he managed to stammer, noting the dreadful look of anguish on their faces.

The brigadier quickly regained his composure. "We have to make sure this never happens again," he stated grimly. "The Huns have to be taught a lesson."

Loreena spoke up. "That is why we decided to open our house. The commandos will be among the first to set Europe ablaze and we wanted to be part of it in some small way." Cain looked at their hardened expressions and realized that they were deadly serious. He understood now that the commando school was more than a training facility; it was the tool that would make the Germans pay.

6

Commando Basic Training Centre, Pistol Range, 0830, 9 August 1942—The section gathered around a bench that was lined with a dozen Webley revolvers. A box of cartridges had been placed beside each pistol. Paper targets stamped with the figure of a German soldier had been set up in front of each firing point.

"Gentlemen," Bourne began, "this is Sergeant McCann, the handgun instructor. He will review the range safety regulations and supervise you during firing." After a brief safety lecture—"For God's sake, don't point the weapon at anyone"—McCann directed the men to pick up a weapon and load it. The Webley was standard issue for the British armed forces but it was the first time that the two Marines had handled one, much less fired the six-shot revolver. Cain hefted the weapon, noticing immediately that it weighed about the same as the U.S. Model 1911 .45-caliber pistol that he was so familiar with. He broke it open, picked up six .45-caliber bullets, and inserted them into the cylinder. He rested the end of the barrel on the edge of the bench and waited for permission to begin firing.

McCann looked up and down the firing line, saw that everyone was ready, and gave the command to fire. Several shots rang out. Novice shooters were more interested in getting the first shot in than hitting the target. Cain assumed the stance that he had learned on the pistol range—body diagonal to the target, feet comfortably spread apart, left hand in his pocket, and right arm extended with the pistol gripped firmly. He settled in, steadied his breathing, and gently squeezed the trigger with the pad of his index finger. The pistol fired, the recoil forcing the barrel of the weapon high and to the right, "just like the .45," he muttered. He thumbed the hammer back, aimed in, and fired. *The trigger pull is about right, but the action is a little tight*, he thought. After firing all six rounds, he broke the revolver open, which automatically extracted the expended cartridges. He placed the pistol back on the table and waited for the "cease-fire" command.

Cain glanced to the right and saw that Montgomery had also completed firing.

"What do you think, Gunny?" he asked.

"I think our .45 is a helluva lot better weapon," he replied, "but this one will do in a pinch."

"Cease-fire," McCann called out, "clear and bench your weapons." He verified that all the pistols were benched. "Check your targets." Most of the men hurriedly rushed forward to see the results, leaving the two Marines to follow along behind.

"Come on, Gunny," Cain said, "usual bet?"

"Yes, sir, I dearly love to drink on your money," he replied smugly. The two had a long-standing competition to see who the better marksman was. Thus far, Cain was two drinks in the hole. They passed several targets and noted that most of the section had scattered bullets all over the cardboard. Several men had only managed to get two or three shots in the target.

"Who fired on targets 11 and 12?" McCann called out.

"We did," Cain said, indicating himself and the gunny.

"This your first time shooting a pistol?" he asked lightheartedly, pointing to the 50-cent-sized shot patterns in the two targets.

"The gunny was on the Marine Corps shooting team," Cain explained.

"And Captain Cain was the team captain," Montgomery injected.

"Well done," McCann said in admiration. The section gathered around the two targets.

"Cor, will you look at that," Finch exclaimed, staring at Montgomery's target. "The Yank's bullets have blown off the German's balls!" Sure enough, the .45-caliber rounds had left a jagged hole where the German's "privates" would have been.

"Och, look at the other," Sergeant Alun Arawn, 1st Battalion Welch Guards, pointed out. "The captain has shot out Jerry's right eye!" There was a hole in the cardboard silhouette instead of the German's right eye.

Montgomery stepped forward to measure the holes in the two targets. He held a 50-cent piece over the hole in his target. One bullet barely hung out. Cain watched closely as the gunny moved to his target and placed the coin over the shot holes.

"Ha," he exclaimed happily, the coin covering the entire group. "Gunny, you need to hold 'em and squeeze 'em better," he gloated.

"The sun got in my eye on the last shot," Montgomery replied straight faced, even though a thick layer of clouds covered the sky.

"Gunny, by the terms of our agreement, you owe me a brew," Cain said quickly, before Montgomery realized that the officer had not paid off from previous bets. "I'll meet you at the Commando Bar, 1900 sharp," he declared. The section exploded with laughter as they listened to the two Yanks banter back and forth.

The lively crowd attracted Colour Sergeant Bourne, who sauntered over to look at the two targets. "Nice group," he added nonchalantly, "but can you do the same with live targets?"

"What a horse's ass," Montgomery muttered under his breath.

The section fired several more relays before McCann announced that the day's shooting was completed. Most of the men had improved, except two corporals, Frank Hunt, 1st Battalion, Coldstream Guards and his buddy Mark Williams, 2nd Battalion, the Gloucestershire Regiment. The two men had never fired a pistol before and just could not seem to get the hang of it, despite McCann's efforts. Finally, in desperation he asked the two Marines for assistance.

"We'll give it a try," Montgomery replied, glancing at the lack of shot holes in their targets, "but we can't promise miracles." The section turned to and policed up all the expended brass, and tidied up the range before falling into formation. Bourne took his position and ordered "Right, turn." This time, the two Marines executed the command flawlessly.

"Well done, Yanks," Finch whispered loud enough for Cain to hear. The section "doubled" back to the cookhouse for lunch before beginning the afternoon training session.

———————

Demolition Course, 1400, 9 August 1942—"Over the next few weeks, I'm going to teach you to blow things up," the demolitions instructor began, "and when I get through, you'll be able to send Jerry to hell!" With that announcement, he pointed to a 15-foot length of thin olive-drab cord stretched between two wooden posts. "This is not your grandmother's clothesline," he said with a smirk, "this is what you'll use to expedite Jerry's trip." He nodded and suddenly there was a thunderous explosion and the line disappeared. The section was staggered by the force of the blast.

"Mother of God," Finch exclaimed, "I sure won't use Granny's wash line ever again." The instructor ignored his comment and went on to explain that what they had observed was "detonating cord," or high-speed fuse. "Detonating cord," he continued, "is a flexible tube filled with explosive that burns at a rate of 4 miles a second." Finch started to say something but the instructor beat him to the draw. "It can also be wrapped around the neck of a smart ass to shut him up."

The instructor and his assistants demonstrated how to safely fuse and prepare the detonating cord for use. The section broke into pairs and spent the rest of the day preparing detonating cord. No one wanted to partner with Finch until Montgomery took pity on him and volunteered to join him. However, the gunny warned him in no uncertain terms, "You screw around and I'll shove a length of detonating cord up your ass and set it off!" Finch turned white and was the soul of propriety for the rest of the period of instruction.

Next, the instructor introduced them to Composition C-2, a malleable plastic explosive. He held up an olive-green wrapped 1 ½-pound block and explained that it would produce an explosion that was all out of proportion to its size. He stopped the presentation when he noticed that Finch was not paying attention.

"Catch," he suddenly announced, and threw the block to the surprised trainee. Finch made a desperate grab and managed to catch it. The instructor smiled maliciously. "Doping off, were we?" To the great surprise of the section, Finch admitted to a momentary lapse in concentration.

"I'll be good, sergeant," he promised contritely.

The section was again divided into pairs and given a quarter-pound block labeled "CHARGE, Demolition, M112" on the wrapper. They were told to prepare an explosive charge using detonating cord and C-2 with a blasting cap as a detonator. An assistant instructor went with each pair to the demolition pits, which were located some distance apart for safety. The men unwrapped the white-tinted explosive and found it was similar but stiffer than a child's modeling clay. They divided the bar in half and were surprised to smell the distinctive odor of marzipan. The instructor showed them how to insert the end of the detonating cord into the blasting cap and crimp it tight with a crimping tool. "Be very careful," he stressed. "If you balls it up, you'll lose fingers or your whole bloody hand!" After the demonstration, each pair prepared their own charges and set them off.

Commando Bar, 1900, 10 August 1942—*Oh no!* Cain exclaimed to himself as he entered the Commando Bar that reeked of stale beer. *I should have known it would be no place to enjoy a quiet drink.* The wooden tables were all occupied and the highly polished wooden bar was jammed shoulder to shoulder with uniformed soldiers loudly demanding "service" from two overworked women bartenders, who were old enough to be their mothers. A cloud of cigarette smoke hung over the crowd, all but concealing the cross-beam rafters. The noise level was deafening. "I'll probably suffer hearing loss," he mumbled, and started working his way through the crush at the bar. He heard a familiar voice call out, "Skipper, over here," and saw Montgomery wave his arm to attract his attention. He was sitting with the members of the section around four hardwood tables they had pushed together. Corporal Finch formally reported that everyone was "present and accounted for," as Cain pulled up an empty chair. Montgomery slid over a pint of Scottish ale. "Don't say I never pay off," he said, "like some people I know."

Cain took a long pull of the brew. "Ah," he said, "that's what I call a good beer."

"Ale," Finch interjected, "it's ale, sir, not beer."

"What's the difference?" Cain asked half-heartedly, not really giving a damn one way or the other, as long as it was cold, wet, and in his hand. Finch's reply was cut off by a tremendous cheer from a crowd of soldiers gathered at the end of the room. *Fight,* flashed through Cain's mind, harkening back to his stints as Officer of the Day spent policing enlisted men's clubs. Another cheer erupted.

"What's going on?" he asked Corporal Hunt, who was sitting next to him.

"Darts," he replied. "They're having a tournament to see who the best player on base is."

"I've got to see this," Cain said, getting up and walking over to the excited crowd watching two men tossing darts at a circular target inside a wooden cabinet fixed to the wall in the corner of the room.

A small lamp illuminated the face of the board. The first shooter had just finished. He left three darts sticking out of the center of the target.

"Is that good?" Cain asked the man at his elbow.

"Are you daft?" the soldier replied. "It's bloody fantastic!"

The next shooter took position, lined up the target using the knuckles of his throwing hand to aim, closed his left eye, and tossed the dart with a smooth, fluid flick of his arm. A roar went up from the crowd as the dart flew straight and true, sticking in the section of the board labeled "20." The shooter took aim again and let fly—another "20!" Cain watched him step away from the throwing line, wipe his sweaty face with a handkerchief, and take his position. All eyes were focused on him as he aimed and threw another perfect "20."

"Tie!" someone yelled.

"Wait a minute," another voice broke in, "he crossed the oche!" The shooter looked down. The tip of his shoe was covering the toe-line.

"Foul," a soldier with a handful of coins yelled accusingly.

"Yer bum's oot the windae," a beefy Scot fired back—and that's when the fight started, or as Finch related later, "the wheels fell off the wagon." Suddenly, the emotionally charged crowd started pushing, shoving, yelling obscenities, and throwing ineffectual punches in the densely packed space. Everyone seemed to be fair game, whether a bystander or not. Cain deftly side-stepped a sucker-punch but took a solid shot to the shoulder that knocked him off balance. An arm reached out to steady him as he started to fall.

"Damn, Skipper," Montgomery shouted gleefully, "just like old times!" The two had been involved in several brawls with the Japs, including one where a Marine threw an obnoxious officer of the Special Naval Landing Force out of the Shanghai Club's second-story window. The official Shanghai Police report absolved any Marine complicity, noting instead that the Japanese officer was drunk and accidently fell. Several Marine witnesses swore that "he committed *hari kari.*"

"It may be like old times," Cain said, "but I think we better get the hell out of here before the MPs get here." They no sooner reached the door when it burst open and a detail of "Redcaps" filed in, led by the massive commando depot sergeant major. The man stood well over 6 feet tall and weighed close to 250 rock-hard pounds. He sported an enormous handlebar mustache that quivered with anger. "What have we here?" he thundered, observing the crowd of brawlers. His command voice penetrated the brain of even the most drunken sod. "Stand to attention," he ordered. Cain would not have believed it if he hadn't been there. The fighting stopped as if someone had turned a switch. The men came to rigid attention. The sergeant major walked back and forth, fixing them with a ferocious stare. "Yer jake-ett's ona slack nail," he said, his voice rumbling with authority. "Other ranks will parade outside, now." There was a mad scramble as the men rushed through the door to get in formation. Montgomery started to follow.

"Not you, Yank, you're free to leave on your own," the sergeant major advised, "and I suggest you get cracking!"

———◆———

McNeal Manor, 2000, 10 August 1942—The light was on in the drawing room when Cain arrived back at the manor.

"That you, captain?" the brigadier called out.

"Yes, sir," Cain replied, stepping into the room. The brigadier was sitting in the overstuffed chair in front of the fire with a book in his lap and a half-filled glass at his elbow.

"Will you join me?" he asked. Cain was ready for a little "pick-me-up" after walking back from the club in the cold. The two men settled in, content to enjoy the mellow feeling that comes from staring into a log fire with a good drink at hand.

The brigadier was the first to break the spell. "How is the training going?"

"The first few days were tough learning the language," Cain replied.

The brigadier chuckled. "Yes, our mixture of English and Scottish words can be a little confusing."

"Other than that," Cain continued, "the training is first rate and the instructors are extremely professional. The men are tough, dedicated, and well-motivated. Most of them are veterans of Dunkirk and can't wait to get back at the Germans."

At the mention of Dunkirk, the brigadier visibly winced.

"I'm sorry, sir," Cain said contritely, "that was thoughtless of me."

"That's all right," the older man replied evenly, "it's something I have to get over. My son would not have wanted me to mope. He was exactly where he wanted to be; leading his Jocks in combat."

Cain sensed that the old man wanted to say more. "Do you know what happened to him?" he asked.

"He commanded a company in my old battalion," he replied. "His company was assigned to hold a section of the perimeter during the evacuation. All we know is that the position was overrun in the final German assault and he is listed as missing in action, presumed dead."

"Maybe he was captured," Cain offered hopefully. "Have the Germans released a list?"

"No, the bastards are true to form, heartless and cruel," he replied heatedly. Cain was taken aback by his vehement response. It was totally out of character for the brigadier, who was always so calm and in control. "It has been especially hard on Loreena," he went on. "The two were very close and she has not fully recovered."

At that moment, Loreena entered the room, tears in her eyes. "This bloody war," she exclaimed in frustration, "when is it going to stop?"

"You should know, my dear, if anyone does," the brigadier answered. Loreena glared at her father in irritation and shook her head signaling him to say no more.

Cain thought to himself, *I wonder what that's all about.*

The old man shrugged off his daughter's annoyance and continued. "The war is going to go on for a very long time," he philosophized, "until we can eliminate Hitler and his fanatics."

"And defeat the Japanese," Cain interjected.

"Yes, quite right," the old man said. "I understand that your president has agreed with Winston that the first priority of the war effort is the defeat of Germany and Italy."

"Yes," Cain responded, "but that doesn't mean we're going to sit on our hands. Before I left the States, there were rumors that the 1st Marine Division was gearing up to be deployed to Australia."

Loreena interrupted, "Isn't that your unit?"

"Yes, the 1st Raider Battalion is attached to the division."

So, you'll soon be in combat, she thought to herself.

"Are the Raiders anything like our commandos?" the brigadier asked.

"Yes," Cain explained, "the two organizations have a similar mission. They receive special training in hit-and-run-type raids targeting specific objectives."

"Our boys have been conducting them since June 1940," the old man interjected. "The No. 11 Scottish Commandos conducted several raids in the Middle East until it was disbanded because of heavy casualties."

Loreena suddenly stood up and fled the room without a word. Cain was quite surprised and turned to the brigadier with a questioning look in his eyes.

"Oh blast, now I've done it," the old man exclaimed. "If you'll excuse me," he said, rising out of his chair, "I've got to go make amends." He quickly left the room, leaving Cain wondering what the hell was going on.

7

Commando Depot, Hand-to-Hand Combat Area, 0830, 11 August 1942—The section formed a half circle around an older gentleman—one trainee thought he looked and spoke like a bishop—dressed in battledress and wearing steel-rimmed glasses. He held an unsheathed bayonet in his hand. Bourne introduced him as Major William Fairbairn, formerly assistant commissioner of the Shanghai Municipal Police. The tall, slender, white-haired man stepped forward.

Finch, never out of character, whispered, "What's the old peeler going to show us, how to collar a thief?"

Fairbairn overheard the remark and pointed to Finch. "I need an assistant to help me," he said mildly, handing the Royal Marine an unsheathed bayonet. "What I want you to do, corporal, is to attack me with this blade."

Finch gulped. "Sir, I can't do that, what if I stab you?"

"Then I've made a serious mistake," Fairbairn replied calmly. "Pretend I'm a Jerry, who just raped your girlfriend." Finch looked at the section, trying to find support for backing down, but all he saw was glances goading, *Go get him, big mouth!*

"All right, sir, it's your funeral," he exclaimed, and charged. He held the bayonet in his right hand and swung it to strike Fairbairn in the midsection.

The "peeler" moved so fast that it was difficult to follow his moves, except to note that Finch ended up flat on his back, gasping for breath, with Fairbairn holding the bayonet at his throat. "You're dead," he said, helping the wobbly NCO to his feet.

"Now that I've got your attention," Fairbairn began, "I teach what is called 'Gutter Fighting.' There's no fair play, no rules except one: kill or be killed," he declared. "In war, you cannot afford the luxury of squeamishness. Either you kill or capture, or you will be captured or killed. You've got to be tough to win, and we've got to be ruthless—tougher and more ruthless than the Jerries."

With that, Fairbairn divided up the section into pairs and started teaching them the fine art of killing in hand-to-hand combat. "During unarmed combat," he began, "if you get the chance, insert a finger into a corner of your opponent's mouth and tear it. You will find the mouth tears very easily." After describing a particularly vicious way of crippling and disabling an enemy, he ended with the remark, "And then kick him in the testicles." Finally, he warned them to use extreme caution during the practice sessions because, he emphasized, "almost every one of my methods, if applied without restraint, will result in death or maiming."

Fairbairn started the session with simple holds and releases, and worked up to throws and blows. Within minutes, Cain felt like he had been hit by a truck.

"Even my hair hurts," he told Montgomery.

"Join the crowd," the gunny responded painfully, as he examined the bruises on his forearms. "A couple of days like this and we'll be in no condition to fight anybody."

"Gentlemen, I need another volunteer," Fairbairn announced, tapping Montgomery on the shoulder.

"Oh boy," the Marine mouthed, "I can hardly wait."

During the rest of the day, Fairbairn demonstrated how to deliver disabling blows, attack sentries, break free from holds, how to break falls, throws, and the use of his specially designed fighting knife, called the Fairbairn-Sykes Commando Dagger. Fairbairn held the knife up and described how he and a fellow Municipal Police officer, Eric Sykes, had developed it in response to street battles in Shanghai's International Settlement. "In close-quarters fighting, there is no more deadly weapon than the knife," he emphasized. "Merely flashing it may strike fear in the heart of a Nazi and make him easy prey."

"Blimey," Harris exclaimed, "he's scaring me and I'm on his side, I think."

Fairbairn's assistants passed out the straight-bladed, double-edged stilettos. Montgomery hefted his and was pleased with its balance. The hilt fit easily into his hand. The 6 ½-inch blade came to a tapered point and was long enough to penetrate even winter clothing. "It's a killing knife," he said.

"Exactly," Fairbairn replied, motioning for him to step forward.

"Once more unto the breach," the gunny mumbled, expecting another rough and tumble go-around with "Dangerous Dan," the nickname Finch had bestowed on the old peeler.

Fairbairn had Montgomery face the section while he came up behind him. "With the knife in your right hand," Fairbairn explained, "edges parallel to the ground, seize the bastard around the neck with your left arm, pulling his head to the left." Montgomery winced at the thought of the blade sinking into his neck but stood manfully as "Dan" continued the demonstration. "Thrust your point well in and then cut sideways," he said, making a motion with his knife, which left no doubt in the minds of the observers that the gunny would be a dead man, had this been real. "I want you to pair up and practice this killing technique," Fairbairn ordered, "and mind the restraint." Two hours later, the section was dismissed, having suffered only two minor stabbings, which were quickly bandaged with only a minimum loss of blood.

The Cottage, 1830, 11 August 1942—Montgomery gingerly walked into the kitchen and lowered himself into a chair.

"What's the matter, sergeant?" Bourne asked maliciously. "Getting old, are we?"

The gunny eyed the Scot with malevolent intent. "If I could get out of this chair," he declared, "I'd strangle you with my bare hands."

The colour sergeant laughed at the gunny's feigned threat. "I know how you feel," he sympathized, "Major Fairbairn used me as a practice dummy and I still haven't fully recovered."

"The man's a killing machine and I still haven't figured out whose side he's on!" Montgomery said with a nod, adding, "I have it on good authority that he's a Gestapo agent on a mission to single-handedly destroy the British Army."

Mrs. Mackinnon interrupted their banter, "Angus, Grace please." After dinner, in what had become a nightly ritual, the three sat down for a "wee dram of whiskey." Bourne filled the glasses with an inch of 15-year-old Glenlivet single malt.

"*Slàinte Mhath,*" he said, raising his glass to them. "*Do dheagh shlàinte,*" they replied, although Montgomery's pronunciation left a lot to be desired.

"Angus," Montgomery began—the two were on a first-name basis in the confines of the house—"tell me about Dunkirk." Bourne hesitated and glanced at the housekeeper. She nodded her head slightly, signifying her approval to go on.

"It's hard to describe," he said. "I was only a ranker in 'the Back Flash' at the time. I remember digging in beside a bridge spanning a canal that was attacked by Jerry tanks and motorized infantry. We fought for two days, but the bastards—pardon my language, Mrs. Mackinnon—finally pushed us back. A few of us made it to Dunkirk."

"What was it like?" Montgomery asked.

"There were thousands of stranded men and hundreds of abandoned vehicles lining the beach waiting to be evacuated," Bourne explained. "The din was infernal. The Germans shelled and bombed us unmercifully; there were bodies everywhere. I lost my weapon in the sea as I waded in water up to my chin. A fishing boat finally came in and I climbed aboard. Even then, we weren't safe; Stukas strafed us several times before we reached England."

"That's how I lost my husband," Mrs. Mackinnon cut in. "It was his boat. When Tom heard about the evacuation, he volunteered to help. On his second trip, the boat was strafed and he was severely wounded." She looked thoughtfully at Bourne. "Angus managed to keep him alive long enough to get him home."

"I wish I could have done more," Bourne voiced sadly.

Montgomery was stunned by her account. "I'm so sorry about your husband, Mrs. Mackinnon," he managed to say.

"He was a good man," she declared, in a voice laced with grief. The three sat quietly, lost in thought for several moments.

What a strange twist of fate, Montgomery thought, silently wondering how the two had got together.

"I don't mean to pry, Mrs. Mackinnon, but how did you happen to come here?"

"I don't have any children," she replied, "so when Angus said he was looking for a housekeeper; I decided to take the position."

Bourne spoke up, "I needed someone to take care of the house after my wife was killed in an air raid."

"Incredible," Montgomery said.

Bourne continued, "My wife was staying with her parents in Edinburgh when a German night bomber dropped incendiaries on the neighborhood. One of them struck the house and set it on fire. My wife couldn't get out. There were over two hundred people killed or injured that night, mostly women and children. It was bloody awful!"

Montgomery simply nodded, at a loss for words.

Bourne slugged down the last of his drink and stood up. "Can you see now why we hate the Germans?" he said heatedly. "We have a busy day tomorrow, so it's off to bed for me," he commented, and abruptly left the room. Mrs. Mackinnon rose and busied herself with cleaning up.

"Let me help you," Montgomery said, carrying dishes to the sink.

"Angus is a good man," she declared, and their conversation ended there.

8

Commando Basic Training Centre, Close Combat Pistol Range, 0830, 12 August 1942—"This morning, you're going to learn to kill with a pistol, using the battle crouch position," Fairbairn explained confidently, looking steadily at the two Marines. "I know that some of you are crack shots on the range, but target shooting is of no value whatsoever in learning the use of the pistol as a weapon of combat."

Cain looked at Montgomery with a raised eyebrow, as if to say, *What the hell is he talking about?*

"Let me explain," Fairbairn continued. "Suppose you're in a dark alley, a poorly lit street, or a room in a blacked-out building. You can hardly see your gun at arm's length, to say nothing of the sights, and suddenly the enemy starts to shoot at you from an unexpected quarter." Fairbairn's descriptive scenario got their attention. They had not thought about shooting in those terms. "Even if you could see your pistol sights, would you take the time to line them and fire at the enemy's gun flash, would you go through all the steps you learned on the range? Of course not. What you will do, is bring the gun up, shove it in the general direction of the enemy, and pull the trigger as fast as you can, making a mockery of all that range training.

"To begin, I'll need two assistants," Fairbairn began, beckoning to corporals Hunt and Williams. "We all know they did not do so well on the pistol range, so they will make good examples." The two stepped nervously forward, expecting another whipping at the hands of Dangerous Dan.

"Come on," Fairbairn chided, "there will be no rough stuff today." The two heaved a sigh of relief and relaxed.

"Take the .45, place it in the palm of your hand, and grip it tightly," he instructed. He checked each man's grip and adjusted it so that the pistol was properly seated. "Lock your wrist and crouch facing the target," he continued. "Bring the weapon up toward the center of your body and when the pistol reaches eye level, start firing." Fairbairn had the men practice several times, until they were comfortable with the technique. "Load your weapons," he ordered. They inserted the magazine containing seven rounds into the butt of the pistol, pulled the slide to the rear, and let it go forward. The slide stripped the first round and pushed it into the chamber, arming the pistol.

"You are cleared to fire," Fairbairn said. The two men crouched in front of their silhouette targets, brought their weapons up as they had been taught, and quickly fired all seven rounds. After placing the weapons on safe and benching them, everyone rushed forward to see if they had hit the targets.

"Blimey," Finch exclaimed, "will you look at those targets, seven hits in each!" Even though the shots were scattered all over the target, Fairbairn complimented them anyway, saying that they would do better with practice.

The two Marines were impressed. "Shit hot," Montgomery exclaimed, knowing that the "point and shoot" technique was no fluke. He and Cain had tried to teach the two soldiers how to shoot but had been unsuccessful. "This is something we've got to implement in the Raider shooting syllabus," Cain vowed.

The Shooting House, 1300, 12 August 1942—"Gentlemen, today I'm going to introduce you to the 'House of horrors,'" Fairbairn told the group. "In the house," he explained, "you will experience a setting as close to actual combat as we can make it."

Finch just couldn't keep his mouth shut and murmured, "Oh boy, I can hardly wait." As soon as he had said it, he knew he'd made a terrible mistake.

"But before we start," Fairbairn began, "we're going to do a little 'gutter fighting' practice. Corporal, would you be so kind as to assist me with a demonstration?" Finch paled but manfully stepped out of the ranks, knowing that he was about to get his ass kicked. "I'd like you to throw a punch at me," Fairbairn said. Finch held back, trying to decide how he was going to keep from getting hurt. Suddenly, Fairbairn lashed out with his foot and kicked him in the groin.

"That's unfair," Finch bellowed with pain and rushed at the older man, intending to teach him a lesson. Fairbairn grabbed his arm, did a half turn, and flipped him over his hip and onto the ground—hard! Finch hit the ground on his back, gasping for breath. The landing had knocked the breath out of him.

"Dangerous Dan" looked down at the stricken soldier. "In combat, there's no fair play; you must show the enemy no mercy and if a kick in the privates gives you the upper hand, take it!" He pointed to two soldiers. "Will you please assist Corporal Finch; he seems to have injured himself. The rest of you gather round."

For the next two hours, the section practiced various "gutter" techniques, until Fairbairn was satisfied with their progress. It only took him another "demonstration" to convince them that he was deadly serious and they had better put everything into the session or suffer the consequences of being his assistant.

During a break, Montgomery flopped down beside Cain. "He's something else," he said, pointing to the old man.

"You got that right," Cain responded, "he's one of a kind. Have you seen the scars on his arms and hands? The brigadier told me that he's been in hundreds of street fights and is an expert in most types of unarmed fighting."

"Gather round, gentlemen," Fairbairn instructed. "As I mentioned earlier, before I was interrupted," he said—looking at Finch, who reddened but kept his alligator mouth shut—"today we're going to do a 'live fire' exercise in my indoor mystery range. The house consists of different rooms containing moving and concealed targets, which you are to take under fire. You will find that we have introduced actual battle sounds, and varying degrees of lighting, darkness, and shadows to make it more demanding. Of course, we have placed some alarming surprises to keep your interest. The house will test you physically and mentally. Are there any questions?" Fairbairn glanced at Finch to see if he had any smart-ass comments, but the young NCO had learned his lesson. "Right," he said, "see the armorer and pick up a pistol and two magazines of ammunition.

"Captain Cain, I'm sure you want to be the first?" Fairbairn asked, knowing there could only be one answer.

"Delighted," Cain responded, stepping up to the entranceway of the House of Horrors, pistol at the ready. At a nod from the older man, he kicked open the door. Pop-up targets imprinted with lifelike papier-mâché German soldiers jumped out at him from three of the darkened corners. *Holy shit*, his mind screamed, as he automatically crouched down and brought the pistol up. Point and shoot, point and shoot; he focused on Fairbairn's mantra. The muzzle came even with his eyes and he squeezed the trigger—twice, before pivoting to face the next target. Six rounds down range, he counted seconds later, mentally ticking off the number of rounds he had left, and one still in the chamber. Cordite hung in the air, stinging his eyes and making it difficult to see. *Back of the room*, he exclaimed, spotting a man-sized dummy holding a gun in one hand and a lighted cigarette in the other in the haze. His pistol barked and the slide locked to the rear.

Cain quickly ejected the spent magazine and inserted another. He started down a long corridor that led off the room. Guttural voices

71

shouted and there was the sound of gunshots. His pulse raced; the room seemed to be closing in. *Steady*, he reminded himself, fighting hard to maintain self-control. *This is not real, it's a test.* He struggled to fight off the claustrophobic sensation and slow his breathing. He stepped close to a wall and tried to spot where the noise was coming from. The lights brightened and a figure popped out of a doorway. Point and shoot! He fired twice. The target disappeared. *Keep moving*, he chided himself. The lights dimmed and the floor moved under his feet. "What the hell?" he exclaimed aloud, feeling his way along a wall. Sounds of battle blared from hidden speakers, filling the corridor with noise, which disrupted his concentration. Another target appeared and he loosed two quick shots. Several cautious steps further along and he felt a drop-off. Just as he stepped over the gap, a third silhouette emerged. Off balance, he fired, hoping to score a hit. The lights came up and a voice ordered him to clear his weapon and step through the exit at the end of the hall. Just as he complied, a fourth target appeared from a trapdoor holding a pistol, followed by a voice that said, "You're dead!" Cain emerged from the building drenched in sweat and sporting a rather dazed look on his face. "My God," was all he managed to say before being led off by one of the instructors to keep him from talking to the men waiting to go through the house.

Commando Bar, 2030, 13 August—Later that night, the survivors of the Horror House met at the Commando Bar to trade war stories. The lively group ordered pints of Belhaven stout and dragged several tables together to serve as their base of operations. "Motor Mouth" Finch, as he was now called by the group, considered it a point of honor to be the master of ceremonies. He looked around the group. "We're one short," he announced, "where's Lance Corporal O'Bryan?"

His roommate shook his head sadly. "Sacked! 'Colors' said he went barmy in the house and had to be taken away." The men stopped talking and thought about their own fears in the darkened shooting house.

Montgomery spoke up, "I don't mind telling you that there were a couple of moments…" and left the rest of the sentence unfinished. He didn't have to complete it; the men knew exactly what he had intended to say. They had experienced the same fearful sensation but up to now had not admitted it publicly.

"Absent friends," Montgomery declared, and held up his glass in a farewell toast to O'Bryan.

The flow of ale continued unabated. Tongues loosened. Finch joked that at one point he had considered "surrender" as the best option after completely missing a target. Hunt admitted, "I almost shite myself when I heard the German voices," which brought a self-conscious laugh from several others at the tables.

"Did anybody shoot the last target?" Cain asked.

There was a chorus of "hell no's," except for Corporal Williams, who smiled drunkenly. "I got the bastard," he said proudly. "I stuffed cotton in my ears and didn't hear the voice tell me to clear my weapon." Everyone laughed; he was the only man in the section who had emerged from the Horror House alive.

9

Commando Basic Training Centre, Assault Course, 0830, 13 August 1942—Captain George, one of the few officer instructors and, by reputation, a real wild man, stepped in front of the formation and announced amiably, "You're on the assault course this morning, my lads." By this time, the trainees had learned to be suspicious whenever an instructor seemed overly civil ... and Captain George fell into that category.

"Oh, oh, we're for it," Finch stage-whispered as the officer took them on a leisurely orientation walk around the course so they could see and appreciate the nightmarish assembly of challenging obstacles. The men likened it to "taking a condemned man on a tour to inspect the gallows."

The timed assault course was a real "ball-buster," requiring physical strength and endurance. The trainees were given 15 minutes to complete it, while decked out in web gear, steel helmet, and carrying a 9-pound rifle, with fixed bayonet. They had to crawl underneath 20 yards of barbed wire in the mud and slime, climb along a slippery 8-foot log ramp that sloped up to a rocky outcrop, jump from the ramp over a 6-foot wire obstacle, climb down a 50-foot cliff using a rope, and finish with a wild bayonet charge into a line of stuffed dummies. To make the course even more challenging, it was laid out with a peat bog through the center. And to add insult to injury, a heavy rainstorm the previous night had made the ground "slippery as owl shit," according to Montgomery. When the preview was over, the men paired up. It was no surprise that the two Americans found themselves together. George casually reminded the group that the course record was 7 minutes, 20 seconds.

"You ready, old man?" Cain teased the gunny, as they stepped up to the starting point.

"Don't get in my way, sonny," Montgomery countered, fixing the "pig sticker" bayonet on the end of his Lee–Enfield rifle. "Remember, we've only got 15 minutes to complete the course," he reminded the officer.

"What'll I do with the extra five minutes?" Cain countered flippantly, despite the butterflies he felt in his stomach. An instructor with a stopwatch in hand shouted "Standby" and "Go!" Cain took off like a shot, determined to set a course record. He hit the ground hard and slithered under the wire, using his elbows and toes to propel himself forward through the slime. Barbs from a low-hanging strand caught his sodden woolen blouse and jerked him up short. Montgomery, in the adjacent lane, gave the squirming officer a Bronx cheer and forged ahead.

Cain tore free, leaving cloth and a little skin behind. Thoroughly pissed at losing the lead, he redoubled his efforts and managed to catch Montgomery just as he scrambled from the barrier. The two reached the pair of 8-foot tree trunks that sloped up to the wire barrier. The trees had their branches and bark cut off, making them slippery as a greased pig. There were two ways to approach the obstacle: either dashing straight up and risking a nasty fall, or crawling up it like a wimp, which was un-Marine like. The two reached the top in a dead heat.

"Airborne," Cain shouted, leaping into space and clearing the wire with a foot to spare. Montgomery's foot slipped as he jumped and he landed short. "Son-of-a-bitch," he bellowed, tearing free of the

75

wire but now several feet behind Cain. The two were so focused; they failed to note that the instructors were following their progress with more than a passing interest. They were wagering money on the outcome. Bourne put two pounds on Montgomery and stood to make a bundle because of the three to one odds. The other instructors favored youth over experience.

Cain was already starting down the knotted rope by the time Montgomery reached it and had slung his rifle. The gunny threw caution to the winds and literally plummeted to the ground, burning his hands in the process, but catching up. The two hit the ground at the same time and scrambled to free their weapons for the final bayonet attack.

"Come on, old man," Cain gasped, his lungs heaving from the tremendous effort, "show me what you've got."

"You ain't seen nothin' yet," Montgomery managed to utter. The two lowered their rifles and charged. That night, the instructors argued long and hard in the Commando Bar over which one of the Yanks had "stuck" the dummy first. In the end, it was agreed to declare a tie and post both names on the course roll of honor for the fastest time.

———✦———

Tarzan Course, 1000, 13 August 1942—Captain George marched the section at the double quick to a grove of soaring beech trees and proudly pointed to his handiwork, a network of ropes high in the upper branches that looked like a giant spiderweb. The average height above the ground was about 25 feet. The instructors weaned the trainees on simple upright ropes, teaching them the fundamentals of gripping the ropes with hands, knees, and boots, then on to the techniques of climbing inclined and horizontal single ropes, finishing with the "cat-crawl."

"This morning, you're going to learn to 'cat-crawl,'" George announced, and pointed to an instructor standing on a platform high in the trees. "Sergeant Gillian will demonstrate the proper technique." The instructor lay flat on the rope, one leg extended backward with the top of his boot curled over the line while his other leg dangled. He then propelled himself rapidly along by pulling with his arms and pushing with his leg until reaching the opposite platform. "See," George said with a straight face, "it's as easy as falling off a log." His attempt at humor fell flat. The trainees looked decidedly ill at ease.

"All right, lads, who's first?" George asked, looking straight at Cain.

The Marine took up the challenge. "I'd love to," he said, and began climbing a makeshift board ladder to the starting platform. He estimated he was about 20 feet off the ground, high enough to severely challenge one's courage. Cain leaned out over the edge of the platform and tried not to look down. He focused on sliding onto the rope. "Son-of-a-bitch," he mumbled quietly, "this is harder than it looks from the ground." He forced himself to inch further out on the wobbly rope until his body was fully extended. He hooked his right foot over the line, with the other leg dangling for balance. Without it, he would have rolled off the rope. *OK*, he told himself, *no guts, no glory*, and carefully pulled himself away from the platform.

Halfway across the rope, Cain began to feel more confident. He realized that the real test of the "cat-crawl" was not mastering the technique but overcoming the fear of heights. The cat-crawl was an imaginative method designed to separate the men from the boys. One by one, the section successfully negotiated the cat-crawl, except Lance Corporal Harris, who seemed rooted to the ground. He refused to try.

George headed for him and the section expected an ugly scene; instead, he spoke quietly. "Lad, all you have to do is climb up there, do the cat-crawl, and come down. I'll be up there with you to help," he said by way of encouragement.

Harris mumbled, "I can't do it."

George looked him in the eye. "You know what will happen if you fail to complete it," he said, "you will be returned to your unit."

Harris shifted from one foot to the other, wrestling with his fear.

"The section is waiting for you. They've all done it but you," George said quietly, playing up that everyone else had completed the obstacle.

Harris looked up at the platform and then at the men silently watching him. Suddenly, he swallowed hard, nodded his head, and made for the ladder. George was right behind him. Up and up they climbed, with Harris glancing nervously down from time to time. When they reached the platform, George quietly and calmly encouraged him to start. Harris leaned out over the stand but couldn't bring himself to go. "You can do it," George urged.

Harris tried again and this time succeeded. He hung on desperately, struggling to overcome his fear. Finally, he reached out tentatively with his hands and pulled, gaining a couple of feet. The act gave him confidence and he began moving steadily until he reached the halfway point. The rope started swaying and he stopped. His face was deathly pale and damp with sweat. It was only a matter of time before he let go and plunged down to the ground. George reached out to steady the rope and kept on talking. "Relax, take a deep breath. Don't look down."

All at once, George shouted, "Now! Go on." The officer's voice snapped Harris out of his fear and he slowly and shakily clawed his way to the platform. As he climbed down from the platform, his knees half-buckled under him when his feet touched the ground. The section swarmed around him cheering and patting him on the back.

George shook his hand. "Good job, lad," he said enthusiastically. "Now up you go again."

Slide for Life, 1100, 13 August 1942—After completing the Tarzan course, the section "doubled" up a ridge overlooking a deep ravine. They were met by an instructor from the Cameron Highlanders who appeared to have been cleaved from one of the ever-present boulders. Easily 200 pounds, he had broad shoulders, heavily muscled arms and legs, and rough-hewn features. Finch immediately named him "Sergeant Mighty" but was careful not to use the nickname within the goliath's hearing. The man delighted in intimidating the would-be commandos by developing fiendish obstacles that tested them physically and mentally. He was thought to be something of an evil genius and his pitch-black eyes had a devilish glint that reinforced their impression. Finch was convinced that the look in his eyes hinted at madness.

Sergeant Mighty called his most devilish inspiration the "Slide for Life," which the trainees immediately dubbed the "Death Ride." It consisted of a 2-inch manila line stretched at a steep angle across a deep ravine. The trainees had to use their toggle rope to slide down the suspended line. It promised to be a hair-raising, high-speed traverse across the gulf.

"Come on, lads," Sergeant Mighty beckoned to the trainees, "it's time to slide for your life." The men stood on the edge of the ravine. Corporal Adair stared at the 50-foot drop. "Blimey, where's me parachute?" he muttered anxiously. Sergeant Mighty ignored the comment and had the section form a half circle to "view a demonstration by Colour Sergeant Bourne," he announced innocently. Bourne's head snapped up at the mention of his name. He had been lost in thought and was not paying attention. It was common for the instructors to play tricks on one another, and this was one of those times. The senior instructor knew how much Bourne hated heights and had planned this little "gotcha" in retaliation for one of Bourne's previous surprises he had been subjected to. The colour sergeant's menacing glare promised massive revenge, which was not lost on Sergeant Mighty, who turned pale after realizing he may have gone too far.

Bourne threaded the wooden peg of his toggle rope through the loop in the other end, put his left wrist in the circle, and placed the rope over the taut manila line. He grasped the free end with his right hand and wound it tightly around his wrist. An assistant instructor—Sergeant Mighty knew better than to get too close—placed a safety line around his chest and attached it to the main line so that it slid loosely. Bourne walked stiffly to the edge of the cliff, closely approximating a man walking the plank. After a moment of hesitation, he stepped off into space holding the two ends of the toggle rope in a death grip. Even though the manila rope was taut, it sagged 2 or 3 feet under the weight of his 190 pounds, giving him the sensation of falling, and sending his stomach into his throat. He let out an involuntary bellow, which the men took to be a shout of defiance and cheered him as he zipped over the gorge. The men were instructed before starting the slide to keep their legs together and extended out in front to stop themselves at the end. Unfortunately, Colour Sergeant Bourne forgot the instructions and smacked face-first into the opposite embankment, much to the amusement of the instructors and students.

Abseiling, 1500, 13 August 1942—Following the successful negotiation of the Death Ride, the section formed up for Mighty's next adventure. "Wasn't that fun," he called out enthusiastically. "I know you're just dying to do it again but sadly we have to move on."

"Is he kidding?" Adair whispered.

"He loves this shit," Finch muttered. "The bloke is around the bend."

"Lads, I know you're anxious to return to your nice cozy huts, so we're going to take a short cut," Mighty announced. The section immediately suspected they were going to experience another one of his inspirations. "It's called abseiling," he explained, "and it's a fast way to go down a cliff." He nodded to an assistant, who took hold of the quarter-inch climbing line that had been anchored to a sturdy tree and prepared to descend the rock face.

The instructor formed a seat with the rope by wrapping it around his shoulder and leg, and then walked backward to the edge of the precipice. He lowered himself to a sitting position with his feet against the rock face. His left hand grasped the rope above his head, thus keeping himself upright, while his right hand let the line slowly play through it, giving him control of the descent. He pushed outward with his legs and at the same time allowed the line to run through his hands. He dropped 15 to 20 feet before swinging into the face of the cliff. Using his feet as buffers, he pushed outward again and made another drop, continuing the technique until he reached the bottom.

"Cor," Finch whispered flippantly, "that sure looks like fun!" An instructor heard Motor Mouth's comment and tagged the chatterbox to be the first "volunteer," much to the amusement of his classmates. He was quickly hooked up, given a few last-minute instructions, and led to the edge of the cliff.

"Nothing to be concerned about, lad," the instructor joked, "it's not the fall that'll hurt, it's just the sudden stop." Finch looked down and paled. His heart was in his mouth as he slowly edged out over the abyss. He had a death grip on the rope and just hung there, suspended over the 100-foot drop. *OK*, he told himself, *let the line play through*. His first bound was only 3 feet but it was a start. The length of his bounds increased as he gained confidence and he quickly reached the bottom. "Damn that was fun!" he exclaimed.

Toggle Bridge, 1700, 13 August 1942—The trainees had to cross the river on the toggle bridge to return to the center even though an iron footbridge stood just a few yards away. The toggle bridge consisted of three ropes suspended over a fast-flowing mountain stream. The trainees walked on one rope while the other two shoulder-height parallel ropes acted as handholds. Toggles were used at intervals to tie the three ropes together. Cain, Montgomery, Finch, Hawkins, and Edwards were the first to cross the bridge. As they edged cautiously along the rope, it began to swing dangerously from side to side. Hawkins, "Charlie the Clumsy," as he was later known, slipped and lost his balance, pulling Edwards into the ice-cold water with him. Their struggles caused the others to lose their grip on the two parallel hand ropes and end upside down in a mesh of rigging. The more they struggled, the worse their predicament became until their strength gave out. Finch was the first to surrender, closely followed by Cain, and finally Montgomery, who swore vengeance on Hawkins before hitting the water with a mighty splash.

McNeal Manor, 1830, 13 August 1942—Cain slowly dragged his bruised and battered body up the stairs to his room when Loreena called his name: "James, Daddy was called away on business, so there will be just the two of us for dinner."

"Great, just what I need," he mumbled. All he really wanted to do was clean up and hit the rack, not chatter with a woman he hardly knew.

"I'll be in the drawing room," she told him.

"Be right down after I clean up," he answered without enthusiasm. Twenty minutes later, he entered the drawing room to find Loreena standing in front of the fireplace, drink in hand, positively glowing with radiance.

"Here," she said, handing him a crystal glass half-filled with single malt, "you look like you need this."

"You are my savior," he replied gallantly, trying hard not to stare at the beautiful woman in front of him.

"Please, sit down," she said, pointing toward the overstuffed chair that the brigadier normally occupied. "I know you must be exhausted."

"I've had better days," he replied, collapsing into the chair's plushness.

Loreena sat down in the chair across from him and raised her glass in salute. "*Slàinte Mhath*," Loreena said. "*Do dheagh shlàinte*," he replied, butchering the pronunciation. Loreena chuckled at his effort. "At least I tried," he said, pretending to be indignant.

"Oh dear," she responded contritely, "I believe I've offended you." The mischievous look in her eyes belied her words.

"Marines are easily offended," he retorted in jest. There was a moment of awkward silence as they sensed a growing attraction toward the other. To cover his uncertainty, Cain took a gulp of his Scotch and immediately regretted it. He choked on the potent whiskey and began coughing. *I'm sure making a great impression*, he thought to himself. On her part, Loreena was worried that she may have really offended the handsome young man sitting across from her. Both scrambled to say something that would restore the mood. "Sorry," they exclaimed at the same time.

They relaxed in front of the fire, sipping the fine whiskey and enjoying each other's company. They eased into small talk, safe ground for two people who were obviously attracted to one another. When Cain innocently inquired about her father's business meeting, she hesitated for a moment before replying.

"Daddy is meeting with several government officials," she offered, but didn't elaborate. Cain was half in the bag and didn't catch her reticence to discuss it further. "Who's he meeting—Winston?" he kidded.

"As a matter of fact, he is," she answered proudly. "My father is a member of Churchill's inner circle and meets with him regularly." Cain was taken aback. *My God*, he thought, *and I assumed he was just an old retired army officer.*

Loreena noted his surprised look. "Daddy doesn't talk about it much, but he and Winston go back quite a way, before World War I, I believe.

"Let's eat in here," Loreena announced, noting that Cain was getting heavy-lidded. She quickly left the room. When she came back with several sandwiches, Cain was slumped in the chair fast asleep. The effects of the alcohol combined with the vigorous activity and little food had done him in. Loreena decided that he needed the rest more than the sandwiches and let him sleep but left the food on a stand. She stood gazing at the sleeping man and decided that she liked him. She took a blanket and tenderly wrapped him in its folds. "OK, Yank," she whispered, "let's see what happens," and headed off to bed.

Sometime in the middle of the night, Cain woke up, saw the sandwiches, and wolfed them down before groggily making his way up the stairs to his room, where he collapsed fully clothed on the bed. Loreena heard him stumbling around and pictured him lying in bed. She smiled to herself as she drifted back to sleep.

Cain's well-developed internal clock woke him up right on time and he sprang out of bed. It took him a second to work out why he was still dressed and then it came to him. "Oh my God," he exclaimed, humiliated by his behavior the previous night, "she'll think I'm a drunk who can't hold his liquor," he moaned. "Just shoot me now and put me out of my misery." He shucked off his wrinkled civvies and hurriedly replaced them with his heavy British battledress, hoping to get out of the house before Loreena got up.

Cain tiptoed down the stairs and was about to open the outside door when he was startled by Loreena's voice. "Sneaking out without breakfast, are you?" she asked sweetly.

"I'm running a little late," he replied gruffly, "and I don't have time to eat."

"I see," she said reservedly. "In that case, I'm glad that I caught you; I'm leaving and I may not see you again before you return to the States." Cain turned toward her, an ashen look on his face.

"Why?" he demanded emotionally.

His change in demeanor startled her and she quickly responded. "My leave is up and I have to return to work in London."

"I'm sorry," he apologized, "I didn't mean to startle you. I thought maybe you were leaving because of my awful behavior last night."

It was Loreena's turn to be surprised. "No silly, I really enjoyed spending the evening with you—well, at least part of the evening," she said, giggling self-consciously.

"I'll miss you," he blurted out, at a loss for words.

"You're sweet," she said, and kissed him lightly on the cheek as he went out the door.

10

Commando Basic Training Centre, Night Assault Landing, 0730, 15 August 1942—"What's the matter, Skipper?" Montgomery prodded. "You've been down in the mouth this morning." He was right. Cain was still thinking of Loreena as he caught up with the gunny on the way to the morning formation.

"Nothing," he said gruffly.

"Right," Montgomery declared, "except that you look like you just lost your best friend."

"I'll be OK," he replied, softening his tone of voice.

"I hope so," the gunny stressed, "because the next 36 hours are going to be a real ball-buster."

The section were practicing for the night assault landing exercise; a terrifyingly realistic reproduction of an amphibious landing carried out under cover of darkness. The exercise called for the trainees to paddle boats from Bunarkaig, a short distance from the school on the shores of Loch Lochy, and attack a heavily defended section of the shoreline. Realism was enhanced by instructors positioned to fire live ammunition, mortar rounds, and explosive charges close to the trainees as they assaulted the objective. The attack was carefully scripted to avoid casualties but despite the precautions, several men had been wounded on previous exercises. On one particularly bloody night, a man was killed and another wounded when their boat veered off course into the fire of a Bren gun.

As might be expected for such a dangerous exercise, preparations were extensive. The section spent hours studying the operational order, maps, and sketches of the objective and sand tables that had been produced showing the precise attack and withdrawal routes. The staff warned that live ammunition was going to be used and anyone deviating from the routes might be inviting a trip to the hospital. "Great," Harris bitched, "I survived Dunkirk and now I have to run the risk of being shot in training." The warning was taken to heart by the section. There were no slackers; the men clearly understood the seriousness of what they were doing and gave it their best shot. They ran through several dress rehearsals, including boat drills in the loch, until everyone was intimately familiar with the plan and had developed a high level of proficiency.

———✦———

Darkness was falling on the big night as the final preparations were completed. The exercise was treated as the real thing and everything was made as grimly realistic as possible, including a personnel and equipment inspection just as if they were going on an actual raid. The two instructors that were assigned to accompany and evaluate the section went over the men with a fine-tooth comb. Equipment was checked to ensure that it was serviceable and free of rattles and noises that might give them away. Pockets were turned inside out to ensure that no incriminating items were being carried that could aid the enemy if they were captured. Identification tags were checked, because on one exercise an unconscious injured man had needed an immediate blood transfusion but was not wearing his ID tag and almost died before the medics could find his blood type. For uniformity, the men were instructed to keep their first aid packets in the pocket on the front left thigh of their battledress.

The school's ordnance sergeant issued blank ammunition for the section's personal weapons. Corporal Williams drew a 20-pound demolitions kit and six blasting caps. He and Corporal Edwards were the designated demo party and were responsible for placing the charge that would blow up the objective. Both men had received extensive training on how to fuse and set the explosives but they were still a little nervous, because the success or failure of the raid was in their hands.

"Got a light?" Finch joshed, as Williams checked the contents of the U.S. Army M37 demolition kit.

"Sure, mate," Williams replied, confident that flame would not cause the C-2 to explode. He tossed one of the 2 ½-pound blocks to the jokester. "Catch," he said. Finch "shit a brick," according to Montgomery, and desperately reached out to catch the deadly explosive. In the process, he dropped his rifle in the mud just as an instructor walked past.

"You're a poor excuse for a soldier," the instructor bellowed. "Pick up your rifle and report to me after the exercise."

"What do you want to carry," Williams asked his partner, "the demolition kit or the blasting caps?" Edwards thought about it for a second. He knew the blasting caps were filled with a high-explosive compound that was extremely sensitive to flame, heat, or shock. "Demolition kit," he answered. "Damn," Williams swore, "I knew you'd say that."

The weather turned ugly as the section formed up in full battle order. Rain squalls pelted the formation, thoroughly soaking them within minutes. The temperature dropped and the wind picked up. "Just great," Harris griped again, "I won't have to worry about getting shot, I'll freeze to death."

Montgomery piped up. "Great commando weather," he said cheerfully, trying to keep up morale. "The instructors will be trying to keep warm. The poor bastards will never know what hit them when we attack."

"Right," Cain pitched in, "let's go kick some ass!" With a chorus of "Up the Marines," the section moved out in an atmosphere of mounting excitement.

"Blimey," Harris whispered, "I feel like I'm off to win the war." The instructors set a fast pace and the column soon reached Bunarkaig, where two Goatley collapsible assault boats were waiting on the beach.

The men lugged the two 330-pound canvas and wooden boats to the edge of the water and launched them into the wind-driven waves. Montgomery was in water up to his waist before it was his turn to climb into the boat. "Son-of-a-bitch," he muttered, as the wind whipped through his wet clothing. "It's cold enough to freeze the balls off a brass monkey."

Cain heard the remark. "Remember, old man, this is great commando weather," he mocked through chattering teeth.

"Yes, sir, I know that you officers are godlike," the gunny replied, tongue in cheek. "But us poor enlisted are only human and right now I'm freezing my ass off!"

It was eerily quiet as they paddled toward the center of the loch in the murky darkness. Moments later, the faint outline of a gap in the trees, marking the landing point, appeared on the shoreline. Thirty yards from the beach, the men started to think they had made it without being discovered. "Maybe the bastards have gone home," Harris whispered. At that moment, all hell broke loose. With paralyzing suddenness, the shore of the loch erupted with gunfire. Machine-gun tracers arched uncomfortably close, explosions rocked the boats, and Very lights and parachute flares bathed the water in a ghostly light. Guttural shouts in German blared from loudspeakers and, in a devilish crescendo, a dozen airburst thunder flashes erupted in an ear-splitting cacophony of sound.

A line of tracers suddenly zipped alongside the boat and shattered Harris' paddle. A sliver of wood struck his helmet with enough force to throw him into the bottom of the boat. "I'm hit," he cried out in fear, clutching his head with both hands.

"Where you hit, lad?" the instructor asked worriedly, and reached out to look at the wound.

"My head, I took a bullet to the head," Harris replied. "I can feel the blood running down my face."

The instructor forced his hands away and looked for the wound. There was enough light from the flares to see that Harris was not wounded, only scared. The wood had embedded in the burlap helmet cover and the blood he felt running down his face was merely sweat. "You twit," the instructor growled, "you're not wounded. Now get off your arse and stop feeling sorry for yourself."

The section had been momentarily paralyzed, shocked by the sudden violence. The instructor bellowed, "What the bloody 'ell are you doing? Get moving! Get out of the boats and hit the beach!" His shouting galvanized the men into action and they leaped out of the Goatleys into the sucking mud. Ear-splitting explosions rocked the sweating, stumbling, slipping, swearing men.

Once off the beach, the men flopped down and took the hilltop objective under fire. Simulated small-arms fire raked the emplacement, while "live fire" from carefully sited instructors snapped overhead. Explosions continued unabated, showering the men with earth and stones.

"What are you waiting for, a bloody invitation?" an instructor shouted at the demolition party. "Get your arse up that hill!" The two demolitionists glanced at each other and nodded. "For king and country!" they bawled, and leaped to their feet.

"Cease-fire," the instructor ordered, as the two men scrambled up the hillside. At the top, they threw themselves against the wall of the simulated bunker. "Next time you carry the demo kit; the bloody thing weighs a ton," Edwards gasped, trying to catch his breath.

"Quit whining and hold the fuse steady while I crimp the blasting cap," Williams replied. Both men knew this was the most dangerous part of the preparation. If it was not done properly, the blasting cap might explode with enough force to take a man's hand off.

Williams carefully tightened the crimping tool around the end of the cap and held it behind and slightly below his waist as he finished crimping it. Satisfied that it was ready, he inserted the fused blasting cap into the C-2 and molded some of the putty-like explosive around it to make sure it was firmly embedded. "Ready, mate?" he asked. Edwards nodded and Williams pulled the ring on the fuse lighter. A slight pop told them the fuse was burning and they had better get out of there. They reached the safety of a fold in the ground just as the 20-pound charge exploded in a gray cloud of debris. The blast echoed across the Highlands.

A white Very light streaked upward, the signal to withdraw. "Pull back!" the instructor shouted. The men pulled back by subsection, each covering the other as they made their way back to the boats through the "enemy" fire. There was no let-up. Explosions and concussion grenades rocked them, while tracers arched overhead. They clambered into the Goatleys, seized their paddles, and in adrenalin-infused frenzy, they propelled the boats away from the madness. Gradually, the firing stopped, replaced by blessed silence as the men padded numbly back in the cold, steady downpour.

Graduation Exercise, 1000, 16 August 1942—The 12-man section mustered on the field in front of the Commando Headquarters in full battle order. The only thing missing was live ammunition. Bourne called the formation to attention and saluted as Lieutenant Colonel Moss approached. He returned the salute.

"Colour sergeant, have the men stand easy," he commanded. "Gentlemen," Moss began, "thus far in your training, you have been challenged physically and mentally by a variety of activities. Over the next three days, you will be called upon to use all of this training to complete the final exercise." He paused and looked each man in the eye before continuing. "You will be tested as you have never been tested before. Good luck," he added. "Colour sergeant, take charge."

Bourne saluted smartly and waited for Moss to march away before escorting the men to the supply warehouse.

A diminutive quartermaster sergeant and an assistant were waiting inside the rough-hewn stone boathouse when the section arrived. Two fully inflated seven-man rubber boats were stacked next to the two men. "Sign here," the QMS said brusquely, thrusting a property receipt into Cain's hand.

"What's this for?" he asked, taken aback by the sudden request. "I've never signed for equipment before."

"Sir, king's regulations state that property must be signed for before being released," the officious little man replied haughtily. Cain fleetingly considered punching the smug little bastard's lights out but decided to surrender rather than start a fight and scrawled a signature on the document. The QMS smiled in victory and strutted back to his warehouse with the clerk trailing in his wake.

"Damn pencil pushers," Montgomery swore, "don't he know there's a war on?"

Bourne spoke up, "Another bloody desk warrior, that one. A quartermaster tried that with Colonel Moss."

"What happened?" Montgomery asked.

"Last I heard, he was counting snow shoes in Iceland."

Cain chuckled. "Don't take it too badly. Wait till that arrogant little shit looks at the signature and tries to find an American named John Hancock. Come on," he urged, "let's get the boats on the truck before the QMS finds out he's been hoodwinked."

———◆———

Coastal Command Headquarters, 1500, 16 August 1942—Cain stood hunched over under the canvas cover in the swaying Bedford lorry, trying to get some feeling back in his aching butt. He had been sitting on the hard wooden bench for over two hours and his rear end had progressed from numbness to painful.

"How much further?" he shouted to Montgomery, who was slouched on the bench across from him.

The gunny looked at his watch. "About half an hour," he yelled above the sound of the road noise. The vibration of the truck's hard rubber tires on the road surface made a loud drone that made it difficult to talk. Most of the section had fallen asleep immediately after leaving the training center despite the cold and uncomfortable seating. They were simply following the age-old custom in the ranks to sleep whenever and wherever possible.

Cain gazed at the sleeping soldiers. The men were jammed together, wool caps pulled down over their heads, swaying with the motion of the truck. Their kit was stacked in the center of the truck bed on top of the two rubber boats, making it impossible to move around to restore circulation. "This is worse than marching," Cain muttered, but then thought better of it, remembering the speed marches he had had to endure. He shivered. The air streaming through gaps in the cover was freezing and he was thoroughly chilled. "Just another shitty day in the Highlands," he muttered, wondering if he would ever be warm again. He glanced at the gray, threatening sky and hoped that the rain would hold off for a few more hours.

Twenty minutes later, the truck slowed down as it approached a sign over the roadway announcing they were about to enter HMS *Lochinvar*, the code name of the Port Edgar training base for the Royal Naval Patrol Service. A spotless White Ensign flew from a tall pole near the entrance. The change in speed acted as an alarm clock and the men came awake. A heavy steel pole blocked the road. A rifle-toting Royal Marine in battledress and a green beret stepped out of a sandbagged guard post and motioned for the truck to stop.

Cain noticed a second armed sea soldier standing off to one side backing him up. "They take security seriously," he said to the gunny, as the sentry carefully studied the transport orders the driver had handed him. Satisfied that the documents were in order, the guard stepped back and signaled to someone in the hut. The gate slowly rose. The sentry motioned the driver to proceed, and with a mashing of gears the lorry drove onto the base along a street that was lined with bizarrely painted buildings. Irregular patterns of black, green, and brown paint covered their sides and roof. *Camouflage,* Cain thought, trying to envision what the scene must look like from bombing height. He couldn't see any evidence of bomb damage, so the paint scheme must be working or, on second thought, maybe the port was not worth bombing.

The truck continued until it reached a boxlike two-story building near the waterfront. Another armed Royal Marine sentry stepped out of the entranceway and told them to get off the truck and follow him inside. The first floor was surprisingly empty except for a large square table covered by a white sheet in the center of the space. Several moveable chalkboards were arranged in a half circle around the table. A stairway led to second-floor office spaces and a viewing platform that ran around the inside of the building. The space was painted battleship gray and was devoid of any decoration, except a large poster of Winston Churchill on the wall with the admonition "Loose Lips Sink Ships," under his pugnacious mien. Altogether, Cain thought it was a cold room, a no-nonsense room—it was a room made for the business of war.

Bourne ordered the men to ground their gear and gather around the tabletop. A commando lieutenant came down the stairway and stood next to the shrouded table.

"Gentlemen," he began, "as Colonel Moss explained to you this morning, this is your final training exercise. It will require you to call upon everything you have learned and all your physical ability to complete it." With that, he dramatically swept the sheet off the tabletop. It concealed a remarkably detailed three-dimensional terrain model.

"This is a relief map of a section of the Highlands about 50 miles from this location," the commando explained. "For the purpose of the exercise, you will consider it to be enemy territory. From this point on, consider yourselves to be operational." He picked up a pointer and directed their attention to a section of the shoreline. "You will land here by two of the navy's light coastal motor torpedo boats. The Special Boat Section lets us borrow them occasionally when they aren't busy probing the French coastline. Once ashore, you'll scale these bluffs and commence the approach to the objective." The officer stopped the brief to allow the men to observe where he was pointing. Cain took a quick look at the map scale. It was the standard military gauge, 1 inch on the map equaled 50,000 inches on the ground. He squatted down so he could look at the bluffs at eye level. He judged them to be 40–50 feet high if the scale was accurate.

The lieutenant continued, using a wooden pointer to indicate the location of the objective. He tapped a section of the map that was unmarked by towns or villages. A single winding road led toward a complex of buildings that was located well inland on the crest of a hill, at least 18 miles from the coast. "This building," he explained, pointing to one of several aerial photographs that were laid out on the table, "represents a radar station manned by an estimated reinforced squad of German soldiers. Your mission is to destroy the radar and bring back its parabolic reflector, a key piece of equipment. Captain Cain, you have 30 minutes to plan and brief your team. Do you have any questions?"

Cain was taken aback. Up to this moment, he had not considered that he would be the mission leader. He assumed it would be one of the British NCOs and that he would simply be a member of the team. He recovered quickly. "I don't have any questions at this time," he said.

"Very well," the lieutenant replied, turning two of the chalkboards around to face the team. "Here is your mission order and coordinating instructions."

"Gather around," Cain directed. "It appears that there's only one good approach to the objective," he said, pointing to a stream gulch on the terrain model that led almost directly to the radar station. "The problem is that we're going to have to cross the river right here." Everyone knew what that meant. It wasn't that the river crossing was difficult—all the commandos knew how to swim—but they would get soaking wet. With temperatures in the high 30s, there was a danger of hyperthermia. "All right, lads," he said, mimicking Bourne, "let's get ready to march." As the men broke up to gather their gear, Cain took time to write down the coordinating instructions in his leader's notebook—radio call signs, pickup times, checkpoints, and emergency signals.

———————◆———————

Motor Torpedo Boat 210, Late Afternoon, 16 August—Cain led the group to the harbor, where several huge barrage balloons tugged at their wire moorings in the light wind. He thought they provided enough protection to discourage low-level strafing but they wouldn't hinder the bombers. The harbor bustled with activity as motor boats and harbor launches scurried about the water carrying out the business of the day. Two battered wooden Vosper motor torpedo boats (MTB) were moored stern first at the end of the pier. It was obvious they had experienced hard use. "Rode hard and put away wet," was how Montgomery described them. Their black and gray camouflage paint scheme was faded and almost completely worn away. In spots, rust streaks ran down their weathered sides. Several new unpainted mahogany slats covered the scars of running gun battles and stood out in sharp contrast to the worn siding.

"Battle damage," Cain said, pointing them out to Montgomery. "This puppy has seen some action," the SNCO replied. Several crewmen in work uniforms were on deck. One glanced up from what he was doing and gave a friendly wave. Lance Corporal Adair waved back. "Friendly bloke," he muttered.

As the group approached the MTBs, their three powerful American-built Packard 12-cylinder supercharged gasoline engines roared to life. Exhaust smoke enveloped the aft section of the boats and the stench of high-octane gasoline hung in the air. Two crew members in dirty coveralls stood ready to let go the mooring lines in preparation for getting underway. Cain led his half-section across the narrow gangway of MTB 210, while Montgomery and the other half-section headed toward the second boat, which had the large pennant number "204" outlined in black paint on her dark-gray hull. A petty officer, wearing a two-piece coverall over a blue jersey and sporting a Webley revolver hanging from his belt, stood nonchalantly at the end of the gangway.

"Permission to come aboard, sir," Cain asked, in the time-honored manner for boarding a ship. The look on the sailor's face seemed to say, *Why the bloody hell are you asking me?*

It was an awkward moment until a voice called out from the tiny open bridge, "Granted." Cain looked up and saw a bare-headed officer in a white pullover wave. "Come aboard!" he shouted. Cain saluted the British naval ensign on the stern and stepped onto the wooden deck.

A tall, lanky man in an oil-stained, brown duffle coat and a salt-encrusted officer's cap greeted him warmly in a broad upper-class accent: "Welcome aboard, captain," he said, sticking out his hand and introducing himself. "I'm Sub-Lieutenant Andrew Bright, the number one, and that scruffy-looking character up there is Lieutenant John McGregor, the boss." The officer waved cheerily from the bridge. "He's busy getting the boat underway," the ruddy faced sub-lieutenant explained. "He wants to be at the landing site just after dark to give you enough time to reach the objective before dawn."

Just at that moment, McGregor pressed a button and bells jangled throughout the ship. Men ran to their underway stations and he bawled, "Cast off all lines." The crewmen responded by tossing the heavy manila mooring lines onto the wharf and quickly stowing the rope fenders that kept the MTB from smashing against the concrete pier in rough water. Depot workers quickly gathered up the mooring lines and coiled them around the steel bollards that were evenly spaced along the pier.

The deck vibrated under Cain's feet as the engines powered up and the boat swung away from her moorings, past the boom-gate at the entrance to the harbor, and headed toward the open sea. She easily slid over the full but gentle swell and within a minute he estimated that the 70-foot craft was doing at least 20 knots and still accelerating into the waters of the Firth of Forth. As the boat picked up speed and the hull lifted from the water, it assumed a bows-up attitude creating a heavy, broad wash that threw twin banks of foam away from the bow. The boat's hull began to plane and take its correct running trim.

Bright noticed Cain's surprise at the fast acceleration. "She can go 40 knots in a pinch," he explained, "and maybe a shade better if Jerry is after us."

"Has that happened often?" Cain asked.

"Only once since I've been aboard, but the skipper is an old hand at dodging German E-boats. Just before I came aboard, the skipper was involved with Lieutenant Wellford's MTB 204 and two others in a night attack on two German merchant ships, escorted by three E-boats," Bright related. "The MTBs attacked and launched their torpedoes before the Germans realized they were there. One of the ships exploded in a huge ball of fire that lit up the area, exposing our boats. The heavily armed E-boats immediately counterattacked and sank one of our MTBs, but the others managed to escape. Our boat was heavily damaged in the melee but the skipper managed to bring her back on one engine. Three of our crew were killed in action and four wounded, including the XO, who I replaced. Since then, we have had several run-ins but nothing like that night." Bright pointed to MTB 204 30 yards off their port side. "Lieutenant Wellford got off rather lightly, only one man killed and two wounded."

Bright pointed to an open space in front of the small box-like bridge. "Captain, you can have your men put your rubber boat and stack their gear there. They can go below and rest in the crew's mess deck. I'll take you on a tour of our little battleship."

Cain passed the word to his men, dropped his pack, and followed the young officer forward to the pedestal-mounted Oerlikon 20mm cannon.

"This is Able Seaman Bender," Bright said, introducing the sailor. "He's the best gunner in the MTB squadron." The diminutive seaman actually blushed at the compliment.

"Thank you, sir, but it's really Winston that deserves the credit."

"Winston?" Cain asked inquisitively.

"We named the cannon after Mr. Churchill, don't you see," Bright replied. "Winston's bark is just as deadly as his bite." Cain nodded knowingly as he recalled hearing Winston Churchill's ringing declarations which had rallied his countrymen to "wage war, by sea, land, and air, with all our might…" Cain then noticed the swastika stenciled on the barrel of the well-greased cannon.

Bender bragged, "Jerry wasn't as accurate as we were." "We downed the ME109 just off the coast when he tried to strafe us." Bright smiled and patted the seaman on the shoulder.

"Come on, let's meet the skipper," Bright said, heading for the bridge. The two squeezed past the port side twin .303 Vickers machine-gun tub into the tiny space occupied by McGregor and the coxswain, who was hunched over the wheel.

McGregor extended his hand to the American with a warm, friendly grin. "How do you like our boat?!" he shouted above the noise of the engines.

"She's quite a battleship!" Cain bellowed, tongue in cheek.

99

The Brit chuckled and leaned closer. "She can take care of herself in a stand-up fight," he replied proudly. "Winston has proved it and we're just waiting for the chance to put one of our fish into a Jerry hull," he said, pointing to the 18-inch torpedo tube adjacent to the bridge. "Our torpedoes were recently upgraded with a new explosive called Torpex and we're anxious to try them out."

Cain studied the officer as he talked. McGregor was in his late twenties and about the same height as Cain. However, whereas Cain was built like a football player, McGregor was lean, like a racehorse. Cain must have outweighed him by 40 pounds. The Brit was all nervous energy and, although he tried to conceal it, his restless fidgeting gave him away. *Can't say I blame him*, Cain thought, *trying to cope with the constant threat of German E-boats night after night would make anyone a little edgy.*

McGregor checked the magnetic compass housed on the forward edge of the bridge and gave the coxswain a course correction. "Steer Nor'-East until we're well clear of the harbor." He then turned to Bright. "Number one, will you take the conn while I brief Captain Cain?"

"I'd love to, John," Bright replied casually. "All right, Andrew, she's all yours." Cain was surprised at the informal relationship between the two naval officers. In the U.S. Navy, he knew if you called your boss by his first name it would be a career-ending event.

"Let's go down to the wheelhouse out of the elements," McGregor suggested, and led the way through a hatch on the port side wing of the bridge. "Watch your head," he warned, as he ducked through the small opening. The charthouse was little more than a large packing box, situated beside the radio room and close enough to the galley to smell the remains of the crew's lunch, which together with the powerful odor of gasoline made Cain a little queasy. He marveled at how much could be crammed into such a small space. A waist-high table filled the center of the space, while long padded seats that folded into bunks and could be used as life rafts lined the bulkheads. Various items of navigation equipment were stowed within easy reach.

McGregor spread a well-worn chart of the coastline on the chart table, which gave Cain a further opportunity to observe him. At 24, the young officer was already a veteran of the brutal East Coast and Channel night-time killing grounds. The first signs of strain were beginning to show on his deeply tanned, angular face. Shallow crow's feet lined the corners of his eyes and marred his otherwise smooth features. *Too much time squinting through binoculars*, Cain figured. McGregor had the look of an experienced sailor and the indefinable air of a combat veteran. The dark blue and white ribbon bar on his uniform coat verified Cain's appraisal. The Distinguished Service Cross, the third-highest award for gallantry in the British Navy, was not given lightly. Cain suspected that the award was for the night action that Bright had mentioned.

McGregor pointed out the landing site on the chart. "I anticipate that we'll be in the objective area sometime after 2000," McGregor explained. "There will be a full moon, which should help you get ashore."

"Good," Cain replied. "I wasn't looking forward to climbing those bluffs in total darkness."

McGregor continued, "My crew will have your rubber boat ready for launching on the starboard side. We'll drop you off about a half mile from the beach. Sorry we can't get you any closer because of rocks. I expect there will be a 1- to 2-knot current running east to west, so we'll drop you off at a point that will allow for the current. Any questions so far?"

"What about our rendezvous?" Cain asked.

"I am to pick you up in 36 hours," McGregor answered. "My orders stipulate that if you're not there, I'm to return to base."

Cain smiled. "We'll make it, have the hot cocoa ready."

"Good man," McGregor replied, "I'd expect nothing less from a Marine." The two men shook hands warmly and parted. McGregor joined Bright on the bridge, while Cain went forward to join his men.

He passed down the narrow passageway, lurching from side to side, as the MTB plowed through the increasingly rough water. The boat rose and fell uncomfortably, up and down, with a corresponding sickening motion from side to side. *Damn*, he thought, *this'll make for a wet ride in the rubber boat.* He stepped through the mess deck hatch just in time to see one of his stalwarts retch into a bucket. The smell of vomit hit his nostrils and for a second he thought he would need a bucket of his own. He just barely managed to control the impulse.

"Welcome to the vomit comet, captain," Finch proclaimed cheerfully. "It seems that a few of the lads haven't acquired their sea legs yet."

Cain looked around the small space and saw that fully half his men were green around the gills. The rough weather combined with the close confines of the cabin and noxious smells—gasoline, grease, and sweat—had sickened them. He noticed that the unaffected men were relishing the condition of the poor sods. They considered seasickness as a "rite of passage" that landsmen had to make in order to be a "real" seaman. Finch seemed to be the biggest dog in the puddle. He kept inquiring when dinner would be served. "Nice juicy pork sandwiches, with plenty of mayonnaise," he chattered gaily, with a malicious grin on his face.

Cain saw what he was up to and interrupted his colorful commentary. "Get these men up on deck," he declared. "Fresh air will do them a world of good." Corporal McTavish was so sick that he had to be helped up the ladder. The rest of the men made it one way or another and collapsed on the deck, much to the amusement of the Oerlikon gun crew. "They don't look much like trained killers," the leading seaman remarked.

———◆———

Motor Torpedo Boats 204 and 210, 1930, 16 August 1942—It was an hour after dusk and the MTBs were close to the launch point. McGregor was hunched over the bridge compass studying its luminous points. Satisfied that he was in the right location, he straightened up and gave the order, "Stop engines." Without the throb of the Packard engines, it seemed unnaturally quiet as the boat drifted to a stop. The air was cold and blustery. McGregor shivered despite the duffle coat and wool sweater. *I'm glad I'm not a commando*, he thought. *It's going to be damn cold on the moor*. He raised his night binoculars and swept the horizon for danger—force of habit even though this was just an exercise—and focused on the shoreline. The full moon provided enough light so that he could make out the landing beach and the tall bluff that backed it. "I'd hate to have to climb those heights tonight," he muttered aloud.

"Did you say something, sir?" the helmsman asked.

"I'm just thinking about the commandos," he replied.

Shadowy forms moved about on the cramped deck. A figure detached itself and climbed onto the bridge. McGregor recognized the burly shape of the Marine officer despite the darkness and the boot polish that covered his face. "All set, Jim?" he asked.

Cain smiled. "Never better," he joked, "I just love this shit!" McGregor could believe it. The Marine seemed to radiate enthusiasm, an eagerness to pursue the job at hand, even in tonight's beastly weather.

"Good show," McGregor said with a laugh. "I'll be thinking of you as I enjoy a hot cup of tea in the wardroom."

"Be careful that you don't burn your lips," Cain responded drily.

"Good luck," McGregor declared earnestly, shaking the Marine officer's hand. "I'll see you in 36 hours," he added.

Cain nodded. "Thanks for the hospitality, John."

Cain stepped off the bridge and joined his half-section waiting amidships for the MTB's crewmen to launch the rubber boat. The sailors muscled the unwieldy 300-pound craft across the plywood deck and slid it into sea. It lurched against the side of the MTB and threatened to get away from the two men holding mooring lines that kept it steady. They were having difficulty keeping their feet in the lively swell that rocked the boat. McTavish, now fully recovered, and Frank Hart were the first men to climb over the rail and jump into the pitching craft. They tried to time their leap to catch the bobbing boat on the uprise but Hart misjudged the timing and landed off balance. He would have fallen overboard if McTavish had not grabbed him. "Going for a swim, were we?" McTavish teased.

"Thanks, mate," was all the shaken man could say. The thought of falling into the cold water had unnerved him.

"Take this," a commando called out from the MTB's deck and passed Hart a rucksack. He and McTavish were responsible for stowing and lashing down the team's equipment and weapons. It was slow work in the dark, which was made even more difficult by the flood of water that sloshed over the spray tubes. By the time they finished, there was a good 3 inches of seawater in the bottom of the boat. Finished, McTavish signaled the others to come aboard. Cain, the designated coxswain, scrambled aboard and the others, one by one, joined him in the jam-packed boat. The men had difficulty getting to their positions. Cain tried to squeeze past another man and his foot caught in a lashing line that threw him headlong into Hunt, who almost went overboard for the second time. "Blimey, what a cock-up," he swore. The training in the calm waters of the loch had not prepared them for the rough conditions they were experiencing. Darkness and rough water played havoc with the inexperienced commandos. Finally, they were all settled in position on the spray tubes with their paddles raised.

"Cast off the bloody lines!" Cain shouted angrily, frustrated by the way the exercise was going. As soon as the lines were in the boat, he ordered, "Give way together—stroke."

The men dug in. Cain stood, gripping the paddle tightly and bracing it against his hip. He angled the face of the blade and steered the boat away from the MTB, which rapidly disappeared into the darkness. "Rest easy," he said, "we'll wait here for the other boat." The men rested the paddles across their laps and used the time to adjust their positions. It was uncomfortable to sit on the spray tube with one leg tucked underneath. It was not uncommon for a paddler to develop painful leg cramps.

A voice called out—"Ahoy, Raider." Cain smiled. *Leave it to Montgomery to use the Marine Raider hail.*

"Over here," Cain responded. A moment later, the second boat appeared out of the darkness. It was almost impossible to spot. It had a low silhouette and a black neoprene covering which absorbed light and blended in with the dark water. Montgomery reported his men were all accounted for and ready to move out.

Within minutes, the only sounds that could be heard were the paddles dipping rhythmically into the water and the rollers surging onto the distant shoreline. The full moon made it possible to see the stretch of beach that had been chosen as the landing site. As the boat got closer to the shore, one of the paddlers spotted a spray of white water cascading off a huge boulder directly in their path. "Dig in," Cain shouted frantically, "rock ahead!" The alarm in his voice spurred the paddlers to put their backs into the stroke. He leaned into the paddle rudder and used all his strength to try to keep the boat pointed away from the "bloody thing." "Put your backs into it, men," he shouted, "or we'll have to swim for it!" The boat gathered speed as a large roller lifted the boat and thrust it toward the boulder. Cain strained with the effort to steer the craft away. At the last minute, the wave broke against the boulder and the backwash angled the boat just enough that it missed the rock by inches.

"Blimey, that was close!" Hunt exclaimed, greatly relieved to have escaped the sea for a third time. Montgomery's boat was far enough behind that it was able to easily avoid the boulder.

The men slacked off after their near disaster until Cain yelled, "Paddle, we're not on the beach yet." They dipped their blades into the water and began paddling with even, strong strokes. The boat caught another roller and rode it through the churning water almost to the beach.

"Over the side," Cain called out. The men jumped into the calf-deep water and dragged the boat to the foot of the bluff, where they concealed it with brush. The second boat came ashore soon after, and was stashed with the first one. The section spread out to provide security while Lance Corporal MacDonald, the best climber, scouted for the easiest route to the top of the 60-foot bluff. He returned several minutes later. "I found a good route, but I'll need all the toggle ropes," he said. They were quickly gathered up and Corporal Williams, MacDonald's climbing buddy, quickly spliced them together, making a 72-foot climbing line.

MacDonald slung his rifle across his back and coiled the line around his shoulder. "I'll tie the line off when I get to the top," he said, and started the ascent. The rest of the section established a security perimeter and prepared to follow. Cain stood at the base of the cliff and watched the Scot scramble up the height until he vanished. *The man climbs like a monkey*, Cain thought with envy, because of his own dread of heights. Minutes later, he heard a muffled shout and the end of the climbing line whizzed past his head. "First section, up you go," he called out, and started to climb. Colour Sergeant Bourne was the second man, followed by Adair, Finch, McTavish, and Hawkins. Montgomery's section—Hunt, Williams, Arawn, Edwards, and Harris—would pull security until it was their turn on the rope.

Cain slung his rifle and gripped the line tightly. He found a toehold and started to climb, using his arms and legs to propel himself upward. The moonlight helped him see the toeholds in the face of the bluff. Erosion had worn down its face, providing crevices and cracks that he could use. The climbing line was a godsend. He used it to help pull himself upward and to take some of the strain off his legs. Halfway to the top, he was breathing like a steam engine from the exertion. His arms strained with the effort but he couldn't rest because Bourne was just a few feet below him. He glanced down to find his next toehold and spotted the end of a rock that offered just what he was looking for. It looked solid. He raised his right foot, placed his boot on the exposed end, and stepped up. It instantly gave way but he had a death grip on the climbing line and instead of falling, he mashed his face into the hard-packed dirt. "Shit," he muttered, more humiliated than hurt, and hoped that no one had seen him.

Bourne was only a few feet below the American and happened to be looking up when the officer slipped. He was instantly showered by a cascade of dirt and pebbles that peppered his head and shoulders. After spitting out a mouthful of mud, he called out anxiously, "OK, sir?"

"Piece of cake," Cain replied self-consciously, as he scrambled to regain his footing. A minute later, he clambered over the rim of the bluff and stepped back a few yards to recover his breath. Bourne soon appeared by his side.

"Tough climb in the dark," the Brit remarked.

"Especially if you're a klutz," Cain responded contritely. Within 20 minutes, the entire section was assembled and prepared to continue the exercise. Just as they stepped off, Sergeant Arawan spotted a blinking light in the darkness.

Lance Corporal Harris, the radio operator, studied the signal for a moment. "It's for us," he said, "we are to return to the boats immediately."

"Are you sure?" Cain asked incredulously, wondering why they were being recalled. The exercise had just started. A series of light flashes confirmed the signal.

Part II

Operation *Switch-Off*

11

HMS *Lochinvar*, **Coastal Command Headquarters, Firth of Forth, Scotland, 0300, 17 August 1942**—Cain stood alongside McGregor on the bridge as the boat slowly approached the entrance to the harbor. A sharp-eyed lookout sighted the black silhouette of a ship off the port quarter. The Oerlikon crew swung the 20mm cannon and the sailor manning the port Vickers pointed his twin .303 machine guns to cover the unknown vessel. McGregor stared intently at it through his night binoculars. "Challenge the bloke," he ordered the signalman. The sailor aimed his Addis lamp at the stranger and sent out the recognition signal, a series of light flashes. A few seconds later, a pinpoint of light flashed out of the darkness with the response. "Boom boat." McGregor explained, "Never can be too careful, might be an E-boat lying in wait."

Cain noticed that the officer seemed quite tense and wondered if it had anything to do with the recall signal. All he was able to get from McGregor upon his return to the boat was that the signal was highly unusual.

"Never happened before," he explained anxiously. "All I know is that we've been ordered to return to base at best possible speed."

The two MTBs approached the pier. Cain was surprised to see Lieutenant Colonel Vaughn standing in front of several commando officers.

Cain glanced at McGregor. "What's going on?" he asked.

"Don't ask me, old man, they're your kind," the naval officer replied.

Just then, the radioman leaned out of the R/T space. "Lieutenant McGregor," he called, "I just received a message from headquarters. You and Lieutenant Wellford are to report to the command center immediately." The two men looked at each other in confusion.

"Must be a flap," McGregor offered by way of explanation.

***

HMS *Lochinvar*, 0700, 17 August—Cain stepped onto the pier and saluted Vaughn, who hastily returned it. "Captain Cain, if you would be so kind as to accompany me," he said without explanation. "The sergeant major will bring your men along." With that, he stepped off at a fast pace, obviously in a rush. Cain was forced to hurry alongside. The rest of the entourage followed along behind. They reached the same building where the exercise brief had been held. This time, however, security had been noticeably increased. Two armed Royal Marines stood guard at the entranceway.

"Sir, may I see your identification?" one asked firmly.

Vaughn was upset with the request but grudgingly handed over his ID. "This man is with me," he said, pointing to Cain.

"I'm sorry, sir, no one admitted without proper credentials," the Marine replied impassively. He had his orders and that was that.

Vaughn's impatience overcame his usual self-control. He barked, "This is the officer who's leading the operation!"

Cain was startled. "What operation?" he blurted out.

"You'll know soon enough," Vaughn replied brusquely. Just as he reached for the door, it flew open and a harried-looking Royal Navy lieutenant peered out.

"Sorry, sir," he said contritely, "a little balls-up with the identification procedures," and ushered them in. The officer guided them toward the same cloth-covered table that had held the exercise terrain model. A single chalkboard covered by a white sheet stood alongside. Several commando officers and two men in civilian clothes were standing around the table in front of a row of chairs. Their eyes were on Cain as he walked toward them.

He wondered what was going on, feeling like a condemned man going to his execution. He also noted that, except for the civilians, he was the junior officer in the room.

"Captain Cain, a moment if you please," Vaughn said, beckoning him toward a corner of the room. "I have a job for you that involves great risk," he began. "You have been selected to lead your section in an operation against the Germans."

Cain was taken aback. "Colonel, what operation?" he asked for the second time.

"I'm not at liberty to tell you until I know if you will volunteer for the assignment," Vaughn replied secretively.

Son-of-a-bitch, Cain thought to himself, *why would I volunteer for something that's high risk without knowing what it is?* But subconsciously, he was intrigued and excited.

Vaughn studied him for a moment. "I know this is highly unusual, captain, but at the moment we need your team for this mission. I can assure you that we have obtained permission from your government to use you and your sergeant, should you both volunteer."

I'm trapped, Cain thought. *I know that Montgomery won't pass up something like this. I'll never be able to face him if I wimp out.* "I'm your man, colonel," he said.

"Good lad," Vaughn replied, clapping him on the shoulder.

Minutes later, the sergeant major brought the rest of the section into the room. "Gentlemen, take your seats," Vaughn instructed. "This briefing is classified Most Secret," he began, "and is not to be discussed outside this room until authorized by proper authority. In two days," Vaughn revealed dramatically, "you men will take part in a raid off the northern coast of France."

Finch nudged his buddy Hawkins. "Blimey, it's about time," he whispered.

"For security purposes, you will not be told the objective of the raid. You will only receive information that is pertinent to your part of the support operation." His statement captured the men's attention. It was electrifying news and brought out a sudden cheer despite the presence of the senior officers. The thought of striking back at the Huns was simply too much to accept calmly.

"As you were!" the sergeant major barked, instantly quieting the hubbub.

Vaughn theatrically whipped the sheet off the table, exposing a three-dimensional terrain model. "This, gentlemen, is a section of the northeast coast of Alderney, one of the Channel Islands that are occupied by the Germans." The finely detailed mock-up showed a stretch of coastline. There was no beach, just a boulder-strewn shoreline that fronted a high bluff, much like the exercise area on the Scottish coast.

Vaughn used his swagger stick to point to a strange-looking structure that looked like a huge upright bedspring. "This is the German Freya surveillance radar station," he said, "and must be knocked out before the raid. Its search pattern extends over 200 kilometers, giving it the capability to pick up our ships in plenty of time before they reach the coast. Our scientists are also keen to get their hands on key components. That's where you lads come in. Your job is to eliminate the German security, dismantle key parts, capture one of the technicians, and bring the lot back home."

For a moment, there was what Cain would later describe as "shocked silence."

Finch, never at a loss for words, finally spoke up. "Piece of cake," he declared confidently.

Yeah, right, Cain thought to himself, *just as easy as climbing a cliff in the middle of the night.*

Vaughn ignored the remark and introduced one of the commando officers who wore the Combined Operations patch on the left shoulder of his battledress. The man was tall and straight-backed. He carried a swagger stick and wore a regulation battledress that perfectly fitted his well-developed frame. The officer was impressive even without the decorations he wore over the left breast pocket of his jacket. Cain noted the Distinguished Service Cross and the George Medal.

"Bugger's seen some action," someone muttered.

"This is Major Grey of the 1st Special Service Brigade," Vaughn stated. "He will brief the intelligence portion of the operation."

"Good morning," Grey began, in a clipped, English, upper-class accent. "Alderney is an island approximately 10 miles off the French coast and 60 miles from the south coast of England. The island is 3 miles long, 1 ½ miles wide, and encompasses 3 square miles. The main town, St. Anne, is located in the center of the island, just south of the harbor, the main port of entry onto the island. We estimate there are about 500 German garrison troops on Alderney, most of whom are based in the capital. They can reach any part of the island within minutes. We have identified four 88mm flak batteries and six 10.5cm gun positions. They are marked on aerial photographs that I will hand out shortly. Their headquarters is located in a multi-story concrete bunker on the outskirts of the town."

Grey proceeded to pass out two sets of aerial photographs. "RAF No. 1 Photograph Reconnaissance Unit took these photos three days ago," he explained. "The weather was a little dicey because of the partial cloud cover but the pilot managed to come back with some fairly good vertical and oblique shots of the installations."

The 9-inch by 9-inch black-and-white photographs were flecked with white spots caused by the clouds but, for the most part, they provided a clear view of the objective. The photo interpreter had made handwritten notations on them to make it easier to identify significant features. A grease-penciled arrow labeled "radar" pointed to the Freya.

"As you can see, the radar installation is rather secluded," Grey pointed out. The installation stood no more than 100 yards from the edge of a cliff in the middle of an open field on a high, rocky promontory bounded by steep bluffs on two sides. It was easy to see that the large antenna array was constructed of rectangular-shaped tubing and why the radar was nicknamed the "bedspring." The base of the radar was partially concealed by a camouflage net, but it failed to screen a wall of sandbags 4–5 feet high that circled the position. "If you look closely," Grey interjected, "you can see the barbed-wire fence that surrounds the site and what we believe to be a shallow antipersonnel minefield. Based on what intelligence has provided us, it appears that the installation is guarded by two dozen Germans, including the technicians that operate the radar."

Cain raised his hand. "Question?" Grey asked.

"Sir, how confident are you about the number of guards?"

Grey looked at one of the civilians for a long moment before answering. "It seems that the Nazis turned the island into a concentration camp for slave laborers and then worked most of them to death. One of them escaped and was rescued by a patrol boat. He was in rather poor shape, as you can imagine. By happenstance, during an interview he mentioned being forced to help build the radar site on Alderney before nipping away. He confirmed that there were two dozen guards and a few technicians."

Cain glanced at the two civilians and guessed that one of the men sitting behind him was the escapee. The man looked strangely out of place among the hale and hearty soldiers. He was tall and stovepipe thin, almost skeletal. His clothing hung loosely on his thin frame, but it was his withered face that identified him as the escapee. His eyes burned with a savage intensity that spoke volumes about what he had endured. The other individual was just the opposite; short, overweight, with a round face and thick eyeglasses. The man looked like an owl, a nickname that the irreverent commandos immediately tagged him with.

The thin man raised his hand. Grey identified him as "Pierre" and asked if he had anything to add.

"*Oui*," the gaunt figure answered. In heavily accented English, he told of being arrested by the Nazis after France capitulated and how he was taken to Alderney, where he was forced to work on building the radar site. Starved, beaten, and overworked, hundreds died and he realized that if he was to survive, he must escape. He managed to slip aboard a truck carrying bodies to the burial pits that had been dug on a beach to the south of the site. He was unceremoniously dumped into a watery burial pit, along with the other corpses, and left to the ravages of the sea. After the truck drove off and the tide came in, he was able to swim undetected out to where a passing British patrol boat picked him up more dead than alive.

"My God," Bourne exclaimed under his breath, deeply moved by the survivor's story. He was no stranger to death after Dunkirk, but he was shocked to hear a first-hand account of Nazi brutality.

Montgomery saw the stunned look on the Brit's face and reached out. "The poor bastards have had it rough," he said compassionately. "Maybe we can pay the Krauts back."

"You can bet on it," Bourne hissed.

Grey handed out a mimeographed drawing of a rectangular building. "This is a schematic of the radar control headquarters interior that Pierre drew for us," he explained. The crude drawing showed two entry/exit doors. One door was located on the south side of the building and the other door faced the main road. Just inside this door was a small room labeled "office and guard room." Four other rooms led off a hallway that ran the entire length of the structure. Each room had a separate door.

"The first room on the left is the actual control room," Grey said, directing their attention to the sketch. "According to Pierre, there is always a radar operator on duty."

"Is he armed?" Cain asked, directing his question to the Frenchman.

"*Oui, monsieur le capitaine,*" the escapee replied in French, and then switched to English. "He has a pistol but there is a rifle on the rack."

Grey pointed to the rooms on the sketch. "This one across the hall from the control room is the commander's office. The next room on the left is the sleeping quarters for the off-duty guards, and the last one is a storage room."

Grey directed their attention back to the photo. "Note the dirt road," he pointed out. A single narrow road ran the length of the headland. It passed by a bunker on the side of the site's entranceway that was labeled "possible machine-gun emplacement." A small nondescript one-story building was tagged "radar control center." Grey pointed to the ground between the building and the radar. "The power lines from the radar to the control center are buried underground and hardened with concrete to prevent them from being knocked out by air." He paused. "Any questions so far?"

"What about the islanders?" Cain asked.

"There were about 1,500 but they were evacuated prior to the German invasion," Grey replied.

"If there are no further questions, I will be followed by Lieutenant Colonel Henry of the Special Operations Executive, who will brief you on the plan's operational aspects."

Grey handed his swagger stick to a fearsome-looking officer whose face and hands were deeply scarred. A patch over his left eye did nothing to soften his appearance. He looked positively frightening. His gaunt, unshaven face and prominent hawk-like nose gave him the appearance of a predatory animal.

"He looks a fright," Finch whispered, unable to contain himself.

The officer overheard the comment and focused his good eye on the Royal Marine. "Trying to start a fight, are we?" he asked in a low, menacing voice.

"No, sir," Finch stammered, for once at a loss for words.

"All right then, let's get started," the officer began, as if nothing had happened. "For this operation, you lot have been placed under control of No. 62 Commando, otherwise known as the Small-Scale Raiding Force. The CO directed me to brief you on the operation." With that short introduction, he lifted the sheet from the chalkboard, exposing the operations order for the mission:

> **Operation *Switch-Off*, Most Secret—Intention:** To carry out a raid on the island of Alderney to recover key parts of the German Freya radar, capture a radar operator, and bring away operations manuals and documents.
>
> **Force Taking Part:** MTBs 204 and 210, two officers and 11 other ranks from No. 62 Commando, and one civilian advisor.
>
> **Outline of the Plan:** It is the intent that the force shall sail from Portsmouth to within a half mile of the northeast coast of Alderney where the MTBs will hove to and launch two rubber landing craft, each containing seven raiding personnel. MTBs will remain offshore until the raiding force returns or two hours after launch. The rubber landing craft will proceed to the landing site. Every attempt will be made to ensure surprise; however,
>
> (a) In the event of the enemy opening fire before the party lands, the boats will return to the MTBs.
> (b) If fired upon while landing, an attempt will be made to reach the objective.
> (c) If the landing is unopposed, the party will attack immediately.
>
> **Date of Operation:** The operation will take place on the night of 18/19 August 1942.
>
> **Withdrawal:** After not more than one and a half hours ashore or on the completion of the mission, MTBs will be signaled from shore and the landing party will withdraw. MTBs must depart objective area no later than one hour before first-light. If at dawn, no signal is seen, the MTBs will return to their base. In the event of the appearance of enemy surface craft, the senior MTB officer will at his discretion engage or retire.
>
> **Allocation of Responsibility:** No. 62 Commando representative will be responsible for canceling the operation during the passage if enemy

(surface/air) action or weather conditions make it necessary to do so. Raiding force commander will be responsible for canceling the operation ashore.

Henry carefully reviewed the operation plan, point by point, and then opened up the brief for questions. The Owl jumped to his feet. "I've not trained for any of this!" he loudly interjected.

"Buck up, lad," Henry replied dismissively. "Captain Cain and his band of merry men will get you safely to the installation, where you will dismantle the parts. After you finish, they will escort you to the evacuation site. Piece of cake, right?" he said, looking straight at Motor Mouth Finch, who had made the earlier wisecrack. "Now, let's go over the plan details." The Owl wanted to say more but after Henry's no-nonsense response, he sat back down, still looking out of sorts.

———◆———

Royal Navy Brief, 0815, 17 August 1942—McGregor waited for Wellford to join him for the half-mile walk to the headquarters building. Instead, they were met at the end of the jetty by an attractive WAAC corporal standing beside a blue navy staff car. Despite the early hour, she smiled and saluted.

"Good morning, gentlemen," she greeted them cheerfully. "I'm to take you to headquarters."

"Right," Wellford responded distractedly. "What's going on, John?" he asked. "I've never been offered a car and driver before. I normally walk to headquarters, rain or shine."

"Don't look a gift horse in the mouth," McGregor said, climbing into the vehicle. Three minutes later, the car pulled up in front of the two-story red-brick building and the WAAF handed him a slip of paper with a room number written on it. They got out wishing the ride had been longer. The driver was a "looker," even dressed in a shapeless brown khaki uniform.

"Have a good morning," Wellford said over his shoulder, as they strode toward the entranceway.

"Gentlemen," the driver called out, "I've been told to wait for you."

Now they were really puzzled; lieutenants do not rate being transported to and fro. *What have we done?* they wondered anxiously.

After presenting their IDs to the Royal Marine sentry, they climbed a flight of stairs to the second floor and walked down a long corridor, past offices that bustled with activity. The night watch was hard at work dealing with the command's 24/7 wartime operations schedule. They found the office with an "Authorized Personnel Only" notice posted on the steel door and pressed a buzzer. A robotic-sounding voice asked for their names. The lock retracted and they entered a small foyer that was almost entirely filled by a large desk, behind which sat an armed petty officer.

"May I see your identification, gentlemen?" The PO took the ID badges and compared them against a list of names on his desk. "Thank you, gentlemen," he said, handing back the badges. "You may go right in," he continued, indicating the closed inner door. They pushed open the metal door and stepped into a large room crowded with officers and other ranks, all talking at once.

A heavyset officer wearing a rumpled uniform stepped forward. The four gold wavy rings on his uniform sleeves marked him as a captain in the Royal Naval Reserve. He looked to be in his late forties but it was difficult to tell under the harsh fluorescent lamps. The light created shadows on his face that made him look older than he probably was. A receding hairline, bulbous nose, and heavy jowls did nothing to soften his appearance. He had an unhealthy pallor that is normally associated with someone who spends a great deal of time inside. The deeply etched worry lines that ran across his forehead gave him the look of a man under a great deal of stress.

"You must be the MTB commanders," he said, holding out his hand and introducing himself before the younger officers could

121

reply. His grip was strong and he looked each of them in the eye as he shook hands. "I'm Hardisty, officer-in-charge of Coastal Forces, and this is my operations headquarters," he stated proudly. The space was a beehive of activity as the occupants reacted to radio and message traffic that was piped into the room. Four lively Wren other ranks were spaced around an outsized chart of the coastline and English Channel that had been fastened to a waist-high platform in the middle of the room. They positioned miniature red and black ship and airplane models around the chart with wooden "rakes," in compliance with instructions from a formidable-looking Wren officer standing on a raised platform overlooking her flock.

She wore a telephone headset and was speaking into a microphone. "E-boat sighted in block E-42," McGregor heard her say. One of the Wrens deftly pushed a red ship model into a square marked with the same number and got an affirmative head nod from the officer.

"How do you like our setup?" Hardisty asked. Before anyone could answer, he continued, "We track all ship and aircraft traffic in our sector from here." McGregor looked closely and spotted the base pier, where two black ship models were positioned. The captain saw where he was looking. "We placed the models there an hour ago after you arrived. We tracked you all the way from the exercise location … and I might say you returned rather quickly. A hot date at the club," he joked. His comment brought a snicker from the nearest Wren, who blushed and quickly turned away.

"Come into my office, gentlemen," the captain said, pointing to a door in the back of the room half hidden by metal filing cabinets. "Tea or something stronger?" the four-striper asked.

"Tea, sir," the two replied, although they would have liked a stronger beverage. "It will keep us awake."

A young Wren brought in two mugs of tea. McGregor took a sip of the boiling hot liquid and wondered again why he and Wellford had been called in.

"I suppose you must be wondering why you're here," the captain said. "Tomorrow night a mixed force of 6,000 British and Canadian infantry, supported by naval and air, will conduct a raid on the French coast." Hardisty paused to let the news sink in.

The two lieutenants were bowled over. Finally, after three years of stalemate and defeat, Great Britain was going to strike back. "So, that's why the exercise was canceled," McGregor said. He immediately asked, "Where do we fit in, sir?"

"I want you to take your commando friends and pay a little visit to a German radar station in the Channel Islands that may be able to monitor ship movements along that area of the coast," Hardisty explained. "Headquarters is afraid the radar will alert Jerry and they'll be ready when our boys hit the beach."

"With the operation on for tomorrow, it doesn't give us much time to get ready," Wellford stated.

"That's the rub," Hardisty replied. "You're on for tonight."

Cabinet War Rooms, London, 0700, 17 August 1942—Loreena McNeal made her way wearily along the narrow, dimly lit, windowless passageway to the map room. She had passed the night in "the dock," a stuffy dormitory that was little more than a cave curtained off from one of the many corridors beneath the New Public Office Building in London's Whitehall area, and was feeling the effects of little sleep after a long, stressful day. The fact that long hours were typical of the assignment did nothing to dampen her enthusiasm. She was proud to work in the Cabinet War Rooms where Churchill and his staff ran the war. On one occasion, she passed the great man coming out of his office-bedroom in his Royal Air Force-blue pajamas. She was shocked but he was unruffled and nonchalantly wished her a good morning. She found out later that the prime minister often worked through the night and used the mornings to read the intelligence reports and dictate correspondence—in his pajamas and bathrobe.

This morning, Loreena was more tired than usual. She had been involved most of the night with tracking the progress of No. 3 Commando in a raid to capture prisoners and destroy a searchlight battery near the French coastal town of Hardelot. The raiders landed successfully but were discovered cutting the barbed wire beach obstacles. Under heavy fire, they were forced to withdraw. On the return, their MTBs engaged German E-boats and in the ensuing sea battle sank two of the Germans and damaged others, with a loss of one MTB and five other ranks. Now she had to write up the usual after-action reports, which would take all morning, and then she had to attend an afternoon brief.

Loreena reached the door marked "Special Operations, No Admittance" and pulled open the vault-like steel blast door. "This bloody thing weighs a ton," she muttered, stepping inside. A frazzled-looking Wren petty officer met her.

"Thank heavens you're here," the woman uttered fretfully. "There's a bit of a flap on and they're calling everyone in." The normally placid working space was bustling with activity. Messengers rushed in and out of the room carrying dispatches which they handed off to harried watch officers, whose desks were littered with messages and files. Wrens hammered away at typewriters, filling the air with an unceasing clatter. A cloud of grayish cigarette smoke threatened to overwhelm the inadequate circulation system. Loreena heard her name called and looked up to see a buxom chief officer beckoning to her from a raised platform overlooking the plotting table.

"Right," she acknowledged, and made her way over to the woman.

"Loreena, the commodore wants to see you in his office immediately."

Loreena stopped in front of the full-length mirror outside the commodore's tiny office to make sure her uniform was "all correct" before knocking on the door. Her smartly tailored jacket and skirt were a bit snug but it was from eating too much probably, she reasoned. The white shirt was fresh this morning but the damn tie always eluded her. It seemed a bit crooked but there was no time to straighten it. "Take me as I am," she whispered to herself, and then giggled at the double entendre.

"Are you coming in or are you going to stand there all day admiring yourself?" a voice growled.

Startled, Loreena stammered, "Yes, sir," and stepped inside the office. Some wags said entering the commodore's office was like venturing into the mouth of a cave to confront an angry bear.

"Sit down," the commodore ordered gruffly, indicating one of the hardback chairs in the sparsely furnished office. "I'll be with you in a moment." The "bear" was sitting behind an old, scarred wooden desk reading a sheaf of messages. Loreena took the opportunity to study the gray-haired senior officer as he scanned them. He was a big man, physically and mentally, a legend in the navy for accomplishing difficult tasks. But he had a hot temper and a reputation for plain speaking that often landed him in hot water with superiors. Subordinates, however, found the commodore's bark worse than his bite, except for an unfortunate few who came out of the cave bearing his teeth marks. Little errors could be forgiven but a major gaff and the wrath of God, or in this case the commodore—his earthly representative—would descend on one's head. It was a mark of some pride to come out of the cave with a rare "good lad" comment from the bear.

This was not the first time Loreena had been in his office. The commodore was an old friend of her father and had taken her under his wing, although he was careful not to show any favoritism. He told her that she had to make her own way at headquarters. "Sink or swim," he counseled strongly. In time, she had developed a reputation for being an extremely competent officer. Within a year, the commodore had assigned her as the director of a new organization tasked with collecting, analyzing, and disseminating tactical information of immediate importance to the commandos. "I'm proud of you, my dear," he told her privately. The organization was the brainchild of the Chief of Combined Operations, Lord Louis Mountbatten, who conceived it after several operations "went terribly wrong." He wanted operational "lessons learned" shared to help prevent bad things from happening in the future. Loreena was given six experienced commandos as staff and told to "get hot."

The commodore finished reading the messages and laid them down. "Loreena, there is to be a large-scale raid on Dieppe by a Canadian division and three British commandos in two days," he began matter-of-factly, as if a raid of this magnitude was a common occurrence. "In support of the operation, a small commando force has been tasked to destroy the radar station on Alderney to keep it from picking up the assault ships." He paused. "Of course, what I have told you is most secret."

She nodded. "Of course, sir."

He continued, "I want you and your team to analyze the operation and prepare a lesson-learned report for my review. Do you have any questions?"

"No, sir," she responded, confident that her section could handle the assignment. They had prepared over a dozen similar reports in the past year and she did not anticipate any problems with handling this one.

"Right, then get to it," the commodore replied curtly, turning his attention back to the messages.

Loreena gathered her band of warriors in the small alcove that served as her office and explained the new assignment. The news caught them flat-footed. *The look on their faces*, Loreena thought, *was somewhere between "Oh, some have all the luck" to "How do I get to go?"* Later, one after another requested to see her privately, begging to be included in the raiding force. Loreena listened politely and then gave them the "You'll get your chance—in the meantime, we have a job to do" speech, which as she suspected fell on deaf ears as she watched them leave the office stiff-backed and disappointed. In the meantime, there was work to be done.

Loreena tasked them with collecting specific information relating to the objective, while she sought out the troop list from operations. She found a watch officer in the brightly lit map room, standing in front of a wall covered with maps and aerial photographs, charting the German positions, the locations of warships, and the often-painful progress of the convoys that kept the nation supplied. It was here that the planners worked on future operations and the intelligence staff pondered the enemy's next moves.

The watch officer greeted her warmly. "What can I do for you, luv?" The two knew each other socially, having enjoyed a rare drink a couple of times in-between shifts at a nearby pub. After telling the officer what she needed, he directed Loreena's attention to a map of the Channel Islands. He glanced at the grease-pencil markings next to Alderney. "Operation *Switch-Off*," he recited, "scheduled for tonight by a section of No. 62 Commando. This op is interesting," he explained. "It's being led by an American."

Loreena was focused on the map when the watch officer mentioned that an American was leading the raid, and it took her a second to grasp what he was saying. *It's him*, she suddenly realized, *Jim Cain is leading the commando operation*. She turned ashen and struggled to maintain her composure, but the watch officer saw the troubled look on her face.

"Are you all right?" he asked, concerned about her sudden distress.

"I'm OK," she managed to say. "It's just that I may know the American. Do you have his name?"

"I'm sorry, I don't have more details to give you," he explained. "We only keep track of the operational code word, the location of the objective, and the size of the force."

"How do you know the American is on the operation?" she asked quietly.

"I happened to overhear one of the senior officers say the unit was being led by an American and they had to get high-level approval for his participation," he replied.

"Please let me know if you hear anything else," she asked earnestly, before ducking out of the office.

Loreena stumbled blindly down the narrow corridor trying to get a grip on her emotions. She was close to tears and so absorbed with her personal problem that she didn't see the commodore coming out of his office. The two collided.

"Sorry, sir," she stammered.

"Are you all right, my girl?" he asked worriedly, seeing the pained expression on her face. "You look like you lost your best friend."

Her eyes suddenly welled up. She couldn't help herself. *What is the matter with me?* she thought, shocked by her loss of self-control.

"Come into my office," the commodore directed, "and have a seat." He shut the door behind them, something he normally did not do when alone with a female member of his staff. "Bad form," he counseled his male officers. "Someone might get the wrong idea."

"What's troubling you, Loreena?" he asked kindly. "I've never seen you like this before."

"I'm terribly embarrassed, sir," she stammered, "I don't know what came over me. I'll be all right; I just need to get some fresh air." The commodore, thinking that it was overwork combined with the claustrophobic atmosphere of the underground bunker, suggested taking a few minutes topside.

"Thank you, sir, I'll take you up on your offer."

"I can't let my staff see me like this," Loreena muttered to herself, and instead of going to her office, she walked directly to the stairway leading to the exit. On the way, she checked the small signboard in the passageway. It showed that today's weather was "sunny," meaning there was no air raid in progress outside. If the "windy" sign was displayed, it meant there was a raid. It was a lighthearted attempt by the underground denizens to introduce a little humor in a desperate situation.

The Royal Marine guard eyed Loreena's pass. "All clear, ma'am," he said respectfully. She made her way up to street level and emerged into one of London's rare summer days. The sun was shining and there was not a cloud in the sky. The streets were jammed with uniformed men and women representing every country in the British Empire, even a few Americans, which started her thinking about Jim Cain again. Tears formed. *I've got to get a grip*, she told herself fiercely.

Loreena let the crowd's movement carry her along until she reached Trafalgar Square, her favorite place in the city. Whenever she could get away, she walked to the square to people-watch and relax from the pressures of work. The square was named after Admiral Nelson's naval victory over France and Spain. A 170-foot sandstone column topped by a statue of Nelson towered over the large expanse of concrete pavement. She walked across the square and sat next to one of the sculptured lions that flanked the column. For a moment, she watched the great flocks of pigeons that restlessly gathered in the open area. Periodically, something would startle the birds and they would take off in a great mass, circle the monument, and moments later, they would land in some other less threatening area. Gray barrage balloons floated high overhead, reminding her of the nightly raids that forced Londoners into the suffocating underground shelters. She glanced at the base of the monument. It was covered by War Savings posters proclaiming, "USSR, USA, US and U, Buy War Savings … it's up to U." There was no escaping the reminders of the war.

12

HMS *Lochinvar*, Coastal Command Headquarters, Mission Brief, 0900, 17 August 1942—The section studied the oblique aerial photograph. Lieutenant Colonel Henry pointed to the northeast face of the bluff. "If you'll look closely, this section appears to offer the best approach to the objective." The photo clearly showed a shoreline that was narrow and strewn with rocks. It could hardly be called a beach; it was more like a shelf.

"Helluva landing site, if there is a heavy sea running," Cain remarked.

"I know it's not ideal, but it's the best approach there is," Henry responded. "It does have an advantage. Look closely and you'll see the gully that runs from the beach to the top of the bluff." The gully was hard to spot because it was not very deep, maybe a meter, and half-concealed by brush, but it would certainly provide concealment for the section as they worked their way upward. The gully had an added advantage; it ran almost to the edge of the German wire barrier and it could not be seen from the machine-gun bunker.

"It's almost too good to be true," Montgomery interjected. "If I was the Krauts, I'd booby trap the damn gully."

"That's my guess also," Henry replied, "so we'll have to be careful."

"We?" the gunny asked, noting that the officer seemed to include himself in the operation.

"Yes, I'll be joining the party as the liaison officer," he replied casually.

Liaison, my foot, Cain thought, taking immediate offense, suddenly believing that they didn't trust him to lead the operation.

Unable to restrain his feelings, he blurted out, "Colonel, with all due respect, I want to make sure I understand your role. I am in charge of the section during the operation, is that correct?"

The atmosphere in the room turned frosty as the men sensed bad blood between the two officers. Henry realized he had stepped on Cain's toes with his slip of the tongue and to his credit immediately clarified his position.

"I have been assigned by my headquarters to make sure you have everything you need to lead the raid."

Cain backed off, realizing that he had jumped to the wrong conclusion. "I'm sorry, sir," he said contritely, and reached out to shake Henry's hand. The men heaved a sigh of relief; the command issue was resolved.

With the command issue settled, the section, under Cain's direction, developed the tactical plan using the standard 5 paragraph order format. The order, known by its acronym SMEAC: Situation, Mission, Execution, Administration, and Logistics, and Command and Signal, was developed to ensure that each team member knew and understood his role in the plan. As the order was fleshed out, it was chalked on a blackboard.

Operation *Switch-Off*

5 Paragraph Order

Situation:

1. Enemy Forces:
    - 500 Germans manning antiaircraft and coastal artillery batteries scattered throughout the island.
    - 12 German (sentries and operators) on the objective.

- Enemy reinforcements can be expected to arrive at objective within 15 minutes.
- A machine-gun bunker is located at the entrance to the objective.
- Sentry walking posts established around the perimeter of the objective.
2. Friendly Forces:
  - 14-man commando section (one liaison officer).
  - Two MTBs armed with (4) .303 machine guns and (2) 20mm Oerlikon cannons.
  - A civilian technical specialist is attached.

Mission: To destroy the German Freya radar on Alderney Island, remove key radar components, and capture a radar operator.

Execution:

1. Concept of Operations: (a) Section will land by rubber boats, move by stealth to the top of the bluff, and assault the objective, eliminating guards and capturing a prisoner. (b) Section will provide security for technical specialist during removal of radar components and withdrawal to MTBs.
2. Scheme of Manoeuvre
   - Boat Team 1 (GySgt Montgomery) will secure landing site.
   - Upon landing of Boat Team 2 (Capt Cain), Scout/Breach Team will commence movement to the top of the bluff using the gully located in the middle of the landing site.
   - On order, Scout/Breach Element (Cpl Williams, Cpl MacDonald) will commence penetration of protective wire and minefield.
   - Support Element (Hunt) will provide covering fire, if necessary.
   - Assault Elements One (Capt Cain) and Two (GySgt Montgomery), on order, will pass through the penetration, assault the command building, and eliminate installation guards.
   - Radar Installation Element (LtCol Henry) will remove radar components and associated manuals and capture a prisoner, if possible.
   - Bunker Element (Sgt Arawn, Cpl MacDonald) will destroy bunker and provide security until ordered to withdraw.
   - On order, all elements will withdraw to the beach.

Organization and Equipment/Weapons:

- Boat Team 1 (MTB 204): Montgomery, Hunt, Williams, MacDonald, Edwards, Harris, and Burns (civilian technician).
- Boat Team 2 (MTB 210): Cain, Henry, Bourne, McTavish, Finch, Arawn, Adair, and Hawkins.

- Scout/Breach Element: Williams and MacDonald. Equipment/ Weapons: 2 wire cutters, 2 Thompson submachine guns.
- Support Element: Hunt. Equipment/Weapons: 1 Bren light machine gun.
- Assault Element One: Cain, Bourne, McTavish, and Finch. Equipment/ Weapons: 1 night binocular, 1 Very pistol, 4 .45-caliber pistols, 4 Thompson submachine guns.
- Assault Element Two: Equipment/Weapons: Montgomery, Harris, Edwards, and Adair. 1 night binocular, 4 .45-caliber pistols, 4 Thompson submachine guns.
- Radar Installation Element: Henry, Hawkins, Burns. Equipment/ Weapons: 1 night binocular, 1 .45-caliber pistol, 1 Thompson submachine guns.
- Bunker Element: Arawn, MacDonald. Equipment/Weapons: 2 Thompson submachine guns.

Administration:

1. Uniform as prescribed: battledress, gaiters, boots, wool cap, Pattern 1937 web equipment, commando knife, toggle rope, water bottle.
2. Exposed skin will be camouflaged with lamp black.
3. Ammunition: 2 No. 36 Mills bombs per individual, 200 rounds Bren gun, 100 rounds per Thompson submachine gun, 28 rounds per pistol, and 5 Very pistol rounds per weapon.

Command and Control:

1. Withdrawal signal: Whistle blasts or 2 white Very flares.
2. Succession of command: Cain, Henry, Montgomery, Bourne.

The plan was completed by early afternoon and the section broke for lunch. The rest of the afternoon was spent gaming each facet of the plan to look for weaknesses, after which the individual elements briefed the rest of the section on their specific role in the plan.

The briefings resulted in several changes being made to the final draft. There was a great deal of spirited give and take during the exchanges, a clear indication that morale was high and the section was ready to go—everyone except the civilian technician. The Owl sat off by himself and would not participate in the discussions. Cain was worried; the man was crucial for the success of the operation. "I need him to be 'up on the step,'" he griped.

During a break, Cain called him into an office, shut the door, and confronted him. "What's going on?" he blurted angrily. "Your head's not in the game!" The man reacted by crossing his arms over his chest and glaring. "I'm not going," he said loudly, "and you can't make me!"

Cain stared at the fat toad, trying to suppress the desire to strangle him. Instead, Cain talked calmly to the Owl for several minutes, attempting to reason with him. "The operation depends on you," he argued, but to no avail. The man refused to listen and started to become belligerent.

Cain stormed out of the room to inform Henry that he had a major crisis on his hands. "Our technical advisor doesn't want to play," he said.

"Not a problem, old son," Henry responded cheerfully. "I'll have a little chat with him."

A quarter of an hour later, the Brit returned with a thoroughly subdued-looking technician. "Tell the Marine officer what you told me," Henry prompted.

"I've agreed to go along on the operation," the Owl said half-heartedly.

"Good man," was all the colonel said, pushing him out of the office.

"How did you change his mind?" Cain asked.

"I told him I would shoot him straightaway, if he didn't accompany us," Henry replied, a wolfish grin on his scarred face. Cain believed him.

———◆———

Motor Torpedo Boat Commanders—The three men were hunched over an Admiralty chart that the operations officer had spread over an empty desk. McGregor used a pair of brass dividers to trace a penciled course and various fixes that he had marked on the chart. The course ran from the Firth of Forth, Scotland to the Naval Base at Portsmouth.

"I estimate it's about 500 miles, maybe a little more if we hug the coastline," McGregor said, noting the skeptical look on Wellford's face. "I know it's a tight schedule but if we maintain a steady 30 knots I believe we can do it."

Wellford nodded in agreement. He jotted down some calculations on a scrap of paper. "John, we'll have to carry extra fuel and then tank up at Portsmouth. That will cost us some time."

"I know," McGregor replied. "We'll radio ahead so they're ready to expedite the refueling."

"John, what about the weather?"

"We're lucky," he responded, "the forecast indicates clear sailing for the next three days. So, if all goes according to plan, we should reach this point by 2330 on the 18th," he said, pointing to a spot about half a mile from the landing point.

Wellford agreed. "That will give the commandos plenty of time to launch their boats, strike the objective, and return before dawn," he added. Both men knew that daylight meant that German aircraft would be up looking for targets.

McGregor pointed to the coastline. "This small cove may be the best place to land the commandos but I don't like the look of those rocks offshore," he said. "They'll be hard to spot in the dark."

"There will be a full moon tonight, which may help you see them," Hardisty replied.

"Yes, but it might also help Jerry spot us," Wellford snapped testily. The captain was surprised by the lieutenant's heated response.

"Sorry, sir," the younger man said quickly. "Guess I'm a little wound up. A few hours' sleep would put me right."

There was a knock on the door and the intelligence officer stepped inside holding a sheath of messages. "Sir, I have the latest information on German ships in the Channel Islands and it's bad news, I'm afraid. The radio intercept station at Chatham has identified the 1st E-boat Flotilla operating out of Cherbourg in the Alderney Island area. Four nights ago, they attacked a homeward-bound convoy and sank a cargo ship before our escort could drive them off. One E-boat was sunk and another badly damaged before the rest broke off the action. The convoy escort, HMS *Campbell*, picked up several German survivors. I have the interrogation report here," he said, handing them copies.

German E-boat "S-38"
Interrogation of Survivors
14 August 1942
<u>Secret</u>

This interrogation is the property of His Majesty's Government
It is intended for the use of Officers generally, and may in certain cases
be communicated to persons in His Majesty's Service below the rank
of Commissioned Officer who may require to be acquainted with its
contents in the course of their duties. The Officers exercising this power
will be held responsible that such information is imparted with due
caution and reserve.

Naval Intelligence Division (NID):

Admiralty
The following report is compiled from prisoners of war information. The statements made cannot always be verified; they should therefore not be accepted as facts unless they are definitely stated to be confirmed by information from other sources.

Interrogation of survivors of *S-38* sunk at about 0225 on 14 August 1942 in position approximately 10 miles east of Alderney, Channel Islands.

1. Introductory Remarks
During the action in which *S-38* was sunk, five men of the crew of 23 lost their lives, while all three officers and seven other ranks were seriously wounded. Thus, only eight men were available for immediate interrogation. *S-38* is the first E-boat from which survivors have been captured. There were no British casualties. *S-38* was commissioned in October 1940 and was assigned to the 1st Flotilla based at Cherbourg (NID report).

Battle Report:
- *S-38*, in company with *S-37* and *S-57*, left Cherbourg at about 1700 on 13 August 1942, and proceeded to the patrol area, arriving at 2130 with the intention of attacking any merchantmen they might meet.

- (NID report) At 0158, HMS *Campbell* and HMS *Garth* sighted three E-boats at a distance of 2 miles.
- Prisoners stated that the first indication of the presence of the enemy was the sight of a destroyer to starboard. The destroyer, indistinctly seen beyond bands of mist, seemed fairly far away, but it was quickly realized that she was actually much closer, only about 400 yards distant and was steaming straight towards them. The E-boat's telegraphist sent a message on the R/T to the other E-boats warning them of the presence of the British ships.
- The commanding officer of *S-38* ordered the ship to be turned towards the destroyer and to fire the starboard torpedo (No. 1 tube). The sailor manning the torpedo tube was not ready, as part of the safety gear was damaged, preventing the firing of the torpedo. *S-38* then turned to port to make off according to the tactics laid down for E-boats after attempting or making an attack.
- A torpedo was then fired as the E-boat turned further to port. There were conflicting statements as to whether this was the port or the starboard tube. But no aim had been possible and there was no chance of the torpedo hitting the destroyer. The Germans then spotted a second destroyer on their port side which they had not seen.
- The prisoners maintain that up to that moment the British had not sighted *S-38*.
- (NID report) *Campbell* and *Garth* were in single line ahead. On sighting the E-boat, *Campbell* quickly opened fire with close-range weapons, hitting the *S-38* on the port side. The salvo wrecked the steering gear, lighting system, and engine-room telegraph. Another shell hit the fuel tank. The bow of the boat and also the starboard torpedo tube were damaged.
- The prisoners stated that their vessel was hit on the port side seven or eight times.
- *S-38* attempted to escape by laying a smoke screen but, owing to the damaged steering gear, could only go round in a circle. One engine was put out of action and a fire started in the fuel tank. Some men jumped overboard immediately after the fire broke out. A seaman ran aft with the intention of dropping depth charges in the course of the pursuing destroyer, but a burst of machine-gun fire from the British discouraged this attempt. The Germans threw themselves flat on the deck, taking what cover they could behind their two spare torpedoes. According to the prisoners, HMS *Campbell* passed immediately ahead of *S-38*'s bow and continued to fire at a range of only 20 meters.
- The Germans did not attempt to use their machine gun.

137

- When the boat was caught in the destroyer's searchlight, the commanding officer ordered the German flag to be hauled down, in a gesture of surrender. An effort was made to move the wounded aft, as the boat was sinking by the bow.
- At 0225, the *S-38* sank, leaving the surviving members of the crew struggling in the cold water.
- (NID report) HMS *Campbell* picked up 18 survivors, including three officers.

McGregor quickly skimmed the section dealing with the sinking and flipped to the page marked **"Tactics and Recognition signals."**

- The prisoners stated that E-boats usually work in threes or in larger numbers. Their usual method of attack is to lie in wait with their engines shut off listening for British ships, then making a coordinated attack with three E-boats; one from either side while the third attacks from astern. They generally launch torpedoes about 1,000 meters from the target.
- The prisoners confirmed that *S-38* carried Very pistols for firing recognition signals and stated that the nighttime signal was usually two or three white Very lights; however, one prisoner stated that the recognition signal changed every 24 hours. Red Very lights were used by vessels as a distress signal. E-boats also used VH/F to pass information from boat to boat.

When the two MTB commanders looked up after reading the report, the intelligence officer handed them another document titled "Translation of a German newspaper account of the sinking of the *S-38*."

"AN E-BOAT DID NOT RETURN"
She daringly attacked three enemy destroyers.

By War Correspondent Ulrich Kurz.
With the German Navy, 15 August 1942
The report of the German High Command dated 14 August announced that three German E-boats were carrying out one of their night operations at high speed. It was a dark night and the sky was overcast. Suddenly, the

moon breaks through. Towards the moon, the sea is illuminated for a considerable distance. With the strength of wind, the swell for the small boats is already fairly heavy. Towards the other side of the horizon lies dark, almost black. From this dark corner, three enemy destroyers suddenly heave into sight; our boats being silhouetted for them against the bright horizon. The enemy at once opens fire with his far superior armament, before our E-boats are able to make use of their torpedoes. Nothing remains for the two boats to do except turn away, in order to get into a better position for torpedo attack.

It is an exciting picture. The enemy fired star shells and tried to catch the German boats in the beams of the searchlights. The two E-boats zigzag, draw away from each other, lay a smoke screen, and lose sight of each other. Now each of them is left to her own devices. The contact with the enemy breaks off. Our boats get into touch with each other by signal and set their courses independently in order to maneuver the enemy into a more favorable position for a torpedo attack, taking into consideration visibility and weather conditions. One of the boats here drew a blank and the other did not return from her last daring attack. A lone E-boat searches the vast sea in vain for her comrade, who no longer replies to signals. The moon had disappeared again and there was nothing more to be seen of the enemy.

"Interesting take on the action from the other side," McGregor declared. "More accurate than the dribble they usually put out."

Captain Hardisty nodded and added, "What is your take on the tactics the E-boats employ?"

"Unfortunately, I'm intimately familiar with the way they operate," McGregor replied. "Wellford and I were part of the escort for two convoys that ran into them. We didn't know they were there until their torpedoes exploded. One of the ships was a gasoline tanker that blew sky high, lighting the ocean for miles and exposing one of them, which we sank. The others got away."

Their discussion was interrupted by the intelligence officer. "Gentlemen, there is one more threat you should be aware of. Headquarters also reported that German inter-island convoys occasionally pass close to the island at night and are usually escorted by two to four patrol boats."

McGregor exploded, "Bloody hell, we could run into the whole Jerry navy." He turned to Captain Hardisty. "What sort of support are we going to have?"

The older man regarded him for a long moment before replying. "Nothing," he said with finality. "You'll have to go it alone. We don't want to alert the Germans to the big show."

13

Schnellboot S-26, **Mooring Berth, Cherbourg, France, 1900, 18 August 1942**—*Oberleutnant zur See* (Lieutenant) Hans Dieter stood beside the helmsman on the bridge of the pearl-gray Schnellboot (S-boat) as it slipped out of Cherbourg's steel-reinforced mooring berth and into the waterway that led to the English Channel. Normally, he would let his executive officer conn the boat but tonight he took her out. The most recent bombing had left the harbor a mass of wreckage and severely damaged the port's repair facilities, storage buildings, and docks. Several ships had been sunk in and around the harbor, leaving only a single channel for the warships. The British target had been the U-boat pens and the *Schnellboot* bunker, but they had failed to destroy either one. Their bombs were simply not big enough to penetrate the thick, vaulted, concrete-reinforced roofs.

As the *S-26* reached the inner breakwater, a lookout spotted the superstructure of a sunken vessel and alerted the bridge. Dieter trained his binoculars on the twisted remains.

"Direct hit," he said, visualizing the death and destruction on the bridge when the bomb exploded. *All over in a second*, he thought, *probably never knew what hit them*. He shook off the thought and ordered the helmsman to give the wreckage more leeway. The two trailing S-boats followed his lead and swung wide to avoid the obstruction.

The three boats of the 2nd S-boat Flotilla had been assigned to intercept the survivors of a supply convoy that had been attacked by a U-boat wolf pack off the coast. The convoy was expected to pass close to the tip of Alderney sometime during the early morning hours. Dieter was excited; this sortie was his first mission in command of the *S-26*. He had been appointed to take over the boat after her former commander was killed in a night attack on a similar mission. The English had set a trap using a convoy as bait. Two British *Tribal*-class destroyers were lying in wait when the S-boats attacked. One boat was sunk, another badly damaged, and the *S-26* suffered a number of casualties, including her commander. Dieter, the second in command, was promoted and made her captain. He was elated, as he planned to use the boat and its crew to advance his career in the *Kriegsmarine* (War Navy).

The death of his former commanding officer could not have happened at a more opportune time for Dieter. The captain had threatened to send him packing after observing several instances of his high-handed treatment of the crew. He thought Dieter was overbearing and arrogant and accused him of being a "Nazi bully," an accusation that would have sent the captain to a penal colony or worse if he had not been a celebrated hero. The official Nazi Party newspaper, the *Völkischer Beobachter* (*People's Observer*), called the captain the "*Schnellboot* Tiger." His picture was featured on its front page being personally decorated by the Führer for leading successful forays against the supply convoys in the English Channel, which was dubbed "S-boat Alley." In honor of their captain, the crew adopted a pennant featuring a growling tiger. There had been nothing Dieter could do; it would have been his word against that of a hero. All he could do was fume and wait for his chance. Opportunity presented itself sooner than he expected, thanks to a British shell that took the "swine's head off."

A product of his time, Dieter was a staunch Nazi with unquestioning faith in Adolf Hitler and a firm belief that Germany would win the war. With his blond hair, blue eyes, and slim body, he was the embodiment of a Nazi "superman." Dieter's first act as captain was to assemble the crew and read them the riot act. He warned them that he would not tolerate the same level of slackness they enjoyed under the previous commander and stated that he expected instant obedience to his commands and complete and total loyalty. Any sign of disrespect would be dealt with harshly. Finally, he eliminated the navy tradition of saluting and instituted the Nazi stiff-arm salute. He ended the assembly by shouting "*Heil Hitler!*" which the crew parroted back with less than an enthusiastic response. The former captain was not only well-liked but admired by the veterans, and Dieter's disparaging remarks about him did not sit well.

The boat's 21-man crew was a mixture of well-trained veterans—many of whom wore the prestigious *Schnellboot* Badge for distinguished service—and inexperienced sailors going to sea for the first time. Several men were professed Nazi Party members, but most were simply German sailors serving their country. Up to the time Dieter took command, morale was good; however, after his speech there was an undercurrent of discontent.

The boat's senior petty officer got wind of the criticism but did nothing to stop it. "*Oberleutnant zur See* Dieter must learn the hard way," he told a friend. Unfortunately, the officer was one who thought he knew everything and that the crew existed only to follow orders … not to think. The high level of efficiency that existed prior to Dieter's assumption of command began to deteriorate.

The *S-26* was designed to be a torpedo delivery system whose basic function was to bring its two deck-mounted, 21-inch torpedoes within firing range of an enemy ship and sink it. Its other weapons were chiefly for self-defense: two 20mm cannons, one mounted well forward low in the hull and the other mounted behind an armored shield just aft of the bridge, provided antiaircraft and close-quarter protection. Each cannon could pump out 240 rounds a minute to a range of 12,000 yards. Two pintle-mounted MG34 machine guns gave her additional protection. Her three 2,500-horsepower Daimler-Benz engines could propel the 90-ton boat at almost 40 knots in an emergency. The engines had recently been overhauled because of battle damage and were at peak efficiency, according to the chief mechanic. For communication between boats, Dieter depended upon a short-range voice transmitter receiver in the wheelhouse. Normally, the radioman was part of the bridge crew.

Schnellboot S-26, **1915, 18 August 1942**—As the three S-boats approached the outer breakwater, searchlights began crisscrossing the sky searching for targets. Seconds later, the 88mm flak batteries erupted with a thunderous roar. "Air raid," Dieter shouted excitedly, "full speed ahead!" Within seconds, the boat surged forward, her engines screaming as diesel fuel poured into the firing cylinders. The deep rhythmic sound of powerful aircraft engines reverberated in the night sky. Parachute flares burst overhead, lighting up the harbor and exposing the three S-boats racing toward the open sea. "Emergency speed!" Dieter screeched into the voice tube as the terrifying whistle of heavy missiles hurtling downward filled the air. Dieter cringed against the side of the bridge, his face a mask of terror. Shattering explosions erupted as sticks of bombs tore into the waterfront's buildings, sending flaming debris high into the air.

A row of geysers boiled up across the path of the fleeing boats. The shock wave from the explosions threw them off course. "What do you want me to do, captain?!" the helmsman shouted, trying to control the boat in the water's turbulence. Dieter was transfixed, unable to react.

"Captain, what do you want me to do?!" he yelled again. Just then, the senior petty officer struggled onto the bridge. He glanced at his officer and knew instantly that the man was incapable of making a decision. "Take her through the breakwater exit," the petty officer ordered.

14

Motor Torpedo Boat 210, English Channel, 2100, 18 August 1942—"Time, sir," Finch announced, lightly shaking the officer's shoulder.

"I'm awake," Cain replied, "are the others up?"

"Yes, sir, and headed to the galley for a little wake up."

"I could use a little wake up myself," he said, feeling groggy from a lack of sleep. The passage down the coast through the North Sea was every bit as rough as expected. The heavy seas relentlessly battered the boats but they came through without major damage. However, to a man, the commandos swore they would never venture on the North Sea again.

"Try this," Finch said, handing him a mug of steaming liquid, "it'll perk you right up."

Cain took a tentative sip. "What the hell is this stuff?" he managed to gasp as the fiery liquid burned all the way down to his stomach.

"It's my own special Pusser's tea," the Royal Marine explained proudly, "a tot of rum, tea, lime juice, and sugar."

Cain took another sip. *The damn stuff tastes awful*, he said to himself, *but it sure woke me up*. "Thank you, Corporal Finch, it's just what I needed." Cain didn't ask how Finch got the unauthorized rum. "Never look a gift horse in the mouth," he muttered to himself.

Cain climbed topside and waited for his eyes to adjust to the darkness. Clouds masked the full moon. A dim figure brushed past him. "Sorry, sir," the sailor apologized, "I didn't see you," and rushed away to man his station for getting underway.

"It's blacker than a sergeant major's heart," the Marine officer chuckled, recalling one of Montgomery's favorite sayings. Not a light showed anywhere in the harbor. Blackout conditions were strictly enforced, unlike on the east coast of the United States, where they refused to turn the lights off. Marauding German submarines lurked a couple of miles offshore waiting for their prey to be silhouetted against the light. The Outer Banks turned into a sea of death when the *Unterseeboots* (undersea boats, U-boats) sank over 70 ships, earning the Carolina coast the unenviable title "Torpedo Alley."

Cain groped his way to the ladder and peered up toward the bridge just as the MTB pulled away from the pier. He felt the deck's vibration increase as the 1,250-horsepower supercharged engines spooled up. *McGregor's like a race driver*, he thought, *speed is his thing*. The screws dug in; seawater boiled angrily astern, exhaust fumes hung in the air, and the white ensign snapped noisily in the breeze. He looked over at Wellford's MTB running close alongside. Her bow cleaved the water, forming a wave that flashed silver in the darkness. Cain took it all in and felt a surge of excitement. He was off to war—no more training exercises, this time it was for real—something he had been preparing for since becoming a Marine officer. The boat motored past the ghostly shapes of several Coastal Commands' warships moored in the anchorage. Three Motor Torpedo Boats and two Motor Gunboats were nestled side by side against the pier. A solitary destroyer showed signs of getting underway to begin the nightly battle to keep the English Channel open for the critical supply convoys.

The signalman flashed the recognition signal from a hooded Addis lamp. A pinpoint of light shot out. The boom boat responded. "Good luck, lads, give 'em hell," it sent.

"So much for security," the signalman muttered. McGregor ordered a course correction. The helmsman spun the wheel in response and the bow quickly swung onto the new heading.

"Action stations, number one," McGregor ordered quietly. He was following standard operating procedure for leaving the harbor. All guns were to be fully manned and ready. Bright pressed a button that sent bells ringing. Cain watched the gunners hurry to their stations and remove the spray shields from the weapons. Able Seaman Bender took his place behind the Oerlikon and attached the waist belt that held him in position. He settled into the shoulder supports while a husky loader removed a heavy 60-round drum magazine from the ready ammunition storage and settled it on the magazine catch gear on top of the gun. Bender swung the barrel from side to side, testing the action.

As the two MTBs reached open water, McGregor ordered that the guns were tested. "Number one, I want every gun to fire a short burst on a safe bearing." Bright passed the word to Bender first. The gunner leaned back in the waist belt, pushed his shoulders into the supports, and pressed the trigger on the handgrip. The cannon erupted in a series of ear-splitting cracks. Cain was startled by the intensity of the noise level. "Enough to wake the dead," he said, covering his ears. He was fascinated by the sight of the tracers arching into the darkness. They looked like they were floating through the air when in fact they were traveling at over 2,000 feet per second. *I'd hate to be on the receiving end*, he told himself, *it'd ruin your whole night.*

Bright ordered the two forward Vickers machine guns to fire. They clattered to life. Cain was near enough to the port gun that he could hear the expended brass hit the deck.

The gun suddenly stopped firing and he heard the gunner swear, "The sodding thing's jammed again," and then a metallic sound as he tried to extract the jammed cartridge. Bright continued to rail about the MTB's maintenance. "We're long overdue for an overhaul, the engines need to be replaced, her bottom needs scraping, and the crew needs a bit of shore leave," he complained. "We've been promised a stand-down for the past month, but nothing has come of it." The young officer suddenly stopped, embarrassed by his outburst. "Sorry, sir, I didn't mean to prattle on."

Cain was about to reply when the other MTB test fired its guns. The boat was close enough that the flash of the starboard machine gun revealed Montgomery standing near the bridge. He waved but the gunny didn't see him.

———◆———

Motor Torpedo Boat 202, 2130, 18 August 1942—Gunnery Sergeant Montgomery was having the time of his life. "I love this shit," the old campaigner bellowed into the wind as the MTB roared across the water. The gunny was happy as a pig in mud. He was geared up and heading into action. It was an intoxicating feeling that stirred some primeval instinct in the tough, hard-as-nails SNCO. He couldn't explain it but combat brought him alive as no other experience. He joked "there is nothing as exhilarating as being shot at and missed." And he had been "exhilarated" many times and hit at least once but the "ding" had not dampened his enthusiasm. He continually volunteered for hazardous duty—two tours in Nicaragua, a stint in Haiti, and duty in China, although he couldn't in good conscience claim the duty in old Cathay was tough. Sure, the Japs were a pain in the ass, but they left the Marines alone for the most part until the war started.

It was the first tour in Nicaragua that made him a combat junky. He was one of ten Marines holed up in the jerkwater town of Ocotal when Augusto Sandino's guerrillas attacked behind a storm of small-arms fire. Bullets peppered the building they were holed up in, killing one Marine and wounding another, but Montgomery was not touched. He was scared and it was not until after the battle that he realized that he felt more alive during the fight than after the shooting had ended. From that point on, he volunteered for every opportunity to experience the rush again.

Unlike most of his peers, Montgomery remained a bachelor. Many a time he counseled lovesick Marines that, "If the Corps wanted you to have a wife, you would have been issued one." The Corps became his life and he devoted himself to becoming the consummate staff non-commissioned officer. He passed this knowledge and experience on to young Marines and those officers he felt worthy. Captain Cain was one of those officers he considered worth the effort. The two had become more than just professional comrades-in-arms, they were friends who shared a love of the Corps.

Motor Torpedo Boat 210, 2330, 18 August 1942—Cain was glad to be in the fresh air after spending two hours on the suffocating mess deck going over the plan. He posted the aerial photos on the bulkhead and carefully reviewed each man's assignment until he was assured they knew everything by heart. It had been drilled into their brains that, in the confusion of darkness and enemy fire, men relied on their training to carry them through. After the briefing, they prepared themselves and their equipment for the mission. Bourne passed around tubes of black grease paint to rub on their faces, necks, and back of their hands. It would cut down on light reflecting off their skin. Cain striped his face.

"Cor," McTavish looked at him and declared, "you look like one of your wild-ass Indians."

Cain laughed. "Watch out that you don't get scalped in the dark, white man."

Each man meticulously taped all the metal parts of their equipment that might clink or rattle and then jumped up and down to check for noise. They cleaned and inspected their weapons for the last time. Bourne reminded them of his old adage that "it was bad form to have a weapon malfunction in the middle of a shoot-out with Jerry." Finally, they drew ammunition and explosives from the ordnance stores that had been brought aboard. In addition to a basic load of ammunition for their personal weapons, each man picked up two No. 36M Mills bombs, a fragmentation hand grenade with a four second fuse, and two half-pound blocks of C-2 plastic explosive. The men stowed the ammunition and explosives in their webbing, along with a water bottle, energy bars, and their trusty Fairbairn-Sykes commando dagger in a sheath strapped to the leg. The dagger had been issued to them just prior to leaving Coastal Command Headquarters on the direct order of Colonel Moss.

Cain shivered in the cool wind that whipped across the deck of the speeding boat, half listening to the muffled growl of the Packard engines. The sea had moderated slightly but not enough to stop the boat from bounding from wave to wave and flinging salt spray the length of the boat. A full moon peeked through a ring of clouds, periodically masking its glow and creating deep shadows on the sea. He took a deep breath to clear his head and glanced at the luminous hands of his Marine Corps issue watch. He smiled, remembering that he never turned it in when he left the battalion. *I'll bet the supply officer is having fits trying to account for it*, he thought. Watches were a highly prized item and often stolen, leaving the supply officer holding the bag. They should reach the island in a few more minutes. The unmistakable sound of metal on metal caught his attention. A helmeted seaman stood at his action station training his Vickers .303 from side to side, diligently searching for the German E-boats that operated along the French coast. The warrior image sent a thrill of excitement surging through Cain's body. He was leading men in combat.

The island rose out of the water, little more than a shadow outlined against the horizon. The MTBs throttled back, maintaining just enough steerage to maneuver closer to the landing site. Bright spotted white froth as angry waves spent their force against a jagged boulder on the starboard beam. McGregor picked them up with his night-glasses and gave instructions to the coxswain to steer well clear of the obstructions. A heavy surge was running off the rocks from a southwesterly swell and he didn't want to fight its pull. The MTB passed the boulders and continued on toward the beach at slow speed. At 800 yards, the cove came into view, dark under the shadow of a ledge, and he ordered "full stop." McGregor passed the word to off-load the rubber boats. With practiced efficiency, the commandos manhandled them over the side and prepared to board. The first men stepped into the boat and balanced themselves. Weapons and packs were passed to them, which they quickly stowed, leaving room for the others to scramble aboard. The mooring lines were cast off and the men eased their paddles into the water. With a whispered "Good luck" from the MTB's crewmen, they dipped their shoulders in the purposeful rhythm that would take them ashore.

Part III

The Raid

15

Alderney Island, 0130, 19 August 1942—Montgomery's boat glided in on a cresting wave, crunching heavily on the pebble-strewn beach that smelled sharply of salt and rotting vegetation. His was the first to reach the narrow strand after being nearly overturned as it passed over a low shelf of rock. The two bow men jumped into the thigh-deep water with a coiled bow rope. They held the craft steady against the water's surge.

The rest of the boat team scrambled out and split up, two men right and two left to provide security for the landing site. Montgomery and the Owl dragged the rubber boat over to a crevice in the face of the bluff and concealed it with brush. In the meantime, the second team landed, concealed their boat, and joined the others at the base of the gully. On signal, the security element joined the group and waited for Cain's order to move out. Up to this point, the landing had been flawless, just as they had planned.

———◆———

Scout/Breach Element—Cain squinted at the narrow brush-lined crevasse in the moonlight and gave the go-ahead signal to the two scouts. Williams and MacDonald began crawling up the steep gully with the main body following along behind in single file. It was slow going in the brush-choked depression. The brittle scrub snapped off easily, making a noise that seemed impossibly loud but was undoubtedly masked by the pounding surf against the base of the cliff. Rainwater had eroded the gully, exposing rocks and gravel that bruised their hands and knees, but it was better than trying to scale the damn bluff. The rough ground dragged at their webbing and clothing, slowing them down.

Halfway up the slope, Williams stopped cold. A thin wire brushed against his hands. Trip wire, his mind screamed. He carefully palmed the loosely stretched wire and slid it through his hands until he reached a metal cylinder half buried in the side of the gully.

"Mine," he whispered urgently, signaling the column. He cautiously felt around the mine, checking for booby traps. The Germans sometimes used them to discourage disarming the nasty things. *It's a debollocker*, Williams decided, using the slang for the German "S" mine's ability to shred a man's groin. He remembered that the tin can-sized mine was activated by stepping on the three-pronged pressure fuse which would set off a propelling charge. The mine would then pop about 2–3 feet in the air before exploding, sending almost 400 steel ball-bearings in a deadly 12-foot radius.

OK, corporal, Williams chided himself, *it's time to earn your pay*, and with that he held his breath and cut the wire. He breathed a sigh of relief when the ghastly thing didn't explode. He now had proof that the explosives manual was correct in stating, "Cutting a slack trip wire will not activate the mine."

MacDonald's face registered fear; even under the black shoe polish he had used to darken his skin.

"You stay here until everyone passes the bloody thing," Williams whispered to him, "and then follow along behind." He signaled the next man in line to follow him and continued crawling. He discovered two more mines before reaching the top. Each time, he had the next commando in line "guard" it until the column had passed.

Williams reached the top of the bluff and peered over the edge, scanning the terrain for any sign of movement or danger. He spotted the formidable-looking barbed-wire entanglement marking the radar facilities' perimeter and just beyond it he saw the roof of the control building. The Germans had placed two rolls of coiled Dannert wire on the ground and stacked another on top, creating a barrier 6-feet high and 6-feet wide at the bottom. The coils were supported by screw pickets and staked down so that they could not be lifted. *Won't keep us out*, he thought, *but it'll sure as hell slow us down.*

There was no sign of a sentry so he broke cover and low-crawled to the wire. MacDonald and Hunt followed but the rest of the section stayed behind in the gully, waiting for the signal to start the assault. Williams and MacDonald attacked the barrier with their wire cutters, while Hunt provided security. "You cut there and I'll cut here," Williams whispered. The two wire cutters quickly discovered that it was a new type. The concertina was square rather than round, and a lot thicker.

MacDonald grunted from the effort of cutting a strand. "Son-of-a-bitch," he muttered. "This stuff is tougher than a woodpecker's lips." Williams couldn't believe the Scot would joke at a time like this. *He's out of his mind*, he thought. MacDonald finally sliced through the top roll. Williams tied it off so that it wouldn't spring back but, in the process, shredded his hands. "I should have brought gloves," he grumbled. MacDonald was able to cut the bottom rolls somewhat faster and the two were finally able to make a gap large enough for them to squeeze through.

Freya Radar Installation—*Soldat* Willi Krause was pissed. The *gott verdammt* sergeant major had placed him on the midnight to four watch for spite. *Just because I was late coming back from town a few times doesn't mean I'm a bad soldier*, he groused, stopping to light a cigarette without bothering to shield the flame. *Smoking on duty is strictly forbidden, but what more can the "swine" do, ship me off to some lonely island and put me on guard duty? Soldat* Krause was the proverbial thorn in the side of his detachment's commander, *Hauptfeldwebel* Schmidt, an old-line, prewar Wehrmacht SNCO who believed that soldiers were supposed to be disciplined and follow orders. Krause didn't see it that way; he questioned authority, lacked discipline, and as a result was habitually on the *Hauptfeldwebel's* shit list.

Krause was supposed to check in with the guard NCO every hour, but he made it a habit to flout the order. He told one of his few friends, "Let the *arschloch* come out and find me." Tonight was no different. Instead of checking in, he casually meandered along the path near the edge of the bluff smoking his cigarette and thinking about the girl in the village who had caused him to be late returning to the base. He had spent several Marks buying her drinks and trying to make time with her, but failed to get more than a goodnight kiss. "Great tits and ass," he said aloud, smiling at the memory. He had just reached the point where the wire intersected the gully that led down to the ocean, when the sound of engines interrupted his reverie. Curious, he stopped and listened closely. The wind was blowing off the water, carrying the sound with it. "What is that?" he murmured, wondering why a boat would be so close to shore.

———✦———

Support Element—Frank Hunt found a good firing position about 5 yards from where his two mates were cutting the wire. It was on a low mound close to the wire barrier but far enough away so that it wouldn't interfere with his shooting. He had good observation because the slight elevation allowed him to see over the knee-high, rough-stalked meadow grass. He scooped out a shallow hole and settled in. The slight depression gave him a chance to lower his silhouette, an important factor in staying alive when the enemy is shooting back. He jammed the bipods firmly in the ground and put the butt of the Bren light machine gun into his shoulder. *Now all I need is a target*, he thought. Minutes later, Hunt spotted a shadowy figure walking slowly along the inside of the wire and lined the form up in his sights.

The figure stopped a few yards away and struck a match to light a cigarette. In the blaze of light, Hunt saw the outline of a German coal scuttle helmet. "Kraut," he mouthed. At this range, the Bren would tear him apart, but the commando didn't pull the trigger. He didn't want to risk jeopardizing the mission by firing his weapon prematurely and alerting the garrison. Instead, he kept the machine gun aimed at the sentry until he passed by on the other side of the wire. *The idiot doesn't have a care in the world*, he remarked to himself. *Wait till he meets Corporal Williams.*

Scout/Breach Element—Williams and MacDonald were concealed in the brush next to a well-worn trail that followed the inside of the perimeter wire. "Sentry path," MacDonald whispered knowingly.

Williams grunted in agreement and muttered, "I wonder where the hell he is?" The sudden flare of a match answered his question. "Speak of the devil," Williams murmured.

MacDonald estimated the sentry would be on them in a couple of minutes and decided they had to take him out. They couldn't risk being discovered. "I'll be the distraction," he said.

The NCO nodded, holstered his pistol, and drew the needle-sharp commando dagger from its sheath. Williams had been selected as one of the "silent-kill" members of the section because of his expertise with a knife.

The two men split up; MacDonald low-crawled 5 yards down the trail, while Williams concealed himself in the grass just off the trail. Minutes later, the pale moonlight revealed the sentry casually walking toward them smoking a cigarette, completely oblivious to their presence. The sentry carried his rifle slung over his shoulder while calmly enjoying his smoke. MacDonald waited until the sentry was at the closest point and then he stood up. At first, the sentry didn't see him, but then did a double take. He shouted something in German, jerked the rifle off his shoulder, and started to point it at him. The German seemed to be totally focused on the Brit and had unknowingly placed himself in the perfect kill position.

Meanwhile, Williams was lying facedown in the grass, trying to control his breathing. Adrenalin surged through his body. Sweat ran down his face. His hands were slick. *Fairbairn made it look easy in training*, he thought, *a little rough and tumble, a "well done, lad," and onto the next demonstration. But here it is not a game, someone is going to die.* He forced himself to concentrate on his memory of the instructions, "Grab the bastard around the neck with your left arm, pull his head to the left, thrust, and cut sideways." The pungent odor of strong tobacco tickled his nose—footsteps—a foreign smell—and the sentry passed by. Williams looked up. The victim stood a few feet away with his back to him.

Freya Radar Installation—Krause tried to spot the location of engine noise but it was just too far away. *Probably a* Schnellboot, he mused. *Those sailors have it good, plenty of food, a warm bed, and no guard duty.* At that moment, he saw the gap in the wire and at the same time a ghostly figure appeared as if by magic on the path in front of him. Krause did a double take and jerked the

Mauser bolt action rifle off his shoulder. "Halt, who is there?" he shouted, half frozen with fear.

Scout/Breach Element—Williams tensed. He slowly and carefully rose to his hands and knees. Suddenly, the German shouted. Now, Williams' mind screamed. He sprang to his feet, took two steps, and grabbed the sentry around the neck, twisting his head to expose the right side of his neck. The man screamed in terror, dropped his rifle, and grabbed desperately for Williams' arm. The two struggled fiercely until the commando tightened his grip and leaned back, pulling the German off balance. Still the man fought. He reached back, frantically trying to gouge the commando's eyes. Williams ducked his head and brought his right hand up. Using all his strength, he buried the dagger deep into the sentry's neck and cut sideways, severing muscles, nerves, and the carotid artery.

Arterial blood spurted from the gaping wound, covering Williams' arm and hand with sticky fluid. Its sharp, coppery scent hung in the air. The dying sentry went limp and the commando let the body slump to the ground. The violent struggle left Williams gasping for air and shaking from the fight and adrenalin rush.

MacDonald ran over to him. "Are you OK, mate?" he asked worriedly. There were deep scratches on the NCO's face.

The commando nodded. "Jerry was a strong bugger," he replied between breaths. "He almost broke free." MacDonald looked at the body sprawled on the trail. It was hard to tell how big the German was but it looked like he was certainly as big as Williams. *You cut him down to size*, he wanted to say, staring at the German's mangled throat, but decided against it. He didn't think Williams would appreciate his attempt at humor.

"I'll frisk him," MacDonald said, and started going through the German's pockets, looking for anything of intelligence value.

He found the man's wallet containing a few *Reichsmarks* and his identification card but little else. He pocketed the items, intending to turn them over to the intelligence folks when he got back. The German's helmet and rifle lay on the path. On a whim, he opened the bolt of the rifle and was surprised to see that the weapon did not have a round in the chamber. *What kind of sentry smokes a cigarette and carries an unloaded rifle on duty?* His thought was interrupted by a loud guttural shout.

"Get down," MacDonald whispered urgently, "there's someone else coming." The two men dropped to the ground and crawled away. There was no time to conceal the body and they left it on the trail.

German Guard Detachment—*Gefreiter* (Corporal) Fritz Hauptman took his job seriously, that's why he was stumbling along the edge of the bluff in the dark looking for the sentry. The small detachment was composed of second-class soldiers who had been declared unfit for front-line combat and had been pressed into service as sentries on this remote island. They had been guarding the installation for months and boredom had robbed them of a sense of purpose. They had become complacent, making Hauptman's job a lot harder than it should have been. Instead of enjoying the war out of harm's way on this nice little island, he was forced to deal with a bunch of poor soldiers. He had learned that *Soldat* Krause had failed to check in again, so he was going to find him and teach him a lesson he wouldn't forget. *A good beating might be just the thing to bring the blockhead around.*

"I should have brought my flashlight," he muttered, stumbling over a rock. The NCO, despite his claim to being a field soldier, was long past the time when he carried a pack and rifle. For the past several years, the only field he had been in was going from his office to the mess hall, and his corpulent figure showed it. His current assignment was based on his administrative abilities, not his leadership skills. He was having second thoughts about tramping around in the dark and shouted in exasperation, "Krause, where are you?" There was no response; all he heard was the sound of the waves crashing against the shoreline. He tried to see the ocean but the full moon provided only enough light to see the rough path. The slope running down to the ocean remained in the shadows.

Hauptman was just about to turn back and roust out a search party when he spied a figure lying in the brush just off the trail. "Krause," he blurted out, and hurried forward to see if it was the missing sentry. He bent over the figure and was so focused that he didn't see the figure rise up behind him. In the dim light, Hauptman failed to see the knife wound in the sentry's neck. It wasn't until he smelled the blood and saw the black splotches on Krause's face, neck, and uniform that it slowly dawned on him that the sentry had been killed. "Oh my God," he stuttered, and rose to his feet. A hard body slammed into him from behind. Stunned, he tried to turn but an arm seized him around the neck and twisted his head to the side. He attempted to shout as a hand clamped his mouth shut. A terrible pain exploded in the side of his neck when he felt something rip his throat. Blood spurted from the wound and he knew instinctively that he was about to die. He grew weak and slumped to the ground alongside the dead sentry. A gurgling sound came from what remained of his palate and throat. Within seconds, he bled out.

———◆———

Scout/Breach Element—"Quick," MacDonald whispered, "we've got to get these bodies off the path before someone else comes along." Williams grabbed the sentry's legs and dragged the corpse into the brush while MacDonald struggled with the other body.

"That fat arse weighed a ton," the Brit muttered after hauling the remains into a clump of bushes. He quickly searched the body but didn't find anything of military value, except for a holstered pistol half hidden beneath the corpse.

MacDonald unfastened the flap of the holster and pulled out the pistol. *All right*, he said to himself, holding up a beautifully maintained Walther P38 pistol in his hand. *Williams will be cheesed off when he sees this*, he thought with a grin. He quickly slid the black leather holster off the stiff's belt and stuffed it and the pistol into his shirt. *Spoils of war*, he told himself. *Besides, the Kraut doesn't need it anymore.*

———◆———

Assault Element—Cain watched the deadly struggles through his night binoculars and when they were over, he led the assault team through the opening in the German wire and headed across the open field toward the blacked-out control building. Halfway there, the assault team split into two subsections. Cain, Bourne, McTavish, and Finch headed for the door facing the road, while Montgomery, Edwards, Harris, and Adair ran for the south door. At the same time, Lieutenant Colonel Henry led Private Hawkins and the Owl toward the radar installation and Sergeant Arawn and Corporal MacDonald headed for the bunker covering the road. The men moved with clockwork precision. The hours spent in planning and rehearsing the attack were paying off.

———◆———

Assault Element One—The team reached the heavy wooden door of the control building and took position, Cain and Finch on one side, Bourne and McTavish on the other. The men were breathing heavily from the dash across the open field but an adrenalin rush had given them a burst of energy. Cain quietly checked the latch. It was locked. He nodded to Bourne, who stepped up to the door, kicked it in, and moved aside. Finch burst past him, with Cain right on his heels. Each man had a sector to clear. Both commandos sprayed the lighted room with bullets from their Tommy guns. A deafening roar filled the small space.

A German talking on the telephone was sitting behind the desk in the center of the room. The impact of the .45-caliber slugs flung him backward against the wall, dead before he hit the floor. A second man started to rise from a chair. Cain swung his Tommy gun and pulled the trigger. The first round hit the man in the belly, the second bullet took him in the upper chest and, as the powerful recoil lifted the muzzle, a third slug tore the top of his head off. The body tipped sideways and fell, carrying the chair with it. Smoke and the sharp bite of cordite filled the air. Bits of wood, shredded paper, and cinder block chips settled to the floor. The deadly fusillade had served its purpose. The room was clear.

Bourne and McTavish took over the assault. The instructors at Achnacarry had taught them to maintain the momentum: "Don't give the enemy a chance to recover." They kicked the next door open and cleared the room with a burst of fire. Cain and Finch darted past them and headed for the second door. McTavish stepped into the hallway. Bourne began rifling through some papers strewn on a table. A floorboard creaked and he spun around at the sound. A German sprang at him and he fell to his knees and took the full weight of the attacker on his shoulders. The Sten was knocked out of his hand. The enemy soldier grabbed his throat, choking him. Instinctively, Bourne fell to the floor, fingers dragging at the commando dagger on his belt. The German tightened his grip and Bourne felt himself blacking out. The dagger came free and he stabbed upward into the attacker's throat. Blood gushed from the wound, the grip loosened, and the German went limp across his chest.

McTavish pulled the dead man off Bourne and helped him to his feet. "Are you all right, colour sergeant?" he asked.

Bourne picked up his Sten and looked at the attacker lying in a widening pool of blood. "He must have been hiding behind the door," he said dispassionately. "Remember that in the future."

McTavish simply nodded, dumbstruck by the colour sergeant's composure after killing a man.

"Let's get on with it," Bourne said, wiping the bloody dagger off on the German's uniform and sliding it back into its sheath.

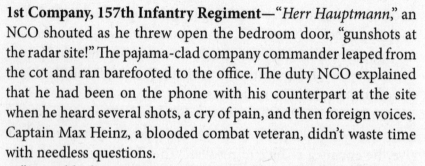

1st Company, 157th Infantry Regiment—"*Herr Hauptmann,*" an NCO shouted as he threw open the bedroom door, "gunshots at the radar site!" The pajama-clad company commander leaped from the cot and ran barefooted to the office. The duty NCO explained that he had been on the phone with his counterpart at the site when he heard several shots, a cry of pain, and then foreign voices. Captain Max Heinz, a blooded combat veteran, didn't waste time with needless questions.

"Assemble the company in the square," he ordered. The 120-man 1st Company was part of the defense force responsible for the radar installation. The company was billeted in several requisitioned private homes in the village and would take some time to form up. Fortunately, the 2nd Platoon had been on a night exercise and had just returned. Its platoon commander was still in the office making a report.

The young officer listened to the conversation with mounting excitement. "Action!" he wanted to shout. "Sir, my platoon is ready," he blurted.

Heinz looked at the eager youngster for a long moment and then made a decision. "*Leutnant* Eberhard, there may be an attack on the radar station," Heinz said. "I want you to take your platoon and investigate. I will follow with the rest of the company as soon as it's ready."

Eberhard snapped to attention. "Yes, Captain!" he shouted, and rushed from the room. Heinz watched the officer bound down the headquarters steps and wondered if he had done the right thing. Eberhard was brand new, having recently joined the company right out of officer training. He dismissed his concern with the thought that everybody has a first time.

Heinz called the battalion headquarters and asked to speak to the commander. The telephone operator said that he was asleep and was not to be disturbed. Heinz saw red. "Get the commander now, or I'll come back there and shoot you," he demanded. Heinz's reputation as a "mean son-of-a-bitch" and not one to screw with had an immediate effect.

"Please wait, *Herr Hauptmann*, while I get the commander."

After several moments, a gruff voice answered, "What the hell do you want, Heinz?"

"The radar station is under attack," he responded brusquely, "and I'm taking my company to protect it."

Such was Heinz's standing with the commander, that he didn't waste time with questions. "Keep me informed and let me know if you need support," he replied, and hung up.

———————

Assault Element Two—Assault Team Two had a slightly longer distance to go and didn't reach the south door until Team One had started their assault. Automatic weapons fire shattered the stillness of the night. "Damn," Montgomery exclaimed, "we're late!" Both teams were supposed to start the assault at the same time. "Hit it," he yelled urgently. Harris, the closest commando to the entrance, put his shoulder down, and launched his bulky 180-pound body against the door, smashing it off its hinges and sending it crashing onto the floor. He couldn't stop his forward momentum and ended up sprawled in the dimly lit hallway after tripping over the shattered door. His three teammates never hesitated for a second. They ran right over him, using his back as a springboard to leap over the obstacle. The team had to keep going. They couldn't give the Germans a chance to recover. Speed and shock were their only chance against the larger force.

The three men raced down the hallway toward the first door on the right leading to the bunk room. Before they could reach it, a German poked his head out and shouted in panic. Montgomery didn't bother to aim; he fired his submachine gun from the hip. The roar of the gun reverberated in the narrow passageway. His first three rounds impacted the wall but the next two bullets struck the enemy soldier in the chest, flinging him back out of sight. The room erupted with panicked shouts and the crash of scrambling bodies. With the element of surprise lost, Edwards pulled the pin from a Mills bomb, yelled "Grenade out!" in warning, and threw it hard into the room. He heard the deadly missile hit the concrete floor and then a metal-on-metal clang as it bounced around inside. *The Krauts will never be able to throw that one back*, he decided.

The commandos ducked back from the doorway and fell flat. An explosion rocked the room, sending smoke and debris jetting into the hallway. Montgomery and Adair leaped to their feet and charged into the darkened room. A jumble of overturned cots, wall lockers, dead, and wounded Germans littered the space. This was neither the time nor the place for mercy. The two commandos opened fire, sweeping their weapons back and forth in a deadly arc. Both men reloaded a second 20-round magazine and fired again. When they backed out of the room, there were no sounds.

———◆———

Assault Element One—Finch kicked in the door and stepped inside, shooting. An enemy soldier holding a machine pistol fell at his feet.

"There goes our radar operator," Cain remarked, looking from the body to the array of equipment stacked on shelves against one wall.

"Sorry, sir, I should have allowed him to shoot me," Finch quipped sarcastically.

"Don't worry, lad," Bourne deadpanned from the doorway, "the night's young." The young NCO paled and then realized the colour sergeant was just kidding, he hoped.

"Come on," Cain urged, "let's get to work." He and Bourne stuffed documents and manuals into bags while Finch and McTavish started wiring the equipment with explosives.

McTavish removed the olive-green plastic wrapping from a 2 ½-pound bar labeled "Charge, Demolition, M112." The C-2 explosive was white, similar to but slightly stiffer than a child's modeling clay. He cut the block in half, releasing the distinctive odor of marzipan, and placed it underneath the radar equipment. Meanwhile, Finch was assembling the fuse. He inserted the end of a 15-foot length of green-colored detonating cord, a quarter-inch waterproof cord filled with high explosive that burned at a rate of 40 feet a second, into a smooth silver tube, 2 inches long and slightly thicker than a pencil. He crimped the blasting cap to the cord with his teeth.

McTavish cringed. "You are a foolish bloke," he chided. "If the cap had exploded, it would have taken your head off."

Finch laughed it off. "Luck of the Irish," he joked, and attached a fuse lighter to the other end of the cord. He inserted the blasting cap between the two halves of explosive and pressed them together.

"Do ya think we've got enough to do the job?" McTavish asked.

"Lad, we've got enough explosive to take the building down," Finch replied confidently.

Radar Installation Element—Lieutenant Colonel Henry and his teammates reached the radar installation before the shooting started. They passed through an unguarded gate in the concertina wire that surrounded the site. "Damn lucky," Henry muttered as they crept up to the housing unit beneath the huge antenna that towered over their heads. Rather than attempt a dynamic entry by kicking in the small metal door on the side of the building, Henry drew himself up to his full height and knocked politely, much to the amazement of Private Hawkins. "Cor, sir," he asked innocently, "what if no one's home?"

Before Henry could answer, the door opened and a soldier peered out. "Yes, what do you want?" One look at the fearsome, black-faced figures pointing submachine guns in his face and he tried to slam the door. Henry stepped forward and shoved it back with all his strength. The door smashed into the German and propelled him backward. Before the dazed soldier could recover, Henry bashed him on the side of the head with his weapon and knocked him down. The German lay on the floor moaning and holding his bleeding head. Henry looked closely at the specialty badge on his uniform. "*Radarbetreiber*," he said gleefully. "Radar operator," he added, noting the blank look on Hawkins' face. "Lash this Kraut's hands," he told the Royal Marine, "we're taking him back with us."

Henry turned to the Owl, who was staring at the blood-smeared face of the German. "Let's get cracking," he said enthusiastically, but the technician appeared to be in shock. "Come on, for Christ's sake, we don't have all day," Henry repeated.

The Owl looked at the officer. "I've never been around violence before," he said meekly, "I'm just a civilian." The two commandos were taken aback. *Where in the hell does the guy think he is; a picnic in Hyde Park?*

"That's all right, mate," Henry replied, "you'll get over it before the night's over. Now up you go, we don't have much time."

Bunker Element—The bunker team was crouching in the grass a few feet from the concrete machine-gun emplacement when the assault team burst into the control building and started firing. Arawn pulled the pin from a Mills bomb, broke cover, and sprinted for the entrance. The door was shut, so he pivoted and moved toward the firing slit in front of the emplacement. He could hear German voices inside, as he stuffed the missile through the opening and dove to the ground. The bomb only had a four-second delay. He heard it hit the floor with a noticeable thump, followed by guttural shouts. An explosion rocked the inside of the concrete, flinging metal fragments through the opening, followed by thick black smoke. Arawn quickly pulled back to where MacDonald waited.

"Nicely done, sergeant," his teammate praised, "but I think we're in for a bit of a challenge."

2nd Platoon, 1st Company, 157th Infantry Regiment—Lieutenant Eberhard's 40-man platoon was split between two Opel Blitz 3-ton trucks. His veteran platoon sergeant suggested they split in case of trouble, but Eberhard had promptly dismissed his concern. After all, the company commander had only mentioned the possibility of trouble and besides, the 2nd Platoon's mission was to investigate the radar site. Personally, he thought it was just another exercise to test his platoon's reaction time.

Eberhard was seated in the cab of the first truck. He used his prerogative as an officer to take the seat beside the driver in the cab—and he was glad that he did. The rutted dirt road was tough on the men sitting in the back on the hard wooden benches, but they should thank him for allowing the driver to use the lights to avoid the worst of the potholes.

The platoon sergeant vigorously protested Eberhard's decision but was immediately rebuffed by the officer. "Blockhead," the NCO swore under his breath; "let the stupid fool learn the hard way." He told his own driver to keep the headlights off and then climbed into the bed of the truck with his men. "Stay alert," he cautioned them, "I don't like the smell of this."

Bunker Element—MacDonald pointed to the headlights coming toward them. "Reaction force, I expect," he said, "we'd better get ready to welcome them." The two split up and took cover on both sides of the road, hoping to catch the approaching vehicle in crossfire. They did not see the second truck because of the darkness and the dust thrown up by the first vehicle. Arawn planned on opening fire with his submachine gun when the vehicle got within 30 yards. At the same time, MacDonald would throw one of the deadly Mills bombs.

The vehicle slowly approached. Arawn steadied himself. "Now," he muttered, and opened fire, sweeping the truck with .45-caliber rounds. Out of the corner of his eye, he saw MacDonald throw the hand grenade. The Thompson's bolt slammed forward. *Empty!* He pressed the magazine release, took the empty out, and replaced it with a full magazine. Before he could fire, the grenade exploded in a brilliant flash. In that split-second burst of light, he saw German soldiers tumble from the bed of the vehicle. The flash also highlighted the second truck.

2nd Platoon, 1st Company, 157th Infantry Regiment—Lieutenant Eberhard leaned forward in the seat trying to spot the entrance bunker. "There," he said, pointing to the low concrete silhouette reflected in the headlights. Everything appeared to be normal. "Like I thought," he muttered, "just another training exercise." The driver was more observant and noticed the thick black smudges around the firing aperture. He jammed on the brakes, throwing the lieutenant against the windshield. The soldiers in the truck bed ended up in a jumble of swearing, angry bodies. "What the hell?!" Eberhard managed to say, just as half-a-dozen steel-cased 9mm bullets penetrated the windshield. One bullet punched through his forehead, blowing fragments of bone and brain matter from his shattered skull against the back of the cab. The driver took two hits in the chest and slumped over the wheel. The truck rolled a few more feet and came to a stop.

At least two dozen .45-caliber rounds scythed into the soldiers jammed in the back of the truck. Five men were hit. Before the Germans could react, there was an explosion that sent shards of red-hot steel flying through the air with devastating results. Three soldiers were killed outright and another four wounded. The surprise attack coupled with the cries of the wounded triggered panic among the rest of the soldiers. They tried to escape the small-arms fire that continued to rake the truck. Two men leaped over the side of the truck but crumpled to the ground. Only one man made it and he fled in terror without attempting to fight back.

At the initial burst of fire, the driver of the second truck slammed on the brakes to avoid crashing into the lead vehicle. The abrupt stop threw the riders crashing into one another but under the lash of their platoon sergeant's merciless tongue, they quickly sorted themselves out and leaped off the truck. Suddenly, the lead vehicle's gasoline tanks exploded, bathing the surrounding area in light and exposing the enemy gunmen. The Germans immediately blanketed them with small-arms fire. One of them was seen to fall but no one could tell if he had been wounded or killed, although the enemies' fire seemed to slack off.

✦

Radar Installation Element—The Owl studied the array of boxes lined up on the shelves. They appeared to be better designed and manufactured than the British equipment he was familiar with. The radar antenna lead caught his eye. He traced it to a large metal box on the middle shelf. He opened the cover and discovered three smaller boxes inside. He smiled. The three boxes contained the bulk of the equipment he was after. "Well?" Henry quizzed, wondering if this was the equipment they had come for.

"It's the mother lode," the technician replied excitedly.

"Then let's hop to it," the officer urged.

The Owl took a camera out of his pack and began photographing the installation while Hawkins tried without success to detach the antenna from the box. Henry watched his futile effort. Finally, he had had enough.

"Cut the bloody thing," he said in frustration, handing the Royal Marine a wickedly sharp clasp knife. After taking the photos, the Owl tried to remove the boxes but the finely engineered equipment gave him fits and he finally had to resort to using a hammer and chisel to pry them loose. While he hammered away, Henry gathered up every document and manual in sight and put them in his pack. Finally, the Owl chiseled the last box free and set it on the floor. It was obvious that each of them would have to carry a box. The Owl looked at the prisoner and then at Henry. "What do we do with him?" he asked.

The officer turned to Hawkins. "Give me the knife," he said viciously. The young Marine reluctantly handed it over, fully expecting to witness a murder.

The prisoner sensed the drama that was unfolding and started to cry. "Don't kill me, don't kill me," he pleaded.

Henry grabbed his arms, raised the knife, and with one stroke cut the bonds. "Thank you very much," the distraught soldier whimpered over and over.

He seized the officer's hand in gratitude but Henry was unmoved and commented, "You're just lucky we need you."

Heavy firing suddenly broke out from the vicinity of the entrance bunkers. Several rounds pinged off the radar array. One high-velocity bullet passed through the side of the building, narrowly missing Hawkins and scaring hell out of the Owl, who ducked behind a steel cabinet.

"Time to go," Henry said, but the Owl didn't budge. "Get up, you bloody bastard," Henry ordered, nudging him in the side with his boot. The terrified man refused to move. "I can't let you fall into German hands, so I'm going to have to kill you," Henry declared.

"You wouldn't dare," the Owl cried meekly. With that, the officer fired a shot into the cabinet next to his head. The demonstration worked. The Owl scrambled to his feet. "I'm going to report you for that," he said indignantly.

In response, Henry threw him a burlap bag. "Fill it," he ordered, pointing to one of the boxes.

The other two boxes were quickly stuffed into bags and the team prepared to leave. "Wait," Henry ordered. He peered out the door and saw a line of German soldiers moving toward the entrance bunker. "Shit," he swore, "they've got our lads pinned down." For a moment, he considered going to help, but it was more important to get the captured equipment back. "All right, you two, let's nip back to the beach."

Bunker Element—"I'm hit!" MacDonald screamed in pain. German fire was heavy and accurate. There was a solid crack of bullets over Arawn's head but he had to get to his mate on the other side of the road. He jammed a full magazine into the Thompson, pulled the pin of a Mills bomb, and got set to heave it. Even though the Jerrys were too far away, the blast might force them down long enough for him to dash to the other side. "Here goes," he muttered, and tossed the grenade with all his might. The missile arched through the air and landed a few yards short of the Germans. Four seconds later, it exploded, and for a long moment they stopped shooting. Arawn leaped to his feet and charged across the dirt road. A few bullets snapped by his head before he made it safely.

MacDonald lay in a depression just off the dirt road. "You're crazy, you know that," he grunted with pain.

"Nothing to it, mate," Arawn answered, "I used to run the hundred in under 12 seconds," referring to his track and field days.

"I'm afraid my track days are over," the wounded man replied, "Jerry hit me in the leg."

Arawn took a quick look at the bloodstained trousers. "Blighty wound," he pronounced. "Now, don't go away, I need to let Fritz know we're still here." He crawled several yards down the road and fired a full magazine at the Germans. Returning, he took his dagger and slit MacDonald's trouser leg. The burning truck gave him enough light to see that the bone had been shattered and was seeping blood. He took a shell dressing and wrapped it tightly over the bullet hole, stopping the bleeding.

———————

Assault Elements—Finch pulled the ring on the fuse lighter and the two men hotfooted it out of the building. The combined assault teams were waiting for them by the gap in the wire. "It'll blow in 10 minutes," he reported.

"Right," Cain acknowledged, and prepared to fire the signal to withdraw. He hesitated because the other teams had not shown up.

The Owl suddenly appeared out of the darkness. "Save me," he yelled hysterically, "that madman is trying to kill me!"

"Who the hell are you talking about?" Cain asked, mystified by the distraught engineer's cry of alarm.

"I guess that would be me," Henry answered, stepping out of the darkness, "and I will if he doesn't do what I say." With that, Henry grabbed the terrified man by the arm and shoved him toward the gap in the wire.

"Do you need my help?" Henry asked.

"Get the boats ready to go," Cain replied. "We'll be leaving in a hurry."

"See you on the beach," Henry called out, leaving the Marine to deal with the immediate crisis.

Cain could see the flames and hear the heavy firing at the entrance bunker, and was undecided whether to send help or withdraw. "We better get cracking, sir," Bourne whispered, sensing the officer's reluctance to leave men behind. Cain considered the options for another moment and then came to a decision.

"You're right, colour sergeant," he said, and fired the two white Very lights, the signal to withdraw.

—————✦—————

Bunker Element—A sudden flurry of shots announced that the Germans were up to something; Arawn looked over the lip of the depression and saw Jerry maneuvering toward them. He unleashed several rounds, which stopped the rush. "Look," MacDonald exclaimed, pointing at two white Very lights, "withdrawal signal!" The lights signified a moment of truth. Both commandos knew MacDonald was not going to make it unless Arawn carried him, and that was out of the question because of the German fire.

"Give me your magazines," MacDonald said. "I'll hold them off until you get away."

Arawn couldn't bring himself to do it. "We'll both stay," he replied firmly.

"Don't be bloody daft," MacDonald swore. "Be a good soldier and do as I say." A heavy burst of fire settled the issue.

—————✦—————

177

Motor Torpedo Boat 210—"Boss, there's the signal," Bright reported excitedly, pointing to the Very lights.

"Right, it's time to go," McGregor replied calmly. "Helmsman, steer course 060 and make speed 15 knots." The MTB quickly picked up speed and turned toward the island. It was a relief to finally get underway. The two boats had been hove to a mile off the landing beach waiting anxiously for the withdrawal signal. The crews had been in a heightened state of alert since hearing the deep rhythmic noise of powerful engines further out to sea. McGregor pegged them as patrolling E-boats. The MTBs' low silhouettes and black-painted hulls made them extremely difficult to pick out against the island's dark outline, so the German boats had passed by without seeing them.

"Keep a sharp watch, number one," McGregor cautioned, "I want to get as close to the beach as possible."

"Right, sir," Bright replied. "I'll go forward to spot obstacles."

———◆———

Schnellboot Squadron—The three *Schnellboots* had reached the intercept point, but all they had seen was the dark mass of Alderney, and even that was difficult to make out. The island appeared to be nothing more than a black hump in the water. The squadron commander ordered the boats to reverse course and continue searching for the missing convoy.

Aboard the *S-26*, *Oberleutnant zur See* Dieter, who had recovered from his earlier paralysis brought on by the bombing, had resumed his arrogant ways. He gave the course correction to his helmsman and then placed him on report for not reacting fast enough, even though the boat executed the order at the same time as the others. He fully intended to have the man transferred by claiming the sailor was incompetent; however, the real reason was to keep the man from talking about his breakdown under fire. The transfer was of little consequence because the crew already knew. The senior petty officer let it be known that they were sailing with a coward. Dieter then turned on the lookouts, accusing them of doping off. As punishment, he refused to relieve them every hour as was the custom of the previous commander, who wanted a fresh pair of eyes on watch. The *S-26* was not a happy boat.

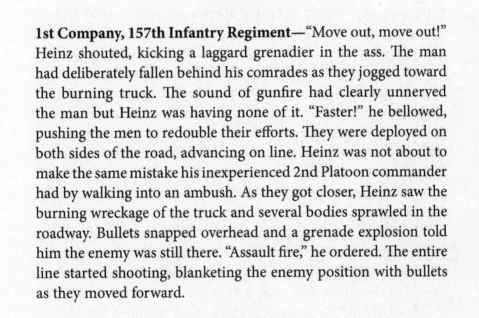

1st Company, 157th Infantry Regiment—"Move out, move out!" Heinz shouted, kicking a laggard grenadier in the ass. The man had deliberately fallen behind his comrades as they jogged toward the burning truck. The sound of gunfire had clearly unnerved the man but Heinz was having none of it. "Faster!" he bellowed, pushing the men to redouble their efforts. They were deployed on both sides of the road, advancing on line. Heinz was not about to make the same mistake his inexperienced 2nd Platoon commander had by walking into an ambush. As they got closer, Heinz saw the burning wreckage of the truck and several bodies sprawled in the roadway. Bullets snapped overhead and a grenade explosion told him the enemy was still there. "Assault fire," he ordered. The entire line started shooting, blanketing the enemy position with bullets as they moved forward.

Bunker Element—Arawn was changing magazines when he was hit. A bullet struck him in the upper shoulder, traveled down the length of his back, and exited his right buttock. It felt like someone had walloped him with a club. There wasn't any pain but the right side of his body went numb and the Thompson slipped from his grasp.

MacDonald realized his mate had been hit. "You OK?" he asked uneasily.

"Now we're even," Arawn groaned back.

"I told you to nip it," MacDonald quipped.

"Too late now, mate. Looks like Adolf is going to have houseguests," Arawn replied, when a German soldier suddenly appeared on the edge of the depression.

———————

1st Company, 157th Infantry Regiment—Heinz was beside himself with rage when he saw the full extent of the ambush. Bodies were strewn around the blazing truck. The most disturbing sight was the driver's grotesque blackened remains hanging out of the cab. He stalked over to the two wounded prisoners propped up against the side of the depression. They were smoking cigarettes given them by one of his men. Heinz bent over the two men and slapped the butts out of their mouths. "*Arschlochs*," he hissed, and kicked the one with the wounded leg. The soldier grimaced with pain but did not cry out, which only served to further inflame the German officer.

"How did you get here?!" he shouted in accented English. The soldiers stared back silently. "Talk!" he shrieked. The commandos said nothing but their faces registered hate. Heinz snapped. He turned to the private first class who was guarding them.

"Shoot them," he ordered. The soldier pointed his MP 40 submachine gun at the wounded men and pulled the trigger. He showed no emotion while murdering them but smiled when one of their daggers was given to him as a souvenir.

After the execution, the bodies were searched. Heinz was disappointed to find little of intelligence value. There was nothing to identify their unit or where they had come from. There weren't even any personal effects, which was strange because most soldiers carried some special memento, a letter, a photograph, a good luck charm. It was their equipment that gave him clues … American submachine guns, a 6-foot length of rope, and most interesting of all, the knives. They were unique. He had never seen them before. Their dagger-like shape and double-edge blade told him they were designed for only one thing—killing. There was no doubt in his mind that the bodies were those of the Englander commandos that had been raiding up and down the coast.

Heinz immediately radioed his commander and gave him a quick rundown of the situation. "The attackers are commandos," he reported, "and must have come by ship. We have taken several casualties but I'm proceeding forward." The last comment was designed to impress the commander with his bravery under fire. *It will look good on the citation*, he thought. He deliberately left out the part about executing the commandos after realizing they would have been a good source of intelligence. The Gestapo would have had a field day wringing information from them.

"*Herr Hauptmann*," one of his men shouted, "the lieutenant wants you to see this."

Heinz rushed forward to the radar housing and peered inside. It was obvious that several pieces of equipment were missing. A thick cable hung from the ceiling, pieces of broken metal littered the floor, and a hammer and chisel lay next to a gap in the equipment shelf. "Radioman!" he shouted. "I want to talk to the commander."

Seconds later, the battalion commander responded.

"The commandos have taken the radar equipment," Heinz reported. There was a moment of silence as the commander tried to think of a way he could explain the loss to his superiors who had assigned him the mission of keeping this sort of thing from happening. There was only one solution. "Kill the commandos and retrieve the equipment!" he screamed.

Heinz heard the commander "loud and clear." Unless he succeeded in retrieving the stolen equipment, he could expect immediate orders to the Eastern Front. Someone had to take the fall and he was the junior man. "Shit flows downhill," he muttered, and shouted for the platoon commander to clear the control facility. At that moment, there was a shattering explosion. Smoke and debris poured from a large hole in the wall of the building. Heinz was incredulous. *How could the Tommies do this and get away?* He was more determined than ever to locate and kill them.

"*Herr Hauptmann,*" the leader of the 1st Platoon shouted, "over there," pointing to the trail of crushed grass that headed toward the perimeter.

"Follow it," Heinz ordered. The lead squad was halfway across the open field when they were hit by automatic weapons fire. Two men were hit and collapsed, while the others took cover and started shooting back. The veteran lieutenant saw the muzzle flashes and knew that it was only one man. He led another squad in an envelopment while the rest of the platoon tried to pin the Englander down.

Support Element—Hunt jammed a second 30-round magazine into the Bren gun's magazine well and pulled the cocking handle back. It only took a few seconds, but in that time a German soldier was able to crawl close enough to throw a *Stielhandgranate* (stick grenade). The deadly missile hit the ground 3 feet from Hunt's position and exploded. Two half-inch steel shards penetrated the Brit's side and ruptured his thoracic aorta. Blood instantly filled his chest cavity and he bled out within seconds.

Assault Elements—The commandos were in the process of launching the first rubber boat when the covering fire stopped. "Come on, lads," Bourne bellowed, "Jerry will be on us in a minute!" But every time they pushed the bow into the water, it was driven back by the waves. Finally, two men jumped into the rough water and held the bow down while the four others clamored in and started to paddle. The two men in the water were hoisted aboard. "Blimey," one jested, "I thought I was going to have to swim home."

"Knock it off and put your backs into it!" the colour sergeant thundered.

The second boat was dragged to the water's edge. "Get in," Henry told the Owl, "and hold onto the equipment." The frightened man hesitated just long enough to get a boot in the ass which sent him sprawling. "And I mean now!" Henry bellowed. The Owl picked himself up and scrambled into the boat. The prized radar equipment was handed to him, which he stuffed under the amidships spreader tube.

Henry turned to the prisoner. "Now you, old son, and don't try anything that might get you killed." The German could not understand English but the fearsome look on Henry's face spoke volumes in any language.

The boat experienced the same problem as the first. It needed to be pulled into the water. Cain didn't hesitate. He jumped into the cold water and grabbed the bow line. Before he could do anything, his feet slipped on the rocky bottom. The 300-pound boat struck him on the head and shoulders and drove him under. It happened so fast that he didn't have time to take a breath and he struggled desperately to get his head above water. Suddenly, a hand reached down and grabbed him by the collar.

"Are you all right, sir?" Harris asked fearfully. In between coughing spells, Cain gave him a thumbs-up. Seconds later, the young infantryman collapsed into the bottom of the boat, the victim of a German bullet.

"They're on the bluff!" someone shouted, as a volley of shots hit the water around the boats. One bullet struck a paddle and wrenched it out of the commando's hands. The hiss of escaping air announced that another bullet had passed through the spray tube. The commandos paddled harder but the water's surge worked against them by pushing them back toward the island. McTavish was hit and fell backward into the center of the boat. *We're sitting ducks,* Cain thought, *unless we can get out of range.*

Motor Torpedo Boat 210—Andy Bright was scanning the landing site with his night-glasses when he spotted muzzle flashes. *What the heck are they shooting at?* he wondered. He looked more closely at the dark water and was finally able to make out the two boats. "John," he shouted to McGregor, "the Germans are on the top of the bluff shooting at the commandos!"

The skipper didn't miss a beat. "Bender," he yelled to the Oerlikon gunner, "are we within shore range?"

"Aye, Mr. McGregor," the seaman replied.

"Take the bastards under fire."

Bender leaned back in the harness, elevated the cannon's barrel, and fired a short burst of 20mm shells. The tracers passed high over the bluff. He lowered the barrel and fired another burst. Bright watched the tracers through his binoculars. "Right on target," he commented, as the shells impacted the edge of the hillside. Bender fingered the trigger and sent a full magazine down range. A moment later, MTB 202 joined in by unleashing a heavy volume of fire from its cannon and machine guns.

1st Company, 157th Infantry Regiment—Heinz looked briefly at the dead British soldier slumped over the machine gun. "*Schweinhund,*" he mumbled. The Englander had cost him several casualties and had held his men up for far too long.

"*Herr Hauptmann,*" a man shouted, pointing excitedly at the base of the cliff. Heinz ran to the edge but could see nothing in the darkness. "There," the man pointed again. The officer strained to see, and finally spotted two boats about 100 yards from the beach.

"Shoot them!" he screeched. "Shoot them!" Most of his soldiers could not see the boats in the darkness, but they opened fire anyway, hoping to get in a lucky shot. A Schmeisser submachine gun added its throaty ripple to the gunfire. Heinz was beside himself with rage as the boats continued to pull away.

Suddenly, a series of flashes from out at sea caught Heinz's attention. Milliseconds later, three red tracers arched overhead, followed by the sharp crack of large-caliber bullets. Many of the German soldiers were combat veterans and instinctively scrambled for cover, but Heinz stood openmouthed, mesmerized by the sight of the tracers. Before he could react, the ground around him exploded under the impact of bullet strikes. The soldier standing at his side screamed and crumpled to the ground. Blood and tissue filled the air, splattering Heinz's face and uniform. The soldier's death snapped him back to reality. He dove to the ground just as an avalanche of cannon and machine-gun fire scythed across the field, pinning his men down by the heavy volume of fire.

Heinz wormed his way to a small depression and got as low as possible. Bullets snapped overhead. The thought of being hit in the face absolutely terrified him. It left him paralyzed and unable to think of anything but his own safety, even as his men were being killed and wounded. The piteous cries of the wounded went unanswered. It was the chance of a man's life to go to their assistance. Heinz covered his head with his arms and prayed, even though he had stopped going to church when he joined the Nazi Party.

––––––––

Motor Torpedo Boats 204 and 210—McGregor had to shout to be heard above the noise of the guns. "Cease-fire," he ordered. The bridge talker relayed the command to the 20mm gun crew, while

Bright passed the word to the machine gunners. The boat fell silent, a welcome relief for the gunners, whose ears bore the brunt of the gunfire. Most of the men had stuffed cotton in their ears but it was not very effective. A few seconds later, MTB 204 followed suit.

"Andrew," McGregor called out, "bear a hand with the boats as they come alongside." Bright acknowledged the order and gathered several members of the crew on the port side.

"Blimey," one of the seamen exclaimed, as the rubber boat slowly approached, "it's barely afloat." Only a couple of inches or so of the spray tubes were visible above the water. German bullets had riddled the floatation tubes, miraculously missing the paddlers. The boat's natural rubber buoyancy was the only thing that had kept it above water.

The commandos were exhausted and had barely enough energy to toss a line to the MTB. The 300-pound waterlogged craft was nearly impossible to propel and they were almost at the end of their endurance. A sailor caught the line and pulled the boat close alongside.

"We've got wounded," Cain rasped. His throat was so dry that he could barely whisper. "Give us a hand." The sailors quickly hauled two limp figures aboard and carried them below to the mess decks, where one of the crew with medical training started working on them. The remaining commandos passed their weapons and the critically important radar equipment bags to the sailors.

"Be careful with the bags," Cain managed to say, "three men gave their lives to get them." The second rubber boat came alongside MTB 204 in somewhat better shape ... at least she was still seaworthy, unlike the other, and was hauled aboard by the crew.

"Lash it down tight; if it gets away, the quartermaster will be after me," Montgomery joked.

"Don't worry, sergeant," a petty officer responded, "when we're through, she won't be getting away." The commandos went below and wrapped themselves in blankets. A sailor handed each of them a tot of rum, saying, "Compliments of the crew."

Cain took his drink and made his way to the bridge, where he was greeted by McGregor. "Glad you're back," he said politely, in typical British understatement. But then he did something totally out of character for the normally unemotional naval officer. He grabbed the exhausted Marine and gave him a bear hug. "We were worried that you'd overstayed your welcome," he said.

"The locals were a bit upset," Cain quipped, but then he grew serious. "I left three men behind." McGregor studied the exhausted Marine for a long moment before replying.

He looked into Cain's eyes. "That's what happens in war and there's nothing you or I can do about it," the veteran said frankly. "We either accept it or get in another line of work. That doesn't mean we have to like it or have less empathy for our men, but when we go against the Hun, we have to be prepared to accept casualties. Now, I've philosophized enough. Get below and rest. We're heading back to Blighty and Jerry may be waiting."

Schnellboot S-26—"*Herr Kapitänleutnant* (Captain Lieutenant)," the telegraphist called out, "the squadron commander radioed that the radar station on Alderney Island is under attack by commandos and we've been ordered to cut them off." Because of her position in the squadron's formation, *S-26* took the lead, with the other two boats following in column. Dieter ordered the speed to be increased and the formation was soon approaching 40 knots. White water curled from the bows as the three *Schnellboots* sliced through the water.

Cabinet Map Room—Loreena was trying to work in her office when she received a phone call from the watch officer. "The raid is underway." Too keyed up to wait for further information, she hurried to the map room. As soon as she opened the door, she could feel the tension. The operations officer himself was standing in the middle of the room nervously smoking a cigarette. The duty section was glued to the radios, except for the watch officer and his assistant; they were studying a nautical chart of the water around Alderney. She saw the assistant point to a spot on the chart and heard him say that a convoy had been attacked several hours ago by two, possibly three E-boats. One freighter had been sunk and another badly damaged before the escorts had driven them off.

The watch officer looked at the distance from the reported attack to Alderney. "Doesn't look good," he said. "Radio the MTBs that E-boats are in the area."

At that moment, they looked up to see Loreena standing behind them. She was tight-lipped and had a stricken look on her face.

"Any word about the raid?" she managed to ask.

The watch officer hesitated—he knew about her American friend—but decided that she would find out sooner or later. He showed her the location of the E-boat attack. "If Jerry stays in the area, the MTBs will have to fight their way through them." Loreena knew what that would mean; the E-boats were more heavily armed and slightly faster than the British craft. No one could predict the outcome. "We're trying to free up an escort to bring them home but we're not sure it can get there in time." Loreena thanked him for the information and decided she would remain in the room.

Part IV

Sea Battle

16

Motor Torpedo Boat 210, English Channel, 10 Nautical Miles West of Alderney, 0330, 19 August 1942—"Three bow-waves approaching from the port side!" a lookout shouted. McGregor focused his night binoculars on the fast-moving objects. They were easy to spot. White spray marked their course. "*Schnellboot*," he muttered to himself. The hours he had spent studying their profiles had paid off. He could identify their shape from almost any angle. "Stay on course, coxswain," he ordered. "When Jerry gets closer, we'll attack." On deck, Bender tracked the speeding enemy boats with his Oerlikon. Bright scrambled amidships to control the torpedo launch. McGregor saw that the leading E-boat had altered course and he ordered the coxswain to follow suit. The boat lurched radically. Below deck, the commandos grabbed something to hold onto.

"What's up?" Cain asked in surprise.

"E-boats," the telegraphist replied excitedly, "we're attacking!"

The Germans continued on the new course, seemingly oblivious to the MTBs. "Standby to fire torpedoes, Andrew," McGregor said through the voice tube.

The leading torpedo man gave Bright a thumbs-up. "Torpedoes are ready to fire," he reported.

"Fire torpedoes," McGregor replied calmly. The sub-lieutenant was amazed at how composed the boss sounded, as if he was ordering fish and chips at the local pub. The torpedoes leaped out of the tubes and splashed into the water. Both fish ran straight and true. "Hard-a-starboard," McGregor ordered, turning at right angles away from the enemy vessel.

Schnellboot S-26—Matrosengefreiter Kraft, a lookout on *S-26*'s starboard side, thought he was seeing things when he spotted the two parallel phosphorescent tracks. He wasn't sure; maybe his eyes were playing tricks on him. He was tired. There had been no relief. *The* kapitänleutnant *was such an idiot keeping us on watch*, he thought. He waited several critical seconds.

"Torpedoes inbound!" he finally shouted, but it was too late. One of the 800-pound warheads slammed into the hull, just forward of the bridge. The second torpedo struck amidships. The explosions collapsed the entire starboard side of the hull, allowing thousands of gallons of seawater to flood the interior. The weight of the water and the boat's forward momentum thrust the vessel headlong into the depths. A large expanse of roiled water, smashed planking, and six life-jacketed crew members marked its watery grave.

Motor Torpedo Boat 210—"My God," Bright exclaimed. The E-boat simply vanished. He couldn't help feel some measure of sympathy for the deaths of the German crew—*there but for the grace of God go I.* Suddenly, a brilliant light burst overhead, and then another and another, bathing the two MTBs in the dazzling white glare of star shells. Red tracers streaked across the sea. McGregor pressed the "open fire" gong. Both MTBs returned fire with all their weapons.

The Vickers gunners never took their fingers off the triggers and Bender's 20mm cannon boomed non-stop. Shell splashes spouted in the water from the Germans' cannon. The boat shuddered from heavy-caliber hits. A gunner on the port side Vickers screamed and dropped down into the gun tub. Two loaders for Bender's cannon were blown overboard. Steel fragments sliced through the thin armor plating on the bridge, felling the coxswain but sparing the two officers. McGregor took the wheel and tried to maneuver the boat out of beaten zone.

Shells pierced the plywood hull in the engine compartment and the MTB's speed dropped off sharply, barely 15 knots. Black smoke seeped from the compartment's hatch. The leading engineer called the bridge.

"The bloody Huns have wrecked the number-three engine and damaged the other two," he reported.

"Very well," McGregor answered. "I'm sending Mr. Bright down to help you." He turned to the sub-lieutenant. "Andrew, go below and see what can be done." The young officer dropped down into the smoky, dimly lit compartment through the bridge hatch. He stumbled over a body, took one look at the sailor's bloodied remains, and almost threw up.

"Over here, sir," a voice called out. He spotted an oil-splattered engineer working on the number-two engine. "Should be up in a minute, sir, but number one will take more time. Best we can hope for is 20 knots."

McGregor maneuvered the boat to throw off the E-boat's aim, but the lack of speed made his efforts only partially successful. German fire continued to wreak havoc. A burst of machine-gun fire swept across the deck. The last Oerlikon loader crumpled. His death left just Bender to service and fire the gun, an impossible situation.

"Bloody hell," McGregor exclaimed, "now we're for it."

Cain suddenly appeared at his shoulder. "I thought you could use some help!" he shouted above the noise of the gunfire.

"Take the gun," McGregor said, pointing to the unmanned Vickers. Cain shoved the dead gunner out of the way and moved into position behind the protective shield of the machine gun. He checked the ammunition for damage and pressed the trigger. To McGregor's surprise, Winston continued to pump out 20mm rounds. He looked closely and saw two commandos serving as loaders.

"Come on, matelot!" Finch shouted, as he reloaded the cannon.

"Hit the bloody thing!" Bender swore, and fired the gun at the E-boat's bridge. Bright flashes blossomed, showing that the Oerlikon was on target. The German boat suddenly veered out of control and crossed directly in front of MTB 204.

The Germans launched another salvo of star shells that bathed the ocean in an unreal greenish glow. MTB 210 was caught in their circle of light and made it a perfect target for the remaining E-boat. McGregor tried to maneuver into the darkness but with only two engines, he was unable to coax more than 20 knots out of them and it simply wasn't enough speed to escape. It was obvious that the Germans intended to sink the boat and then destroy the other. Torrents of machine-gun bullets and cannon fire streamed across the water. Down in the R/T compartment, the telegraphist frantically transmitted a distress call.

"This is MTB 210, Mayday, Mayday," he tapped in Morse code, and added the boat's approximate position. "German E-boat has us under fire. Request emergency assistance," he added.

Motor Torpedo Boat 204—"Ram him!" Lieutenant Wellford bellowed. The coxswain spun the wheel and the MTB headed directly for the German ship at over 30 knots. Wellford hit the collision alarm and braced for the crash.

"What the hell is that noise?" Montgomery shouted, just as the MTB slammed into the E-boat. He was thrown the length of the mess deck and ended up with the other commandos in a pile against the forward bulkhead. The Oerlikon loaders were thrown off their feet but the gunner was strapped in. Despite being shaken up, he had the presence of mind to lower the barrel of the cannon and rake the Germans' topside from stem to stern.

The MTB struck just forward of the enemy's bridge with a terrific crash. The boat's forward momentum carried the 40-ton vessel's bow up onto the Germans' deck for a brief moment before sliding off.

The crash staved in three of the MTB's mahogany cross braces below the waterline. The water-tight traverse bulkhead held but it was cracked and leaking badly. By the time the battered and bruised commandos untangled themselves, there was 3 inches of water on the deck and it was steadily rising. A petty officer forced his way through the crowd. "Come on, lads," he yelled, "help me shore up the bulkhead!" The commandos pitched in and braced the weakened bulkhead with spare pieces of timber the boat carried for emergencies. The temporary fix slowed the water but didn't stop it.

The collision opened up a large hole in the E-boat's hull that extended from the deck to the waterline. The crash knocked out its engines and it slowly drifted away. The MTB was in somewhat better shape, but the weight of the water in the mess deck and forepeak forced the bow down and brought the rudders out of the water, making it impossible to steer. Wellford was not ready to give up capturing the German boat. He tried to swing the MTB around using the engines to pivot but it proved to be too difficult. "Only one thing to do," he told the coxswain, "full speed astern!"

With the water rising steadily, Montgomery led the commandos out on deck. One of the E-boat's machine guns opened fire, coming uncomfortably close. "Son-of-a-bitch," Montgomery exclaimed, diving behind the protective shield of the machine-gun mount. The forward 20mm cannon emptied a full magazine into the offending automatic weapon and Montgomery had the satisfaction of seeing the gunner disappear in a spray of gore. The distance between the two boats steadily decreased until there was only a few yards separating them. They were close enough to see the damage caused by the Oerlikon. The bridge and all the weapons stations were shot to pieces. Bodies were scattered about the deck. The boat appeared to be abandoned. A British sailor prepared to throw a grappling hook. Before anyone could react, a German leaned out of a hatch with a Schmeisser submachine gun and shot him at point-blank range. The sailor screamed and toppled into the water. "That's done it," Wellford shouted, "board the bloody Hun!"

Shots rang out and the German submachine gunner fell backward into the hull. A grapnel sailed through the air and thudded onto the E-boat's wooden deck. Several British sailors grabbed the line and pulled the two boats together. The commandos rushed forward with a cheer. Montgomery ran straight for the bridge, a .45-caliber pistol in one hand and a hand grenade in the other. Two bodies filled the small space but he clambered over them and pulled the pin from the grenade. He hurled it through the hatch that opened to the charthouse. Three seconds later, a muffled explosion blew smoke and debris out of the opening. McTavish brushed past him and started to go through the opening.

Montgomery grabbed him by the shoulder. "Don't go in," he said, "they'll come out. The boat's sinking."

The E-boat gave a sudden lurch and settled further into the water. "Pull back," Montgomery shouted, "she's going down." The commandos scrambled back aboard the MTB just as several Germans climbed out of the wreckage and jumped into the water. Almost immediately afterward, there was a small explosion and the E-boat went down in a shower of sparks. "Damn, they scuttled her," Wellford exclaimed.

Cabinet War Rooms—The radio intercept station on the coast picked up MTB 210's transmission and immediately relayed it to the operations center. A radio operator copied the message and handed it to the watch officer, who took one look at the flimsy and hurried to the director's office.

"Sir, I believe you should see this at once," he said.

The director quickly scanned it. "What is the position of the destroyer?" he asked.

"Sir, the last word we had was that it was approximately 5 miles from the MTB's position."

"When was that?" he asked impatiently. "We don't have time to play 20 questions."

The watch officer gulped; he had never seen the director so upset. "Sir, I'll check," he answered.

"Never mind, I'll find out myself," the director said angrily, and with that he stormed out of his office and into the operations center.

Loreena noticed the commotion and saw the director stalk over to the plotting board.

"Why hasn't this been plotted?" he demanded, holding the message in front of the watch officer's face.

The poor officer knew when to surrender and fall on his sword. "No excuse, sir," he stammered, although he wanted to say that they hadn't had time.

"Well," the director said angrily, "plot it!"

By this time, Loreena had positioned herself to see the plotting board. A Wren placed pasteboard ship symbols in position on the board. She saw that the destroyer was not close enough to help. "Dear Lord," Loreena muttered to herself, "they are on their own."

17

MTB 210, English Channel, 15 Nautical Miles West of Alderney, 0355, 19 August 1942—McGregor spun the wheel just as a 20mm round tore into the bridge. It struck the bulletproof steel plating and splintered into fragments. He felt a sharp blow in his side and knew instantly that he had been hit. "Mr. Bright to the bridge," he called weakly into the voice tube. *Got to hold on*, he told himself, leaning heavily against the wheel, but his strength gave out and he slumped to the deck beside the body of his coxswain. The last thing he remembered before blacking out was the open staring eyes of the young petty officer.

Another fragment ricocheted and struck Cain in the back of his right shoulder and exited out the front. The force of the blow knocked him against the gun mount. His entire arm went numb and he couldn't raise it to grasp the machine gun. For a brief moment he couldn't figure out what had happened … and then the pain started. "Shit," he exclaimed, "that hurts!"

Bright tried to climb through the hatch from the wheelhouse but it was blocked by a body. He pushed harder and succeeded in opening it wide enough to squeeze through.

"John," he exclaimed, recognizing McGregor as the one blocking the hatch, "are you all right?"

The officer moaned and tried to sit up. Blood covered the front of his duffle coat. "Take the conn," he whispered, and passed out again. Taken aback, Bright wrestled with the sudden change of fortune—second in command to commander—for a brief moment and then grabbed the wheel. *Which way?* He glanced at the compass and brought the boat to a westerly heading.

———◆———

Motor Torpedo Boat 204—The petty officer stood halfway down the ladder shining his flashlight on the dark water and floating debris that covered the mess deck. "How deep do you think it is?" Wellford asked worriedly, looking over his shoulder.

"I'd guess about 3 feet," the petty officer replied. They turned their flashlights on the damaged bulkhead and saw that the cracks had widened and it was now leaking like a sieve.

"Any chance to stop it?" Wellford asked.

"Not a chance in hell, sir," the PO responded knowingly. "It'd be like pissing against the tide."

"Right then," the young officer said, "pass the word to the crew to assemble on deck with their life jackets." The two men quickly climbed out of the oppressive space, spurred on by the sound of sloshing water that gave vent to a sailor's claustrophobic fear of being trapped below decks. As Wellford passed the R/T office, he leaned in and ordered the telegraphist to send a distress signal. "Say we're shipping water and need help immediately."

"Aye, aye, sir," the radioman responded, and immediately began pounding the brass telegraph key.

The damaged bulkhead finally collapsed under the weight of the water and the boat sank lower and lower. It was only a matter of moments before she went under.

"It's time," Wellford said to the senior petty officer, "the old girl is going down. Pass the word to abandon ship," he declared sadly.

The order was passed from man to man and they quickly gathered amidships each with their yellow "Mae West" life vest. The vest was designed to be slipped over the head and held in place by waist straps. Two cords, when pulled, triggered the release of carbon dioxide from small carbon dioxide cartridges. The gas instantly filled the vest's air pockets, providing the man with a dependable floatation device. A small emergency light was attached to the vest, and when activated a small red light glowed in the dark, which assisted rescuers in locating the survivors.

Montgomery grabbed Edwards by the shoulder. "Give me a hand," he said, pointing to the rubber boat. He took his dagger out of the sheath and started sawing on the line that held it to the deck. It was hard going because the blade was meant for stabbing or thrusting, not for cutting through rope. "I should never have challenged the sailors to snub it down tightly," he muttered to himself. With a final effort, he cut through the line, but Edwards was having difficulty with the second lashing. The boat sank lower.

"I'll finish it," the gunny said. "You get ready to go."

Edwards joined the others who were busy stripping off their equipment and unnecessary clothing. In a concession to regulations, they stacked their weapons on the deck but kept their daggers and toggle ropes. They also neatly lined up their boots by the rail. One commando said the deck looked like a shoe store display. Montgomery kept his .45-caliber pistol. He stuffed it into his battledress. "I'd feel naked without it," he rationalized, "and besides, there might be sharks." No one had questioned him on how he expected to keep the underwater man-eaters at bay.

A wave rolled over the bow and still the crew hesitated to leave the false security of the wooden craft. Many of them couldn't swim and were badly frightened. The thought of abandoning the ship in the darkness, far from land with only a thin rubber floating device, had paralyzed them. Several loud cracking noises rose from below and the ship immediately began to settle.

Finally, Wellford gave them an order. "Over the side, lads, and good luck. Remember to stay together," he warned. Immediately after they abandoned ship, he had them sound off to make sure everyone was accounted for. One man was missing, the telegraphist. He had last been seen at his station frantically tapping away.

Montgomery had cut halfway through the lashing when he felt the boat start to go under. He jumped over the side just as it slipped bow first into the depths in a swirl of escaping air bubbles and floating debris. He lost his dagger when a piece of wood struck his hand and he dropped it.

"Damn," he exclaimed, shaking his soon-to-be bruised hand.

"You all right, gunny?" a voice called out.

"Neptune just got my knife," he bitched. Several of the crew were lucky enough to find large pieces of plywood to hang on to, but most of the men simply bobbed up and down in the swells, held up by their Mae Wests. Almost immediately, several of the men discovered that their vests leaked. They were either old, stored improperly, or the seawater and gasoline had affected them.

Within seconds of the boat going under, the commandos' rubber boat shot to the surface. The partially severed lashing had parted under the pressure of the compressed air in its tubes and thrust it upward. The boat's miraculous appearance set off a frenzied rush to reach the haven of safety. The mob of panicked sailors kicked and clawed each other in an attempt to climb out of the icy water into the boat. Incensed by the breakdown of discipline, Montgomery pulled the pistol from his battledress blouse, drained the water from the barrel, and fired. The unexpected roar of the handgun was more than a shot in the dark, it stopped the disorder.

"Knock it off!" he roared. "You're Royal Navy sailors, not a bunch of thugs!" His furious outburst shamed them into silence and restored discipline. Wellford set up a rotation system; half the crew rode in the raft, while the other half floated in the water, holding on to the boat's lifelines. Every half hour, they switched positions.

Montgomery gathered the commandos together and had them use their toggle ropes to tie themselves together, so they wouldn't drift apart. He then formed them into buddy teams.

"Aloneness kills," he emphasized. He knew from his experience at Pearl Harbor that the physical presence of another human often made the difference between life and death.

"Check on each other," he stressed. They had only been in the water a short time when they started experiencing physical problems. The water was covered with a thin film of gasoline and those who had swallowed the foul mixture became violently ill. The fumes attacked their eyes and caused their eyelids to swell. They made it worse in a vain effort to wash it off. The vapor also irritated their lungs, initiating coughing fits. One of the commandos coughed so hard that he took in a mouthful of seawater that choked him. His buddy kept his head out of the water until he slowly recovered.

Despite Lieutenant Wellford's warning to stay together, a few crewmen drifted away in the darkness. Every time the officer crested a wave, he noted the survivors' red emergency lights seemed to be further away. Wellford leaned on Montgomery and the commandos to help him keep the sailors together. The strongest of them started corralling the drifters like swimming cowboys bringing back the strays. They paddled around the group, talking to each man and assuring them that help was on the way.

At one point, a sailor grabbed Montgomery's arm. "Did you hear that, sergeant?" he blurted out, "it sounds like an explosion." Off in the distance, the Marine had heard the faint reverberation of gunfire.

———

Motor Torpedo Boat 210—Bright did his best to dodge the German fire as he headed west toward home, but the E-boat's superior speed gave it an ability to dodge in and out of range, avoiding most of the MTB's return fire. The British boat was slowly being shot to pieces. Several crewmen had been killed or wounded, and a second engine had been damaged, reducing its speed to barely 15 knots. Bender and his commando loaders were keeping the Germans at bay, but it was only a matter of time until they were overwhelmed. *Jerry certainly wants that radar equipment badly to follow us this far away from the coast*, Bright thought. Suddenly, there was a loud bang and a thick gout of black smoke poured out of the engine compartment. The boat drifted to a stop, wallowing heavily in the swells. "That's bloody done it," Bender swore, "we're at their mercy."

Below deck, Cain sat in a bunk watching the sickbay attendant wrap McGregor's wound with a shell dressing. The attendant had stopped the unconscious man's bleeding but he was worried that he was bleeding internally. "Finished," he said, tying off the bandage. "Now it's your turn," he said, examining Cain's shoulder.

"Doc, I can hardly wait," the officer replied, using the Marine Corps' term for a corpsman. At that point, Cain was feeling no pain, thanks to a shot of morphine.

"You're lucky," the attendant said, after looking at the hole in his shoulder, "it's a through and through wound. No bone damage. A few weeks and you'll be right as rain." He replaced the dressing just as the engines stopped.

Cain got shakily to his feet and staggered topside. Bright was on the bridge looking through his night-glass. "Here he comes," he said resignedly.

Cain looked up and could see a necklace of white spray marking the course of the E-boat. "The bastard is going to wait until he's right on us before opening fire." Cain glanced at the battered remnants of the 20mm cannon. Bender was hanging lifeless in the gunner's harness and the two commandos were being carried below for treatment.

"Happened a minute ago," Bright said emotionally. "The Krauts got them after Winston jammed."

"Anything we can do?" Cain asked.

"Nothing but wave a white flag and hope they honor it. I've sent a man to find something white that we can wave." The E-boat continued on course, heading directly for the MTB. Cain estimated it was a mere 500 yards away.

Suddenly, a white star shell blossomed, bathing the area in brilliant light. The scream of an incoming shell ripped through the air over their heads. A mammoth geyser erupted 100 yards short of the speeding E-boat. Both men swiveled around. They saw a flash and then heard another shell pass overhead to explode closer to the German boat.

"My God, it's ours!" Bright screamed, thumping Cain on the wounded shoulder.

"Son-of-a-bitch," Cain swore, almost falling to his knees.

"Damn, I'm terribly sorry," the young officer expressed after realizing what he had done. "Look, Jerry is turning away!" he yelled. The German boat had reversed course and was maneuvering wildly as it sped away. Several more shells cascaded around it but somehow the boat managed to escape into the darkness.

———————

HMS *Gurkha*—HMS *Gurkha*, a Tribal-class destroyer, pulled alongside the severely damaged MTB. "Do you need assistance?" an officer inquired over a loud-hailer.

"We have wounded that need medical attention," Bright responded, "and we could use a tow. Our engines were knocked out." Within minutes, the destroyer's crew had lowered Stokes litters. McGregor was to be the first hoisted aboard because of his severe injuries. He had regained consciousness, and as they lashed him into the wire rescue litter he asked to speak with Bright.

"Well done, Andrew," he said weakly, "you brought us through and I'll see that you're recognized for it." The young officer was taken aback. He thought that he would be held responsible for the loss of the crew members and damage to the boat.

"Thank you, sir," he said at last, "I'll get her back in fighting trim before your return." Just as a crewman signaled the hoist operator to haul McGregor up, the Owl popped out of a hatch sporting a bandage around his head, and ran across the deck screaming that he should be the first to go aboard the destroyer.

Before anyone could stop him, he threw himself on top of McGregor, who cried out in pain.

"Stop him!" Bright shouted. Two crewmen grabbed the frenzied man and tried to pull him off the injured officer.

"Help, help," he screamed, "I'm wounded!" The deck crew crowded the destroyer's rail to watch the unfolding drama.

Lieutenant Colonel Henry walked purposefully across the MTB's scarred deck and looked down at the Owl. "Mr. Burns," he said sternly, "be a good man and stand up, you're hurting the officer."

The Owl tightened his grip on the basket and shouted, "Save me!" He cried out, "This man is going to kill me."

Henry leaned close to his ear and whispered malevolently. "Right you are, Mr. Burns. If you don't get up right now, I intend to cut off your head and shite in it." Coward that he was, the Owl was no fool. He knew that Henry meant what he said, and stood up, although he still insisted that he had been injured.

Cain and Finch were the last of the wounded to be hoisted aboard. Finch's legs had been peppered with shrapnel and he was heavily bandaged but alert. The normally irrepressible commando was down in the dumps but not because of his wounds. "I told that matelot he couldn't hit the broad side of a barn," he blurted out. "And look what happened to him, he got kilt." Tears streaked his cheeks. "The bloody fool saved us."

Cain reached over and patted the distraught man on the shoulder. The three bags containing the radar equipment were the last things they hoisted aboard. Henry immediately escorted them below and had them placed in a locked cage, under guard.

Bright and two crewmen cut Bender's remains out of the harness and placed him in a mattress cover. They laid him alongside four of his shipmates on the deck. There was no time to do more than that. Bright then made his way to the bridge to report.

"Commander," he said, "the other boat was sunk and the crew are waiting for rescue." The two-and-a-half-striper looked at him and shook his head.

"I'm sorry, sub, but my orders are to return to base as soon as we have whatever you took off the island."

The young officer was dumbfounded and blurted out, "You mean you're going to leave our men out there to drown?" His comment hit home. Half the men on the bridge, including the commander, had been rescued at one time or another from a watery grave.

"Right," the officer announced, "as soon as your wreck is ready for towing, we'll pick up your mates. By the way, Bright, well done! If you hadn't come toward us, we'd have never reached you in time."

———◆———

Cabinet War Rooms—"Sir, message from *Gurkha*," the Wren petty officer said, handing the form to the watch officer. He looked at the neat script—the message takers had to have good handwriting—and noted the time it had been sent.

They should be on their way back, he thought. The ship had reported the safe arrival of the packages and the rescue of the crew members, several of whom were wounded. "Good show!" he exclaimed. But as he continued to scan the text, a line caught his attention. "HMS *Gurkha* currently searching for additional survivors."

"Damn," he swore, "the boss isn't going to like this."

"What won't the boss like?" Loreena interjected. He handed her the message.

"The good news is that *Gurkha* made contact and picked up the radar equipment. The bad news is they're continuing to search for survivors. She was supposed to return immediately. I can't believe the stupidity of that commanding officer, risking everything for a few seamen."

His comment shocked Loreena. Her face turned brick red and she fought the temptation to slap him. Instead, she asked, "Have you ever been to sea?"

"No," he answered, "I've never had the opportunity."

"I thought so," she replied bitingly, and stalked away.

18

20 Nautical Miles West of Alderney, 0500, 19 August 1942—An hour after they had abandoned MTB 204, a sailor screamed that something had bumped him under the water. His shout prompted another to see a fin and yell "Shark!" Panic gripped the survivors, fearing that they were about to be attacked by the man-eaters. They desperately thrashed the water, hoping to keep them away. Wellford tried to calm them but he was ignored and the panic continued.

"Shut up," Montgomery thundered, "and listen to me! There're no sharks anywhere near us, so calm down!" The gunny's furious outburst stopped the imaginary shark sightings and helped the men regain a measure of self-control, but it was a tenuous hold.

"How did you know there weren't any sharks around?" Wellford asked quietly.

"I didn't," Montgomery replied, "but we had to stop the panic."

The officer shook his head in disbelief. "You sure had me fooled."

A long rolling swell caught the group and carried them above the surrounding sea. In the brief moment that they floated on the crest of the wave, a sailor spotted a huge shadow plowing through the water.

"My God," he yelled, "there's a ship bearing down on us!" The fading moonlight revealed the gray-painted hull of a Royal Navy destroyer.

———————

HMS *Gurkha*—A sharp-eyed lookout spotted a cluster of red emergency lights dead ahead and reported the sighting over a sound-powered telephone. "Hard-a-starboard," the commander instinctively ordered. The 2,500-ton warship heeled to the right, missing the men in the water by a scant 50 yards, but the bow wave swept over them, upending the rubber boat and tossing the men into the water. The commander breathed a sigh of relief. "That was too close," he muttered. He then turned to a petty officer. "Pass the word to the master-at-arms, an extra tot of rum for the lookout," and then ordered, "Full speed astern." The ship lost way as the two 18-foot propellers bit in and gradually reversed her course. "Stand by to pick up survivors," sounded over the ship's loudspeaker. The crew quickly broke out a scrambling net and lowered it over the side so the swimmers could climb aboard.

———————

20 Nautical Miles West of Alderney—The black hull of the *Gurkha* appeared out of the darkness and hove to close to the overturned rubber boat. To the men in the water, the ship that loomed over them was like a steel mountain that would have to be climbed to reach safety. The survivors hastily abandoned their temporary refuge and swam toward the side of the ship. The first two appeared to be in good shape until they reached the net and tried to climb it. The net was difficult to grab because the ship was rolling from side to side in the waves. One minute it would dip into the water and the next it would be in the air. The trick was to catch it at the right moment. The two finally managed to grab the net and pull themselves up. One ran out of gas about halfway up the side and fell back into the water. Fortunately, no one was below him when he hit. The second man made it to the top but didn't have the strength to climb onto the deck and begged for help. A huge boatswain's mate picked him up by the seat of the pants and the scruff of his neck and hauled him onto the deck. Within minutes, the scrambling net was crowded with climbing figures. The few men who were too weak to make the climb were thrown ropes which they tied around their waists and were hauled aboard.

Montgomery spotted a sailor who was feebly attempting to pull himself up out of the water but each time he fell back. He reached out to the exhausted man and dragged him closer to the net. "Hold on to my arm and I'll pull you up," he said, holding onto the net with one hand and extending the other. The man was totally worn out and couldn't hold on. "Damn," Montgomery swore, and jumped back into the ocean. He tried to push him up the net, but all he succeeded in doing was going under himself. A deckhand spotted the two struggling men and threw down a line. Montgomery tied it around the sailor's chest and he was hauled up like a limp sack. The gunny looked around and saw that he was the last man. He pulled himself out of the water and grasped the rope net. "No sweat, I've done this a hundred times." But as he said it, he looked up. The rail seemed like it was a mile away and then he realized how tired he was.

"Come on, old man," a voice nagged. Montgomery looked up and saw Bourne looking down at him from the rail. "You want me to come down and pull you up?"

"It'll be a cold day in hell before I let that Limey son-of-a-bitch help me," he muttered heatedly, and started climbing the net. The anger carried him halfway up the side before his strength gave out from physical exhaustion. He couldn't hold on to the rope and he started to fall backward. A hand reached out and grabbed him by the shoulder.

"I've got you, mate," Bourne declared, "just hold on." Edwards and Adair grabbed him by the belt and started hauling him up. Seconds later, they lifted him over the edge of the deck. Bourne leaned over the exhausted man. "We couldn't let our favorite Yank sergeant feed the fishes now, could we?"

———————✦———————

Cabinet War Rooms—The Wren petty officer knocked on Loreena's office door. "McNeal," she said, "we have received another message from the *Gurkha* that she's picked up several more survivors and is now on her way back."

"Is there a list?" Loreena blurted out, before she could stop herself.

"No, ma'am," the petty officer responded sadly. The entire office staff now knew about her feelings for the American Marine.

Loreena thought for a moment and then made a decision; *to hell with what people think.*

"Please check with the motor pool and see if there is a car available to take me to Portsmouth."

———————✦———————

HMS *Gurkha*—"Sir," the officer of the watch reported, "the lookout reports men in the water off the starboard quarter."

"Bloody hell," the captain exclaimed, "who are they?"

Bright, who had remained on the bridge, replied, "I believe they are off the E-boat we rammed."

"They'd better hurry," the captain replied, "I can't stay here much longer."

Six German sailors swam to the side of ship and begged to be rescued. A dozen crewmen were detailed to bring them aboard. They threw lines tied with a simple bowline loop on one end to the men in the water. All the swimmers had to do was step into the loop, grip the rope, and the crew would pull them up. *Oberleutnant zur See* Dieter was not a strong swimmer and was the last German to reach the British ship. Four of his crewmen had already been rescued and the fifth was getting ready to be hauled aboard. Desperate to be saved, he grabbed the young sailor by the shoulder and yanked him away from the rope. The frightened man briefly resisted, but he was no match for the officer's frenzied assault. He was pushed under the water and barely managed to get away. Dieter ignored the angry shouts from the British seamen and grabbed the dangling rope. He signaled that he was ready to be pulled up. Instead, the rope went slack and splashed into the water beside him. Uncomprehending, he looked up and saw one of his rescuers gesture and yell something he couldn't understand. One of the Brit sailors pointed to the attacker. "A right bloody bastard," he swore. "Get away from the line," he yelled. "Sod off," another yelled. Other crewmen joined in, threatening to leave him in the water, but the German ignored their warnings.

"Fuck him," a line handler barked, extending his middle finger and then throwing the rope overboard.

"Swim, Kraut," he added, before turning his attention to the other German. He and his mates quickly brought him aboard.

"Torpedoes," a lookout shouted into the sound-powered telephone, "dead ahead!" The captain trained his night-glasses on the two phosphorescent tracks heading directly for the ship's bow, "down the throat" in naval parlance.

"Sound the collision alarm," he ordered. *At least the crew will have a chance to grab something to hold onto before they hit.* He held his breath waiting for the inevitable. There was nothing he could do. Whatever launched the torpedoes had waited until the ship stopped to rescue survivors, and now she had no chance to maneuver out of the way. "Wait!" He stared at the torpedo tracks and suddenly realized the bloody things were going to miss. They passed along the sides of the ship, leaving a trail of vapor bubbles in their wake.

The captain leaped into action. "All ahead full speed," he ordered, just as the radar operator reported a contact and gave the range and bearing to the target. The gunnery officer quickly relayed the information to the forward mount and told the gun captain to fire a star shell. The 4.7-inch QF (quick-fire) cannon fired, and seconds later the round burst over the water, illuminating an E-boat maneuvering at high speed. The gunnery officer ordered the two forward mounts to take the boat under fire. Their first two salvos bracketed the German and the next two left it a blazing wreck.

"Good shooting, gunner," the captain declared. "Now it's time to go home."

Oberleutnant zur See **Dieter**—Dieter was treading water close to the side of the British ship when it got underway. "*Schweinhund!* (Pig dog!)," he shouted angrily. And then the realization that he was being abandoned sunk in. His anger was immediately replaced by panic. "Don't leave me!" he shouted, but no one heard him; the men at the rail had disappeared. The ship gained speed and as the stern got closer, he could feel the pull of the water increase. "My God," he screamed, "the propellers!" He tried to swim away from the hull but the suction was too strong and he was dragged under.

His Majesty's Naval Base (HMNB), Portsmouth—Loreena and three members of her team stood pier-side waiting for the gangway to be lowered into place so they could board the *Gurkha*. After a wild hour-long ride from London in the Wolseley staff car, they arrived a few minutes after the ship tied up at the pier. They were fortunate that the commodore had signed a special pass authorizing them to make the trip. Without it, they would never have been able to pass through the Home Guard roadblocks that dotted the route. The "old farts," as her team called them, were only too willing to exercise their authority over non-essential traffic. As they neared the base, the roadblocks were manned by regular troops, who closely scrutinized their pass and ID cards.

"Security is certainly tight," one of her companions remarked.

"Portsmouth is one of the debarkation ports for the Dieppe raid tonight," Loreena replied.

After receiving clearance from the sentries at the gate, they drove past a long line of heavily armed Canadian troops. The men seemed to be in good humor, smiling and waving to the good-looking girl in the staff car. They were finally able to reach Clarence Pier, which was lined with landing craft and warships of every description, and park across from two Royal Navy ambulances. The sight of the "blood wagons," with their cargo doors open, sent a chill through Loreena. She had been unable to find out the names of the casualties and she prayed that James was not one of them.

"Come on," she urged impatiently, "get the bloody gangways in position."

One of her "chair-bound warriors," as they called themselves, heard her comment. "I'm sure he's all right," he said.

She cursed silently, wondering if everyone knew her personal business.

"Thank you, Tommy," she replied coolly, and then reminded him to start interviewing the commandos as soon as they debarked.

An officer at the top of the gangway signaled the stretcher bearers and they immediately started down with their load of blanket-wrapped wounded. Loreena moved closer to see them but she was shooed away by a sailor.

"Please, ma'am, stay back so they can load the injured," he ordered. Now she was too far away to see their faces. A bedraggled sub-lieutenant appeared helping to carry a stretcher. He stood aside as the medical orderlies loaded it into a vehicle and then looked around, as if he was lost.

"Are you OK?" Loreena asked.

He stared at her for a moment before replying. "I'm fine," he managed to say, "but there're too many that aren't."

At that moment, Loreena saw Cain at the top of the gangway and her heart skipped a beat. "James!" she shouted, and ran to meet him.

Her shout caught the attention of two sailors, one of whom remarked to his mate, "If I had a girl like that waiting for me, I'd never go to sea again."

Casting military decorum aside, she threw her arms around him just as he stepped onto the pier. She felt him pull back.

What's the matter? she thought. *Maybe he doesn't feel the same way about me.* She took a step back and for the first time saw the bandages under the battledress that was draped over his shoulders.

"Oh my God," she gasped, "you're hurt." The grimace on his face explained why he hadn't returned her hug.

"I'd better sit down," he said, through gritted teeth.

Loreena guided him to an ambulance, where an orderly took one look at the bloodstained bandages and ordered him inside. "Just a minute, doc," Cain said, turning to Loreena, who had tears running down her cheeks.

He took her arm with his good hand. "I want to see you again," he declared. "I've never known anyone like you…" Then he hesitated, not knowing what to say next.

"Oh, James, I've been so worried," she sighed, and kissed him on the cheek.

The orderly cleared his throat. "Sir, please get in, we've got to get to the hospital."

"I'll see you as soon as I can," Loreena called out as the doors shut.

Two heavily armed Royal Marines led the blindfolded E-boat survivors to a truck, which took them to a holding area where they would be interrogated for several hours before being transported to a POW camp.

Lieutenant Colonel Henry, the Owl, and the German radar operator walked to the headquarters building, where they were met by a colonel from Special Operation Executive, a pair of German-speaking interrogators from the Secret Intelligence Service, and four radar specialists. A party of sailors carried the valuable classified equipment and Henry's pack with the radar documents. After dropping off the equipment, the working party was unceremoniously shooed out of the building. "Blimey, not even a thank you," the senior rating groused.

The German prisoner was immediately taken to a small room in the basement. The only furniture was a desk with two chairs. A large two-way mirror covered half of one wall. An interrogator welcomed him in a friendly voice and invited the young prisoner to sit down and relax. He was offered a cigarette and asked if he would like something to eat. This opening gambit was simply the first step in an interrogation process that was designed to wring every bit of useful information from the naive youngster.

Meanwhile, the Owl had pigeonholed the colonel from SOE and was trying to lodge a complaint about the abuse he had suffered when Henry strode by. "That's him," he pointed excitedly, "that's the man."

The colonel looked up and smiled. "I see you're up to your old tricks," he said, and shook Henry's hand. "Well done," he added, "the general will be pleased."

"Couldn't have done it without Mr. Burns," Henry replied generously. The Owl's mouth dropped open in disbelief.

"I'm sure he'll receive a suitable reward from a grateful government," the officer went on, "even though the operation was so secret that nothing will ever be made public. Don't you agree, Mr. Burns?" The Owl looked at the two hard-boiled officers and immediately understood that discretion was the better part of valor. If he didn't keep his mouth shut, he might end up in confinement for the duration of the war.

While this was going on, Loreena's chair-bound warriors rounded up the unwounded commandos and led them to an empty room in one of the warehouses close to the pier. They presented a formidable sight as they marched along the pier—Bourne and Montgomery leading each file—despite their disreputable appearance—shoulders back, arms swinging in unison, bare feet slapping the concrete—through a gawking crowd of sailors and dockworkers. "Don't fuck with that lot," a grizzled old dockworker was heard to say, "they'll eat you for breakfast."

Loreena met the group and hugged each one, a highly unusual military greeting but one that was greatly appreciated by the surprised commandos. Her uniform was soon wet through and smelling of high-octane gasoline, but she thought it was a small price to pay for welcoming them home. The commodore, "bless his soul," had called ahead and had the room stocked with eats and, more importantly, a large tub of iced Guinness.

"I've died and gone to heaven," Edwards announced, snapping the cap off a bottle with his belt buckle.

"Wait!" Bourne growled, stopping him in mid-sip. "Come on, lads, grab a bottle," the colour sergeant ordered. When everyone had opened one, he raised his bottle. "To our fallen comrades," he toasted.

"Fallen comrades!" the men repeated, manfully struggling to control their emotions.

After the toast, Loreena and her staff got down to the business at hand. She apologized for delaying them, but she explained that the interview would form the basis for an after-action and lessons-learned report which would be immediately circulated to the operating forces. It was important to gather the information while it was still fresh in everyone's minds. "The things you learned might save lives," she added. The commandos were dog-tired but willingly participated. Each man was individually interviewed by one of Loreena's staff and then participated in a group session. The process took four hours and by that time the men were physically and mentally exhausted. On the long drive north to Achnacarry, the men slept the sleep of the dead.

19

Royal Naval Hospital Haslar, 0845, 19 August 1942—Cain remembered lying down on the ambulance stretcher and nothing more until a white-coated figure started removing the bandages from his shoulder in the hospital triage.

"Damn that hurts," he mumbled. The shot of morphine he received on board the ship was wearing off.

"Sorry," the figure replied. "I'm afraid the dressing is stuck to your skin." Cain gritted his teeth. "That's got it," the medical assistant said, dropping the blood-soaked mass into a container. "Don't go away, a doctor will be here shortly."

Right, Cain thought, *like I'm going to skip right out of here*. His shoulder hurt like hell and he was cold to boot. He couldn't stop shivering. He had been stripped from the waist up to work on the hole in his shoulder. A passing medical orderly saw his condition and placed a blanket over his bare shoulders. "Thanks," he mumbled.

Cain gradually became more aware of his surroundings. The triage was filled with medical personnel tending to the wounded, who lay on stretchers placed on metal waist-high sawhorses. Metal carts holding medical devices and supplies stood next to each stretcher. Each one had a slender pole holding a bottle of plasma that dripped into a plastic tube inserted into a wounded man's arm.

"Needles," Cain complained, staring at the needle taped to the inside of his arm, "I hate needles." His needle phobia was well known among the corpsmen in his old Marine unit. At one point, having dodged a required inoculation for several days, the chief corpsman had cornered him in his office. "Do you want it easy or hard, captain?" he asked, pointing to a dozen tough-looking corpsmen standing outside.

"OK," Cain replied, "let's do it the hard way." The chief nodded and the sailors moved in.

"Just kidding," the officer said meekly, offering his arm for the injection.

Cain turned his head just in time to see a sheet being pulled over the adjacent man's face. "OK," a doctor voiced solemnly, "take him away." Medical orderlies lifted the stretcher and carried it out of the room. "Nothing more we could do for the poor devil," the physician said absently.

"Doctor, over here," someone called. The physician straightened his shoulders and quickly walked over to attend to the next man.

Cain was among the last of the injured to be treated. His wound was not as serious as some of the others, so he was placed near the bottom of the treatment priority list. He found out later that this was the function of triage—to prioritize the injured and treat the most seriously wounded first. A doctor bent over his shoulder, inspecting the wound.

"I know you lads are tough, but this may smart a little," he said, as a medical orderly lifted his shoulder off the stretcher.

"You're right, doc," Cain muttered through clenched teeth, "they can't make it tough enough for a commando but you're sure approaching it."

"Right you are," the young doctor replied. "I believe you have the perfect wound—no bone or nerve damage—but I'm sending you to X-ray just to be sure. I expect you should be fine in a few weeks."

Commando Basic Training Centre—"All right, lads, up and at 'em," Bourne called out, as the lorry neared the training center entrance. He had sensed the truck slowing down and forced himself to open his eyes. The men were still half asleep when the center's sergeant major appeared at the vehicle's tailgate. "Right," he thundered, "you lazy buggers have exactly 10 seconds to get off this vehicle!"

"Oh my God," Williams moaned, "we're back in training."

No sense in fighting city hall, Montgomery thought, and jumped down from the back of the covered lorry. The others followed but not fast enough to suit the sergeant major.

"Fall in, and be quick about it!" The men formed two short ranks facing him. "Straighten up; you look like a bunch of rag pickers." They did their best but after hours in salt water their uniforms hung on them like bags, their bearded faces still had remnants of camouflage, and they were groggy from lack of sleep. In short, they were a far cry from the guard at Buckingham Palace. The sergeant major's testy comment stung. Even Bourne, the ultimate parade soldier, resented the way they were being treated. "Little better than recruits," he muttered under his breath. He expected better treatment after all they had been through.

The lorry drove away, and for the first time, the section could see the road into camp. It was lined with platoons of trainees at rigid attention. Lieutenant Colonel Moss and his staff stood in the center of the roadway. The pipe major, dressed in his colorful regimentals, was off to one side. For a moment, the section gawked at the scene and then the realization hit them. The sergeant major was putting on an act, and a good one at that. The entire training camp was assembled to welcome them back. A feeling of immense pride surged through the section—backs straightened, chests thrust out, heads snapped up.

"That's it, men," the sergeant major urged. "Show them what fighters you are."

Montgomery, as the senior man in the section, looked knowingly at Bourne. "Take it," he whispered.

The Brit nodded. "Sergeant major," Bourne called out in his best parade voice, "Cain's commandos are all correct." The hint of a smile appeared for an instant on the older SNCO's face and then he brought them to attention. "Forward march," he commanded. Three paces from the colonel he ordered, "Halt!" The section's steel-plated ammunition boots rang out as one on the asphalt roadway. The sergeant major's arm whipped up in a parade ground salute. "All present and accounted for, sir," he reported.

The colonel returned the salute. "Welcome home, commandos," Moss bellowed—the signal for the pipe major to swing into action. He filled his cheeks with air and blew into the blowpipe and squeezed, producing the first notes of "Scotland the Brave."

"Forward march!" the colonel commanded, and the entire detail—his staff, the pipe major, and the section—stepped off together. As the colonel passed the platoons, he was saluted—and much to the utter amazement of the section, the salute was held until after they passed by. *Bloody hell, I wish the rest of the section could see this*, Williams thought with pride.

Cabinet War Rooms—Just as soon as Loreena entered the operations center, she saw that something was terribly wrong. One of the Wren petty officers near the door was quietly sobbing into a sodden handkerchief. The watch officer stood motionlessly next to a map of the Channel. His face was ashen and his whole demeanor spoke of calamity.

"What's wrong?" Loreena asked.

"The bloody Dieppe landing's a disaster," he snapped. "The Canadians have had tremendous casualties and the general's ordered a withdrawal."

"What happened?" she asked.

"We don't know, except that the Germans were ready for us." At that moment, the operations officer entered the room and took one look at the despondency that had infected the duty section.

"That's quite enough, everyone," he said forcefully, "we have a job to do, now let's get to it." He turned to the senior Wren and pointed to the distraught female petty officer. "Please get a relief for her."

"Yes, sir," she responded, and then as an after-thought, added, "Her fiancé was in the raiding force."

The operations officer spotted Loreena and called out, "Lieutenant McNeal, a moment, please," and motioned for her to follow him to his office.

"Loreena, I didn't mean to be so formal, but at times like this we have to maintain military bearing and discipline."

"Yes, sir," she replied. The officer was an old hand at dealing with crises. He had been in charge during the Dunkirk evacuation and his steadiness under pressure was legendary.

"Loreena, I would like you to assume the duty as an assistant watch officer until the present crisis is over."

Officers' Ward, Royal Naval Hospital Haslar—Cain was bored to death. For the first three days after being admitted, he lay in bed swathed in bandages and hooked up to an IV that drove him up a wall. The damn thing was taped to his arm, forcing him to lie on his back. He grumbled to the ward nurse, known as the "old battleax." "I sleep on my side," he moaned.

She fired back, "Captain, think of the lads who are in much worse shape than you. They're just glad to be alive." Embarrassed by the truth in her words, Cain told himself to stay calm. By the fourth day, however, he was climbing the walls and determined to get out of bed. He pestered the "old battleax" until she finally surrendered and rigged a portable IV stand just to get him out of her hair.

His first attempt to get out of bed taught him a lesson in humility. As he sat up and tried to swing his legs over the edge, he almost passed out, much to the amusement of the old battleax, who never said a word but the *I-told-you-so* look on her face spoke volumes. The second attempt was better and he shakily made his way to the head unassisted—*What a relief!* He had trouble "handling" business with only one hand, but it was certainly less embarrassing than sitting on a bedpan. Following the successful leak, he made his way into the other ranks ward, determined to find his boys.

"May I help you?" a pretty young nurse asked.

"Yes," he replied, "I'm looking for the wounded commandos…" and before he could say anything more, she grimaced.

"They've been placed in isolation back there," she said tightly, pointing to a closed-off section. "The one they call 'Motor Mouth' has been a bad boy." Cain took another look at the lovely girl and guessed what she meant by a "bad boy."

"Hey, lads, look who's here," Finch called out cheerfully as Cain shuffled into view. Hawkins and McTavish greeted him warmly, but Harris was too badly wounded to respond.

"How you doing?" Cain asked.

"Hell, sir, every meal's a banquet and every night's a Saturday night," Finch responded lightheartedly.

"Let me rephrase that," Cain said. "How's everybody feeling?"

"Not so good, sir," McTavish interjected. "The bootnecks took a spray of shrapnel in the legs. They won't be dancing for a while." Cain believed it. The two Marines were each bandaged from crotch to ankles. They looked like pincushions—drainage tubes ran from their legs to bottles on the floor, and IVs were taped to their arms.

"How's Harris?" Cain asked, eyeing the unconscious commando.

"He took a round through the lung and may be surveyed out," McTavish responded sorrowfully.

"Damn, I'm sorry to hear that," Cain said. "Does he know yet?"

"No, sir," the Scot replied, "Hawkins overheard the doctors talking."

"What about you? Where did you get hit?" McTavish hesitated. Finch piped up, "He got shot in the ass."

"I understand you've been a bad boy," Cain quipped to Finch.

"Me, sir?" Finch responded with mock sincerity, "I've been the soul of propriety."

"I'll bet," Cain said with a laugh. "Anything I can get you boys?"

"How about a date with the nurse?" Finch inquired wishfully.

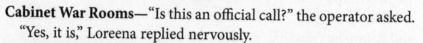

Cabinet War Rooms—"Is this an official call?" the operator asked.

"Yes, it is," Loreena replied nervously.

"Standby," the voice said.

I can't believe I'm doing this, Loreena thought, fully aware she should not be using an official line for personal business.

"Ma'am, I have the hospital on the line," the operator announced, interrupting her thought.

"This is Lieutenant McNeal calling for Captain James Cain," she declared self-consciously. The hospital operator told her that it would take some time for the patient to get to the phone.

What will I say to him? she asked herself, suddenly at a loss for words. *What if he doesn't want to talk with me?* The wait seemed interminable—and then suddenly his voice came over the wire.

"Loreena, I can't believe it's you!" he exclaimed. All her anxieties disappeared as soon as she heard his voice.

"James, I miss you and I can't wait to see you."

"You're all I've thought of since I've been here," he responded.

Suddenly, the operator's voice cut in, "I have a priority call, I'm sorry to cut you off."

"James, I love you," Loreena blurted out, just as the line went dead.

Royal Naval Hospital Haslar—Lieutenant Colonel Moss stormed into the building as if he was assaulting a German machine-gun position. Bourne and Montgomery trailed along behind. The hospital administrator barely had time to meet them in the entranceway. "Where are my commandos?" Moss demanded loudly.

"Sir, if you would mind waiting, I will have them brought to you," the administrator replied.

"Nonsense," the colonel exclaimed. "Point me in the right direction and I'll find them." And with that, he proceeded down the main hallway toward the patient wards, the sound of his cleated heels striking the deck echoing off the walls. As he opened the door to the officers' ward, he was confronted by the old battleax.

"And who do we have here?" the head nurse demanded defiantly, blocking his way with her formidable girth. Moss was taken aback by the woman's cheek.

"I'm Lieutenant Colonel Moss and I've come to see my commandos," he fired back.

"I'm the head ward nurse," she replied forcefully, "and these are my commandos, so back off, colonel."

Stalemate, until Bourne stepped forward from behind the door. "Why, you old battleax," he exclaimed, and wrapped his arms around the surprised nurse. Moss stood openmouthed, not knowing if the embrace was a prelude to a fight or a test of strength.

"Angus!" the nurse cried happily. "How are you?"

"Fit," he replied, stepping back to take a good look at the heavyset matron. "You're as pretty as ever."

"What a bundle of pish," she snorted, but her face flushed red with embarrassment. Moss was amazed to see that the tough old bird actually blushed.

"Well, lass, will you let us pass?" Bourne asked.

"Anything for you, Angus," she replied, stepping aside to let them pass. "Just don't upset my little darlings."

"All right, colour sergeant, what was that all about?" Moss asked, after they walked further down the hallway.

"Nurse Deirdre took me under her wing after I was wounded at Dunkirk," Bourne explained. "And put me back together. She's extremely protective of her brood and woe be it to anyone who poses a threat. The lads will be well looked after under her care."

"So, her bark is worse than her bite?" Moss asked.

"No, sir," Bourne answered, "she barks just before she bites!"

Moss laughed. "Remind me to stay on her good side."

"Here we are, sir," Bourne announced, as they reached the curtained cubicle. He stepped aside, allowing Moss to enter.

Finch was the first commando to spot the senior officer. "Attention on deck!" he shouted automatically. Cain, who was visiting, shot to his feet, while the others stiffened in their beds.

"Carry on," Moss said at once, rather embarrassed at the reaction. He was here to honor their bravery, not to inspect.

Cain, now unencumbered by the IV, hurried forward to greet him. "Sorry I wasn't at the door to meet you, sir," he apologized, "I didn't know you were coming." The last remark was aimed at Montgomery, because he thought the gunny should have let him know the colonel was going to visit.

"That's all right, Cain, I didn't know I was coming until this morning. Now, if you don't mind, I'd like to talk with your men," and with that, Moss turned toward Finch's bed. The commandos held their breath, not knowing what Motor Mouth would say. Finch had a tendency to speak first and think later. Bourne said he had an affinity between his foot and his mouth! To their surprise, Finch did them proud; he was the embodiment of a Royal Marine non-commissioned officer. His responses were crisp and respectful, interspaced with appropriate "Yes, sirs" and "No, sirs." Cain breathed a sigh of relief when the colonel started to move on to the next man—but it was too soon.

"Anything I can do for you, Corporal Finch?" Moss asked.

"Yes, sir," he replied. "Could you put in a good word for me with the delicious-looking nurse?"

"Oh my God," Cain muttered. He shouldn't have worried; the colonel was an old campaigner and just laughed. "I noticed her myself, Finch. You have good taste."

Moss went from patient to patient, chatting them up. Finally, he nodded to Bourne, who took several items from a box that he was carrying. The colonel stood in the middle of the cubicle.

"Normally, we would award these after completing the commando course," he began, "but after your recent experience, you have more than earned it." With that, he presented each of them with a green beret. "Now that you are officially commandos, it gives me great pleasure to recommend each of you for the Military Medal for exceptional bravery in action against the enemy. Well done, lads," the colonel said, and with that he strode out of the cubicle.

"I'm a bloody hero," Finch preened.

Cain followed the three men to the exit.

"I understand you're going to be released in a couple of days," Moss said.

"Yes, sir," the Marine responded. "With your permission, sir, I would like to take a few days leave in London before returning to Achnacarry."

"Fine," Moss replied, "I'll let the adjutant know. Have a good leave, you deserve it," he added, and patted him on the shoulder. Without thinking, Cain tried to salute. *Not a good idea*, he decided, as the pain radiated down his arm. Moss joined Bourne and Montgomery in the staff car and they drove away.

Three days later, Cain received a message directing him to report to Combined Operations headquarters for temporary duty on or about 1200 on 5 September. *I wonder what that's all about*, he thought. The message went on to state that he was authorized a five-day leave before reporting to Achnacarry for duty. "Thank you, Colonel Moss," he whispered with a smile.

20

Combined Operations Headquarters, Richmond Terrace, London, 1100, 5 September 1942—Cain's taxicab pulled up in front of a nondescript stone building in Whitehall, the heart of the British government's quarter in London. *This can't be commando headquarters*, he thought. There weren't any signs, no armed guards—nothing to indicate that the multi-story structure housed the men and women who were responsible for setting Europe ablaze.

"Are you sure this is the place?" he asked the driver.

"Guv', I've been driving young men like you here for over a year," the cockney driver replied. "Trust me, this is the place." Cain paid the fare and added a little extra. "Thank you, sir," the cabbie expressed, and added a "good luck" before heading back out to look for another fare. Cain smiled as the driver pulled away. The "old timer" was extremely proud of his Austin Low Loader taxi and had given the young officer a rundown on its pedigree. As a car enthusiast himself, Cain enjoyed the distraction from the grim realities of war as they passed rows of bomb-damaged buildings.

"Back to business," he mumbled and headed for the ground-level headquarters entrance, which like most government buildings had sandbags stacked around it to protect the inhabitants from bomb blasts. A large black enamel placard, with a white letter "S" in the center and the words "SHELTER HERE," was posted at the entranceway.

A passerby saw him looking at the sign. "Public shelter," the gentleman offered. "The basement is supposedly bombproof."

"Does it get much use?" Cain asked.

"Not much during the day, but Jerry can be a real pain in the bum after dark. Three nights ago, a 2,000-pounder went through the roof of a building two streets away."

"What happened?" Cain asked.

"It failed to explode and one of our bomb-disposal lads disarmed it and took it away," the man explained casually, as if a ton of high explosive slamming into a building was a common occurrence. Cain greatly admired the fortitude of the population under the German bombing campaign.

Cain entered the building and saw a sign labeled "COHQ" with an arrow pointing down a marble staircase to the lower levels. He reached the first landing, where a formidable-looking concierge manned a desk.

"May I help you, sir?" he asked firmly but politely. The man's demeanor marked him as military. *Probably has a pistol within easy reach*, Cain assumed.

"I've been assigned here on temporary duty," he said, and handed the man his orders. The gatekeeper examined the document carefully.

"We don't see many Americans down here," he said, returning them.

"I expect you'll see a lot more of us in the not-too-distant future," Cain replied.

"We can use you," the man declared, and then directed Cain to an office halfway down the hall.

"I say, old boy, you're a bit early," a familiar voice called out. Cain turned and was surprised to see Lieutenant Colonel Henry standing in a doorway.

"Good to see you, colonel," the Marine replied, wondering what he meant by "a little early." "I didn't expect to see you at headquarters," Cain stated.

"I'm here to attend an awards ceremony," Henry explained. Cain mentioned that he was there for temporary duty but he didn't know what it was.

"Well, come on," Henry said, "I'll show you where you need to go." The two men walked down the hall and entered a room that Cain took to be some sort of briefing room. A dozen chairs were arranged in rows in front of a raised platform that held a Union Jack and the Combined Operations flag. *This must be where the awards ceremony is taking place*, Cain thought.

"How's the wing?" Henry asked suddenly.

"On the mend," Cain answered. "The doctor said I should be able to discard the sling in a few more days."

"Any long-term damage?"

"None, I was very lucky." The colonel started to ask another question, when Lieutenant Colonel Moss entered, followed by Montgomery, Bourne, and the five unwounded members of the raid. Cain was thrilled to see them. After a quick round of handshaking and backslapping, Moss interrupted. "We were concerned that you'd be late."

"I don't understand, sir."

Moss looked at Henry. "Didn't you tell him?"

"I thought I'd leave that to you, Rupert," Henry answered.

Just then, a harassed-looking staff officer entered and announced that Lord Mountbatten would be a few minutes late. Lightbulbs went off in Cain's head. He turned to the two senior officers.

"Gentlemen, would you tell me what's going on?"

Moss held up his hand in a sign of apology. "James," he explained, "you and Gunnery Sergeant Montgomery are to be decorated for Operation *Switch-Off*."

Cain was taken aback. "But, sir," he started to say, just as Mountbatten, two senior officers, and a big well-dressed man in civilian clothes entered the room.

Everyone snapped to attention. The chief of combined operations went around the room shaking hands with everyone and then mounted the stage. Before he spoke, an aide guided Cain and Montgomery to the middle of the platform. "Gentlemen, please take your seats," he told the audience. "It gives me great pleasure this afternoon to recognize the bravery of two of our American allies." He nodded to an aide, who proceeded to read the first citation. When he had finished, Mountbatten stepped in front of Cain and pinned the Distinguished Service Order on his blouse. "Well done, captain," he said, shaking the Marine's left hand. "You have done a great service for England and brought great credit to your Corps."

Mountbatten then nodded to his aide, who read the second citation. "For conspicuous gallantry on 17 August 1942, while on a special mission in the Channel Islands, Gunnery Sergeant Leland Montgomery, U.S. Marine Corps, showed remarkable courage and contempt for danger by leading a half-section of commandos against a hostile enemy force and later materially assisting in the rescue of several commandos." Mountbatten pinned the silver Distinguished Conduct Medal on Montgomery's blouse and shook his hand.

"I understand you're a crack open ocean pistol shot," he joked. For once, the gunny was at a loss for words. "Good show," Mountbatten added. Then his aide whispered some message of urgency to him; he apologized, "Gentlemen, I regret that I have to return to my office. Again, thank you for your service to my country." And with that, he left the room, followed by the entourage of senior officers. The civilians remained behind, but stayed in the background amidst the backslapping and boisterous chatter of the commandos.

The entire ceremony, from beginning to end, lasted no more than 10 minutes, but for the chief of combined operations to conduct the ceremony despite his hectic schedule spoke of the importance of Operation *Switch-Off* and the participation of the Americans in special operations, an undertaking that Churchill was particularly keen on. He was pressing Roosevelt to develop the same type of force. The establishment of the Marine Raider Battalion was partially the result of Churchill's prompting. Mountbatten also wanted to use the success of Operation *Switch-Off* to help take some of the sting out of the Dieppe raid, which had been an absolute disaster.

The congratulatory exchange among the commandos died down and the civilian took the opportunity to introduce himself. "I'm Jack Kelly," the soft-spoken man said, sticking out his hand and handing Cain a business card. The Marine glanced at the simple pasteboard card. It only had three lines. *Jack Kelly, Office of Strategic Services, 70 Grosvenor Street, W1.* "I don't want to take up your time now, but would you mind dropping by tomorrow for a little chat? Say around 1000?"

Cain recognized Kelly's statement as more than a casual invitation; it was a request that should not be ignored. "Yes, sir," he replied, "I'll be there." They shook hands and the mysterious Kelly left.

"Who the hell was that?" Cain asked. No one knew.

"I guess you'll find out tomorrow," Montgomery said.

Office of Strategic Services Headquarters—Cain was a little blurry eyed stepping out of the taxi. Colonel Moss had been good enough to give the commandos a night of liberty after Montgomery swore he would have them at the train station for the early run to Achnacarry. Bourne had led them to an after-hours pub that still served the "good stuff" and they had partied most of the night. The regular patrons were proud to support the war effort by providing free drinks to the "fighting forces." Edwards pointed out that there were two heroes in their midst, much to the chagrin of the two Marines, who insisted that the young commandos were the real heroes. In any event, Cain was able to snatch a couple of hours sleep in a room Lieutenant Colonel Henry had snagged from a wealthy widow who had donated her house to the government for the duration of the war.

The OSS address was smack dab in the middle of the wartime American compound, halfway down the street from the U.S. Embassy. 70 Grosvenor Street was a nondescript five-story brick office building, drab and unpainted, betraying four years of wartime neglect. The U.S. military headquarters was on the opposite side of the square. Cain entered the building through the street-level entranceway and found himself facing a security checkpoint manned by two heavyset armed guards in civilian clothing. They didn't seem overly impressed by Cain's rank, nor were they as polite as the soldier at the Combined Operations headquarters. In fact, they were downright rude. "What's your business?" one demanded brusquely.

Typical ugly American, Cain reflected, and had the greatest urge to tell them he was here to blow up the building. But he figured they wouldn't think it was funny and would probably shoot his ass. Instead, he said politely, "I'm Captain James Cain and I have an appointment to see Mr. Kelly."

One of the gorillas checked a list, found his name, and pointed to a circular staircase to the upper floors. "Third floor, fourth door on the right," he growled.

"May I help you, sir?" a pretty WAC receptionist asked, as he walked into the office. Her polite greeting helped soothe his anger over the encounter with the animal act at the checkpoint.

"Yes," he replied, "I have an appointment with Mr. Kelly."

"He'll be right with you as soon as he finishes a meeting. Please have a seat." Cain had hardly settled into a chair before the inner office door opened and Kelly appeared.

"Come in," he said, "I'm sorry to have kept you waiting." Cain was impressed. He had expected to wait a minimum of half an hour as a reminder that he was a lowly captain. He entered the office and was surprised to see a uniformed Marine. Kelly introduced him. "This is Colonel Bill Eddy, the head of our operations in North Africa." The two Marines shook hands and exchanged courtesies. Kelly offered the men chairs and then turned to Cain. "Thank you for coming," he said, which Cain thought was kind of him to say, considering that the invitation was almost an order. "You're probably wondering why you're here," he voiced. "I'll get to that, but first, do you know anything about the OSS?"

Cain told him bluntly that he didn't have the foggiest idea.

Kelly smiled. "Most people don't know who or what we are, so let me give you a quick overview. The organization was created in 1942 by President Roosevelt to centralize the collection of intelligence. Up to this time, there wasn't any national intelligence agency. It was all in the hands of the various military services. The president selected Colonel Bill Donovan to be what was then called the coordinator of information. Are you following me so far?"

Cain nodded and Kelly continued. "As you can imagine, the FBI, the State Department, and the military were not too happy about its formation, but Donovan has the ear of the president, so the organization has grown."

Colonel Eddy interrupted, "Gentlemen, unfortunately I have to leave for a meeting. I'm glad to have met you, captain, and if you decide to join our little band, I think you will find the assignment exciting." With that he shook hands and left.

Cain turned to the OSS officer. "What did the colonel mean?"

"I was just coming to that," Kelly replied. "You have been recommended to join the OSS by the Brits because of the way you handled Operation *Switch-Off*." Cain suddenly remembered Henry's questions about his wounded arm. The probing had been more than just an interest in his well-being; it had been to find out if he was going to be physically OK. "OSS has an interest in sending combined British and American special operations teams into France to work with the Resistance. Would you be interested?"

Cain was taken completely by surprise and did not immediately respond. He felt a surge of excitement. What an opportunity, he thought. The idea of working with an elite force was a strong incentive—but then again, he was already in an elite Marine unit—and going into immediate action had a strong appeal. He was torn. "I am certainly interested but I need some time to think about it before I make a decision," he finally replied.

"I understand you have a few days' leave," Kelly replied. "Let me know at the end of it."

———

Cabinet War Rooms—Loreena was mentally exhausted. She had been cooped up in the underground bunker for over a week. Her 14-hour days had worn her to a frazzle, which she finally realized after severely mauling a young Wren for some petty mistake. Five minutes after storming back to her office, she couldn't even remember what the slipup had been. *I need to get out of here*, she decided, *before I lose it completely*. She called in the section's chief petty officer and told her that she was going outside for a breath of fresh air to clear her mind. "About time," the petty officer acknowledged, "you've scared the girls so much they can't do their jobs correctly." Loreena started to respond angrily and then suddenly realized the older woman was right, she had been taking her frustration out on the staff.

———

Trafalgar Square—The crowd in Trafalgar Square was at its height during lunchtime. Hundreds of government office workers and Allied military milled around, enjoying the midday sun while munching on sandwiches. It was difficult to find a space to sit down but she finally found a vacant spot between two of the four lion statues. She took off her cap and threw her head back to let the sun's rays bathe her face. "God, this feels good," she sighed, taking a deep breath of air that for once didn't smell of sweat, dampness, and mold. For the first time in a week, she could think of something other than reports of death and destruction. "James, where are you?" she murmured, suddenly feeling a great sense of loss.

After leaving the OSS headquarters, Cain decided to think about the offer and do a little sightseeing to clear his mind. The thought of going back to the lonely room had no appeal. Besides, the weather was absolutely perfect for a little stroll. He meandered along the street, letting the crowd dictate his path, and soon found himself in the center of the city. One of the ever-present barrage balloons caught his eye. It seemed to be hovering over a tall column in the center of a large open square. *What the hell*, he thought, *I might as well see what the damn thing is*. The square was quite crowded and he almost turned back; crowds were not his thing. He plunged on until he reached the base of the column, where he stopped to admire the four bronze plaques. He strolled along, marveling at their rich detail, and was so engrossed in studying them that he accidentally bumped into a British servicewoman. "I'm terribly sorry," he stammered, "I wasn't watching what I was doing." The woman turned to face him. "James!" she exclaimed.

Cain stood openmouthed, spellbound by the sight of the beautiful girl.

"Loreena," he whispered, and impulsively took her in his arms and kissed her passionately. "I can't believe it's you," he breathed into her ear. The two finally broke apart, slightly embarrassed by their embrace in the midst of the crowd. Passersby simply took the hug in stride and smiled good-naturedly—after all, there's a war on, you know.

Author's Note

Commandos is a work of fiction, and the author has taken some liberties with historical details to aid the story. The characters are products of the author's imagination and any resemblance to any person, living or dead, is entirely coincidental. That said, there was a Commando Basic Training Centre located at Achnacarry in the Scottish Highlands. A contingent of U.S. Marines did undergo training there in 1942 in preparation for the Allied landings in North Africa.